The Machine Society

Rich or poor. They want you to be a prisoner

The Machine Society

Rich or poor. They want you to be a prisoner

Mike Brooks

COSMIC
EGG
BOOKS

Winchester, UK
Washington, USA

First published by Cosmic Egg Books, 2016
Cosmic Egg Books is an imprint of John Hunt Publishing Ltd., Laurel House, Station Approach,
Alresford, Hants, SO24 9JH, UK
office1@jhpbooks.net
www.cosmicegg-books.com
www.johnhuntpublishing.com

For distributor details and how to order please visit the 'Ordering' section on our website.

Text copyright: Mike Brooks 2015

ISBN: 978 1 78535 252 2
Library of Congress Control Number: 2016934226

Design: Stuart Davies

Printed and bound by CPI Group (UK) Ltd, Croydon, CR0 4YY, UK

We operate a distinctive and ethical publishing philosophy in all
areas of our business, from our global network of authors to
production and worldwide distribution.

For Christine, Joey and Lizzy.

Acknowledgements

Thank you to Christine Kirkham, Peter Parr and Sheba Sultan
for support and suggestions.

For more on Mike Brooks, visit www.brooksbooks.co.uk

Part I: The Perimeter

'We must rid ourselves of the notion that humanity is an error.
It is not. Even so, it is for each of us to work out what his life
is for.'
Erich Vinty

Dean Rogers snapped awake, his heart beating hard, a stabbing pain in his stomach. With his eyes wide, he listened, dreading he'd missed the siren.

There was only silence.

Sighing, he pulled up the thin sheet and fidgeted, trying to relax his aching body on the hard mattress. Brilliant sunshine streamed in through the uncovered window. He lay on his back, arm across his eyes, and slipped back into his dream, the recurring dream, the one at his grandma's house, in the back garden, childhood days when the sunshine was softer…

Then came the siren, wailing like a banshee. He shot out of bed. With two quick strides he was at the sink in the corner, checking both taps were fully turned on, then grabbing two plastic cups from the glass shelf. A cup in each hand, he stood, tense, waiting; aware of a sharp dryness in his mouth, the stultifying heat in the room, and the sweat on his naked body. He avoided looking in the mirror. He hated the dark rings under his eyes: he used to try and cover them using a cosmetic stick – male grooming – back when such things could be bought. Looking down at his thin body, he saw his stomach was flat; funny to think he'd once tried to get this effect through tortuous hours at the gym; now he'd achieved the same thing through involuntary adherence to the government's 'Watch your Health' campaign, which roughly translated as almost bare supermarket shelves.

A grinding, metallic clunk came from somewhere in the pipes behind the walls, winning back his full attention. The left tap spluttered. Water fizzed and spat out: a good clarity today. He waited for the first cup to almost fill up then, without missing a drop, switched cups. While the second cup filled, he emptied the contents of the first into a bucket underneath the sink. The water kept flowing. He jiggled his feet, suddenly desperate for a piss. When the second cup filled up, he switched again. Three, four, five cups… half-way through the eleventh, the water stopped abruptly with an airy splurt. He continued watching the tap, willing it to come back to life, but no more came. Not a bad day – nearly two litres.

At some point the siren had stopped. After emptying the last half-filled cup into the bucket, he stood in the silence, trying to ignore the sharp pain in his bladder. Then, with one last look at the taps, he dashed over to the toilet in the opposite corner of the room. He sat down to piss, something he'd started doing recently, he didn't know why, maybe because sitting down felt like resting. He looked around his tiny flat – bed, chair, sink, toilet. It was small, but he had his own space. At least his job covered the rent so he didn't have to doss down in those dormitories on the outskirts of the city, close to the Security Wall. If you were in one of those dormitories and you lost your job, there would be nowhere else to go, just over the Wall, never to be seen again. He felt the dryness in his mouth and tried to ignore it; he would save his own water for later. Best to wait until he got to work, then he could drink their water. Even so, maybe a little sip wouldn't hurt? But that would be giving in: without self-control what have you got?

He ought to get going soon, he realised. Work didn't start for over an hour, and most days the journey took only twenty minutes, but the bus route was always changing, and if he was late it would be instant dismissal. He grabbed his overalls off the chair and put them on, sniffing quickly under each arm and grimacing. Snorting, he quoted out loud: 'We must rid ourselves of the notion that humanity is an error. It is not. Even so, it is for each of us to work out what his life is for.' He loved that book, *The Machine Society* by Erich Vinty. He'd read it maybe fifteen years ago – before the Security Wall went up. The militant atheists had accused Vinty of being a 'religionist' and called for the death penalty. The last he'd heard, Vinty had been held in detention for his own safety and then he'd suffered a mental collapse.

He sighed. Always alone: at home, at work. He thought about her again. Kneeling down, he reached under his bed and found the picture frame. Sitting on the floor with his back to the wall, he looked at the happy couple in the photograph. With his finger he traced around her face. They would have gone mad sharing a room like this. Why did he torture himself? Why didn't he throw the picture away? Their final conversation still haunted him.

'Working for who?' he'd yelled. 'I don't believe this. Last week you were agreeing with me that Krane Media are peddlers of lies and propaganda. Why are you being so two-faced?'

'Forget it,' Jane shouted, her eyes wet. 'You're right. I have sold out. But we need money, don't we? Your job hardly keeps us in the lap of luxury.'

That hurt. He'd spoken out on behalf of a bullied colleague at the school where he taught and got sacked for his trouble, along with his colleague. A job as a shop storeroom attendant in the Better Life Complex was the only work he could find. So what if it didn't pay well, at least it was a job. He'd started thinking about having a family and he didn't want Jane to work – then she'd announced she'd taken a job as a deputy assistant producer with Krane.

'What happened to your principles?' he said. 'And what happened to talking these things through? Isn't that what a marriage is about?'

'Oh, like the discussion we had before you got yourself sacked?' Jane pointed at her husband. 'You know, you talk about equal rights and all that, but deep down you're no different to other men. You're jealous because I'll be earning more than you.' Her gaze swept across the lounge as though she didn't recognise it. 'All your socialist beliefs aren't going to pay the bills. I'd rather be with a regular bloke who treats me like an equal than a right-on liberal who treats me like a shiz.'

'Frack you!' He'd spat out the words, shocked by the sound of his own venom. He'd never spoken to her like that before. She stared at him in disbelief, grabbed her bag and ran out of the house. That was the last time he saw her.

Dean put the photo back under the bed.

'Fracking work!' he said. Standing up, he checked in his pocket for his ID-card, then hurried out the door.

* * *

The bus weaved through silent back streets. Every day a slightly different route – that way the driver reduced the likelihood of encountering roadblocks. Dean had seen reports of hijackings on TV, though he'd never experienced one or met anyone who had. And what could anyone use to block the road? The streets were bare. Since the oil ran out, only a few electric cars had remained, and you needed a special permit to run one of those. The Safer Streets campaign was the government's rationale for removing all vehicles. But safer streets for whom? People stayed inside. When was the last time he'd seen a child playing outside? It was too hot and there was poison in the rain. And he rarely saw a cyclist. But no one argued against the government's edicts. What difference would it make?

He watched grey towers of concrete sliding past, entrances filled in with breezeblocks, windows boarded up, everything covered in graffiti, dust and decay. Despite the stifling heat, those buildings still looked cold. He winced and rubbed his chest, his heart tightening.

Not so long ago the bus would have been crammed full. Where had everyone gone? It didn't bear thinking about. No one made eye contact any more. No one spoke. There was nothing to say; each person reflecting the other's emptiness. His hand tightened around the card in his pocket, squeezing it until the plastic edge hurt his palm.

The journey dragged. These streets once teemed with life. Images like that could still be seen nightly on TV, if you could find a bar that had one. But where was this bustling life? Not in this part of town. Women in figure-hugging business suits rushing to work carrying take-away coffees, men with their brief-cases, women in supermarkets with shopping trolleys full: where? A fracking lie! It must be. But so brazen? Dean detected the early warnings of a migraine – on top of everything. No respite. His dry mouth prickled and he thought about the water dispenser at work.

The bus juddered and slowed down as the driver negotiated an impossibly tight bend. Coming to a near-standstill, it then sped up dramatically as it came out of the turn. It reminded Dean of car chases in the action movies he loved when he was a boy.

Rounding the next corner, the dome of the Better Life Complex came into view: New London's central mega-domicile: recreation and consumption from cradle to grave, for the elite who could afford it. The passengers stirred, sitting up, stretching, bracing themselves for the disembarkation procedure. They plunged into an underpass and soon they were pulling into the Complex's underground terminus. As they came to a stop, Dean checked his watch, relieved it was still early. He shuffled down the aisle and stepped out onto the security platform, automatically raising his arms for the tedious routine of checks and searches. He looked away, hating to see the malevolence in the guards' eyes. These guys were probably paid little more than he was, so why did they treat backroom workers like criminals? They might as well push them along with cattle prods. But then all workers hated anyone in a different grade, either envying those in a higher category or lording it over those in a lower one. When he started at Harding's Emporium, he had not fully appre-ciated how the pecking order worked. But he had learned quickly enough. Amazing how your fortunes can reverse: one day it was coffee and croissants in the staff lounge and saving up to splurge on a box seat at the Citadel Palladium; the next day you're glad of the first job you could find, with barely enough for a beer in a shizzy bar at the end of the week.

* * *

Dean sat in the corner of the storeroom at Harding's Emporium. The front-of-shop staff rarely came in here, and he'd never been into the shop; it was out of bounds. As long as he kept the storeroom neat and everything ran smoothly, the manager would leave him alone. Sometimes he'd catch a glimpse of someone through the goods hatch, but otherwise he could go for hours without seeing a soul. Except, of course, Jones, the delivery driver. But he wouldn't see Jones today. He sat close to the water dispenser: it was his water, as many as four cups for the day, and a kettle to heat it in. He shuddered. The storeroom hadn't fully warmed up yet. He thought about the adaptability of the human body and how it could acclimatise to massive changes in temperature – there was a time when he'd find 32 degrees unbearably hot. Not so now. Cradling the mug of hot water, he closed his eyes and felt a sudden urge to sleep, but something in his gut kept him alert, always ready for instructions relayed to him on the computer-com. Forcing his eyes open, he scanned the dimly lit room, taking in the grey metal shelves stacked high with sealed boxes of trinkets and gaudy gifts: *'Recreate the ambience of historic sophistication in your home with luxury facsimile reproductions of genuine works of art in 100% plastic.'* Glorified tat! The cheapest of these gifts cost double his weekly salary. But he didn't care about that. Just as long as he had a job. You had to count your blessings, and trust you couldn't possibly fall any lower.

At that moment, the storeroom door opened, making him jump. Little Clare stood there, a silhouette in front of the bright light streaming in from the shop.

'Hello!' he said.

She let out a shriek, then quickly put a hand to her chest and composed herself. 'Sorry, I didn't realise someone was in here.'

Standing up, he scratched the back of his head. 'It's OK. I guess I'm early today. I didn't mean to make you jump.' He wanted to say more but small talk didn't come easily.

'Quiet.' She put a finger to her lips, like a child caught creeping about the house after bedtime. 'Don't let the boss hear.'

'It can be our secret,' he whispered. What are you doing? Trying to flirt? He chastised himself. He'd already been down this road and discovered it went nowhere. When he'd started at Harding's – before he knew the rules, before he'd learned about the pecking order – he'd presumed it was OK to talk. He'd felt lonely in the backroom and Clare had looked the most friendly of the shop girls, in fact the only friendly one. Her style was less dramatic. The only thing she did with her hair was to wrap it in ribbons, which was nothing compared with the lacquering the others went in for.

'I was looking for something,' she said apologetically. She knew the storeroom was his patch: the pecking order worked both ways.

'Hey, it's fine,' he said. 'I mean, I don't mind. Is there anything I can get you?'

She cleared her throat. 'The New Deco clocks. It's for a front window display.' Her words speeded up. 'I've got this idea: just clocks. I mean, all the same clock. All set at different times – not the ten-to-two smiley face – different times. It could look really good if we...' She stopped speaking. She'd said 'we'. There was no 'we' anymore.

He opened his mouth to speak, then froze. He remembered, on his first day at Harding's, the look the manager had given him when he caught them talking. The implication was clear enough: *Know your place!*

'Listen, no worries. They're up here.' He rolled a ladder into place and climbed up, reaching to the back of the top shelf to pull out a large box. It always pained him to handle these pseudo antiques. He had a degree in the History of Design and an Advanced Degree in ceramics. He knew all about Art Deco and the work of Clarice Cliff and Pavel Janak, but what did that matter now? People didn't want facts anymore. 'Don't let the facts get in the way of a good story,' his university lecturer had said. 'Focus on the romance, the violence, the sex.'

Balancing carefully, Dean climbed down the ladder, one arm wrapped around the box, then stood before Clare. This was the closest he'd ever been to her.

'Thank you,' she said.

He glimpsed her parted lips, noticed her softness, her clean smell. She took the box, and he stood back, letting his gaze fall to the floor while she left the storeroom. Looking up, he saw her glancing back before she closed the door.

Locked in again. He'd reckoned Clare didn't struggle like he did; she didn't get the bus like him each day. That meant she must live somewhere in the Complex. How on earth could she afford that? Rich parents, no doubt. She seemed capable of a lot more than shop work. She could probably afford to have aspirations. So could he, not so long ago. He remembered running home to see Jane. 'I'm going to get a post at a decent university,' he'd announced as he walked in the door, throwing down his coat and striding into the kitchen. 'I've been thinking about it for ages. But today I realised I should just go for it. I want students who really care about the subject. It'll bring in a good steady income. I can lecture part-time and get stuck into research. Maybe it could lead to a book? I could get a few papers published first, make a name for myself. We can rent somewhere bigger, somewhere with enough room for kids...'

'Kids?' Jane turned round, apron on, her hands covered in flour. The alarm in her voice silenced him for the rest of the evening.

Shaking his head, he returned to his seat next to the water dispenser and finished off his mug of water, now tepid. He felt his stomach churn. He'd once read there is only happiness in the present, if you 'live in the moment'. But how do you do that? He closed his eyes and felt the emptiness in his belly and the broiling tension. There was something lurking there, something he kept trying to ignore. This time, rather than ignoring it, he reached for the hidden feeling. He could sense himself getting nearer. Be patient. What is it? Now very close... *It's fear.* The realisation hit him physically. He felt the knot in his stomach loosen slightly. *But fear of what?* An image came into his mind: the Security Wall glimpsed through the gaps between skyscrapers, always in the periphery. It was fear of the Wall. Not the Wall itself but whatever lay on the other side. Then he knew: he was afraid of annihilation.

* * *

Dean stepped off the bus and slunk along the pavement, his hands in his pockets, dawdling, waiting for the other passengers to disappear. He watched the men and women in overalls scurrying towards the high rises and getting eaten up by the concrete jaws of the towering apartment blocks. Standing still, he listened to the electric hum of the workers' bus fading out of earshot. Alone again. He shivered despite the heat – someone walking on his grave. There had been more screams last night. In the still darkness, he'd heard muted voices rise in tempo, then explode into shrill, pleading cries. These episodes were becoming more frequent, perhaps every fortnight now. In the early hours, foggy from sleep, it was difficult to discern the direction and distance the sounds were coming from, especially with the apartment walls so thin and the windows open. It felt like the screams were getting nearer, closer to his block, his floor, his apartment. Everyone knew the debt collectors favoured working in the night, when people were drowsy and less resistant.

He remembered the day the lights had short-circuited at the Emporium and he'd been sent home early. A CleanCo van was parked outside his block. Men in white overalls had passed him in the atrium, carrying black bags. He'd decided to take the stairs, peering through the glass doors on each landing. On the third floor he saw buckets outside one of the apartments. Pushing open the door, he listened. No sound. No footsteps behind him. He hurried down the corridor, slowing down as he reached the apartment. The door hung off its hinges like a broken neck. Inside, the apartment was like his, but in disarray, the bed upturned, grey overalls and a bedsheet trampled on the floor. He looked at the doorframe and inspected the charred latch. The black liquid by his feet must be blood. He knelt down to scrutinise the bloody lump of gristle in the pool of blood, nearly gagging as he did so. He could make out a fingernail, white bone: a finger cleanly severed, lasered presumably. Voices in the stairwell made him jump and he fled, sprinting to the far end of the corridor and round the corner.

Dean tried to shake off the memory by breathing deeply as he stared at his home: a cold, grey block standing blankly, like a sentry on duty. He thought about his tiny apartment and the grimy sheets that were long overdue a wash – he was trying to save up enough water. Looking around, the streets were deserted. He thought about beer, turned round and headed for Pete's Bar.

Pete's Bar squatted in the basement of one of the oldest apartment blocks in the sector, hidden down a short flight of stairs. The neon sign above the doorway had stopped working. The corrugated iron door completed the impression of dereliction. Inside, the only lights came from the table lamps, a single fluorescent strip behind the bar and the glow of the TV. Dean shuffled up to the bar and pulled out a 1,000 credit note, which was all he had to last him until the end of the week. As long as he stuck to a single beer, he figured he'd still have enough left over for a loaf of Carbohide-Right, even if he couldn't afford any Margadreame.

He slid the note across the bar top. 'Bottle of green, please.'

'Coming up.' The barman swiped the money away and

organised the drink, unlocking the refrigerator and pulling out a label-less green bottle. He poured the frothy liquid into a glass and slid it in front of Dean, followed by a handful of notes and coins.

Dean filled his pocket with the change before taking a sip. The beer had an instant impact, both shocking and relaxing. Leaning forward with his elbows on the bar, he looked up at the TV.

...another record day on the stock market. Goldthorn Plastics are up five points. Hanning Entertainments are up four points thanks to massive sales of Perry's music-bytes...

The announcers' manic commentary fizzed over a dizzying flow of images: factory production lines, sequined cabaret dancers.

...meanwhile, this week's vote is in and again the public is calling for no change in administration. This is an overwhelming vote of confidence for President Afini's ongoing efficiency cuts which will ensure a further massive boost for the economy...

Dean twisted round on his bar stool and surveyed the room. The place was empty except for an old man sat proud and upright at a small round table, his arms flat on his legs, a half-drunk glass of beer in front of him.

'Hope your shares are up.' The man smiled.

Is this guy crazy? Dean thought to himself, glancing across at the barman, now sat at the far end of the bar staring impassively at the giant TV.

'Come and join me,' the man called out, raising his glass and taking a drink.

Dean stared at him, trying to make out the expression that lay behind his thick, white beard.

Then the man called over to the barman. 'Two more drinks over here.'

The barman sorted out two drinks and took them over to White Beard's table.

'Come and join me,' said the old man. 'This drink's on me.'

Dean climbed down off his bar stool and walked over.

'Take a seat. Talk to me! Don't worry, what can I do to you? I'm old. I'm weak. There's hardly any life left in me.' He finished off his drink, then pushed one of the two fresh glasses towards Dean.

'Thank you.' Dean mustered a shy half-smile and sat down. 'I'm afraid I can't buy you one back.'

'No problem. Can you remember when it wasn't weird to have a conversation in public? I don't blame you for thinking I'm strange.'

'I don't,' said Dean, avoiding the man's gaze.

'Well, thank you, but I wouldn't blame you. You know, apart from the barman there, I haven't spoken to anyone in six weeks, not since I lost my job. Been cooped up in my apartment trying to figure out what comes next. I'm just glad my wife didn't live long enough to see this day.'

'I'm sorry about your job.'

'Yeah, well, maybe it was a blessing. I hated that job anyway. Complex. Surveillance monitor operative. They told me my eyesight was shot. But that's crap. The boss had a friend who needed a job. One time I would have taken legal action – I was a fighter in my day. But what hope would I have now? No, when your number's up...' He took a long drink.

'I don't know what to say. You're taking it very well. I mean, jobs aren't easy to come by.' Talk about stating the obvious. Dean lined up his two drinks. 'I work at the Complex.'

'Oh, yeah? Whereabouts? Maybe I've seen you on the monitors?'

'I shouldn't think so. I'm in the storeroom at Harding's Emporium.'

'Storeroom, hey? You seem too bright for that. If that fool of a manager you've got can run that place then I'm sure you could.'

Dean couldn't help laughing out loud, then, self-conscious, he looked over at the barman, who was still staring at the TV. 'You've got the measure of my boss, all right.' He squinted inquisitively at his drinking companion; his father would have been around the same age if he'd still been alive.

'So, who are you really? What's your line?'

'I used to teach design at West London Starbucks University. Seems a long time ago now.'

'Ha! Starbucks University. They were called high schools in my day. Then everything got re-branded. Schools became universities. A five-year-old kid at university, the parents loved that! I remember Starbucks too and their shizzy coffee. The good old days!'

The two men sat in silence, drinking their beer. The incessant monologue of the TV newscaster couldn't distract Dean from his thoughts. He cleared his throat and looked at his companion. 'Excuse me, could I ask you something?'

'No need to be so formal! Go ahead.'

'Yes, sorry. It's just I haven't spoken to anyone for so long, and you seem pretty clued up. The thing is…' He clinked together his glasses of beer and lowered his voice. 'What do you think's going on? I mean, all of this? The boxes we live in. The way our bosses treat us like criminals. No one speaking anymore. I mean…' He stopped. He could feel his face reddening.

The old man smiled. 'You're spot on. Trouble is, no one's asking questions anymore because we've all fallen asleep. The way I see it, they got us while we were down, while we were all traumatised. First came the Great Recession, then global warming kicked in, the poisonous rain, then the Internet went down. One disaster after another. We were helpless. Afraid. Then the people at the top made their move. Total lockdown. They put up the Security Wall.' He made a sweeping gesture with his hand. 'They claimed the Wall was for our protection.'

Dean looked over at the TV. 'Protection,' he said out loud.

'They've turned our brains into mulch. All this bollocks about the Big Democracy. Voting on some hyped-up issue every week. When was the last time you voted?'

'Erm, I wouldn't like to say,' said Dean, looking again to see what the barman was doing.

...do you lack pep in the morning? Try spreading your toast with new formula Margadreame. Tests show it will make you 14 per cent healthier...

'All I know is, I've never voted! Not since they introduced the New System.' The man placed his hands flat on the table. 'We used to vote for people, for political systems, for ideas, for change. At least, that was the theory. Then they introduced Total Democracy. A referendum for every new policy. But no one has the slightest understanding of the issues they're voting for, so why bother? That box of lies in the corner is the only source of information we have: soundbites and sex – that's all we want, that's all we need! They've won.' He picked up his drink and downed it in one.

Dean wiped his hand across his forehead. 'I feel ill,' he said.

'It's the beer. They poison it,' the old man said matter-of-factly.

'I'll be fine. I think I should go.' He stood up, but didn't move. 'Empires all fall in the end, don't they?'

'We'll see.'

Dean breathed out heavily and pointed at what was left of his beer. 'You can finish mine.'

The old man raised his glass in salute. He looked like the last man on the Titanic.

'I've got to go.' Dean turned and headed for the exit. On the way out he saw the barman jotting something down on an old e-pad. Dean quickened his pace, almost running up the steps outside, then stopping to catch his breath. The TV was loud, he thought, surely the barman hadn't heard them.

Back home, lying on his bed, he went over his conversation with the old man. He closed his eyes and tried to imagine how tomorrow could be different.

* * *

Next day, Dean sat in the corner of the storeroom with his head in his hands. The night before had brought the familiar dream: back at his grandma's house, at the bottom of the garden, the gate and the wood beyond. Only, this time, when he put his hand on the latch of the gate there was no one calling him back, so he went through. He jumped over the gurgling stream, it felt exhilarating, the freedom, the prospect of adventure. But the deeper he got into the wood, the darker it became. Fear bubbled up. He turned round to make his way back but didn't know which way to go. He started running, sensing that the further he went, the more lost he would become.

Dean sat bolt upright in his chair, trying to forget the dream, the fears, and everything else: the old man in Pete's Bar and the screams in the night. He stood up and looked at the boxes of merchandise piled up around him. Sedatives, distractions, he thought.

The computer-com started blinking, calling him to attention. He went over to read the screen: 'Hologram Seascape G607: Ref 43.2.4.5.' He placed the flat of his hand on the screen prompting the computer to give a Storeroom Location Code. He turned and started hunting for the right box. The backs of his eyes throbbed as he checked the codes on the metal-frame shelves. The box he needed was right at the top, stuck away at the back. *Always at the fracking back.* He climbed up the ladder and felt his back twinge as he tried to manoeuvre the right box down with the least amount of re-arranging other containers. Then he carefully navigated his way back down, balancing the item. He put it down by the serving hatch and tapped the reference number into the panel on the side of the box. When he'd done so, the hatch slid up.

'About time,' said Coleman, the boss, waiting on the other side, only visible from the neck down to the waist.

Dean remained silent, digging his fingers into the sides of the box as he thrust it towards Coleman.

'Careful, you Peri!' Coleman bent down, eyeing Dean with contempt. 'It'll come out of your wages if there's any damage.' Coleman yanked the box away and strode off.

Dean hated the term 'Peri'. Anyone who didn't live in the Complex was a 'Peri', short for Perimeter. But behind the insults lay people's fears. That thought was some comfort.

Protocol dictated that storeroom assistants close the hatch immediately after handing over merchandise, but he saw Clare over near the shop entrance. He watched her, liking the way she gestured with her hands while she talked to an obese afro-haired woman with orange skin. Clare's enthusiastic tones sounded to him like life-energy. So rare. But whatever she was saying, the fat woman looked unimpressed; either that or she was pulling a poker face to try and drive a hard bargain. Suddenly, he became aware of someone creeping up to the hatch. A child, maybe aged around nine, was pointing a green plastic laser gun at him.

'You're a Peri!' said the boy with a sneer. 'I heard what that man called you. You're a Peri and I'm gonna kill you. You naughty Peri!'

Dean's jaw clenched while he weighed up his options. Snatching the stupid gun and snapping it in two was one. He held his breath and let the anger pass. Then a jet of water hit him in the face. He stared wide-eyed at the boy. *A water gun! Water! What stupid parent would let their child waste water like that?* Reaching out, he snatched the gun and – he couldn't stop himself – squirted the boy in the chest. The boy burst into tears, screaming as if the gun had been real, and ran towards the orange woman with the afro.

Dean stood there, helpless, as he watched the drama unfold, the green gun clutched tightly to his chest. Coleman was trying to mollify the orange woman, her face a knot of anger. The child was pointing in Dean's direction. Now Coleman was looking at him too, his eyes full of malice.

* * *

Coleman could have gloated more. When he handed Dean his papers he simply pointed at his watch and said, 'Work 'til five, then go and don't come back.'

Working until the end of the day was like walking slowly towards a cliff edge. They could have pressed charges, but maybe they wanted to make sure he left quietly. They even let him ride home on the workers' bus. The Emporium would have a replacement by morning. Dean would have nothing.

Walking from the drop-off point to his apartment block, Dean felt his numbness starting to thaw. He wished he'd smashed that gun – or fired it in the kid's face. He should have fired it at Coleman instead. No, he should have leapt through the hatch, punched Coleman in the face and smashed the place up. What difference would it make, anyway? A small crime, a big crime, it all ended the same fracking way. He could feel the Security Wall getting closer. The back of his neck prickled. He vowed to drink every drop of water when he got home. And that tin of tuna he'd been saving: his mouth filled with saliva at the thought of devouring it. He had no savings, nothing of value. The debts kept piling up in some unfathomable way: his rent, income tax, the government democracy charge – everything was worked out daily on the basis of constantly fluctuating interest rates. All he knew was, no job meant no life. Did he have days, hours, minutes? Perhaps Jane could help him get another job. But how could he find her?

Arriving at his apartment block, he decided to take the stairs. His thin shoes scraped on the chalky concrete steps, echoing in the tomb of the stairwell. He examined the flaking paint on the stairwell walls. *Everything, from the moment it is created, is in a process of decay.* Pausing by the door on the third floor landing, he peered through the panel of reinforced glass. He tried to remember the exact apartment where he had seen the finger, and wondered who lived there now. But what did it matter anyway? One faceless clone is much like another.

Back in his apartment, he headed straight to the sink, took one of the plastic cups, and knelt down to dip it in the water bucket. He closed his eyes and tipped the water into his mouth. After just half a cup, to his surprise, he felt like he'd had enough. Not the ecstatic experience he'd imagined. Putting the cup back, he moved over to sit on the edge of the bed. Even the tuna didn't interest him now. Why was life so disappointing? They lied, cheated and manipulated. They controlled you and you could do nothing to stop it. Life was supposed to be so precious but, when it came down to it, you didn't really know what to do with it. Falling sideways, he curled up on his bed, foetus-like, a wave of tiredness finally calming his restless thoughts.

* * *

The groceries on the kitchen table, tins and packets, were stacked and piled high, like a wall.

'Jane. Why did you go?' he asked out loud.

The world had turned black and white, and it was getting hotter.

'I haven't gone. I'm right here!'

Dean turned and looked at his partner. 'But you left me?' He felt himself shrinking, becoming tiny, helpless.

'I didn't leave you. You left me.' Jane spoke the words, but they were his words too, spoken in unison.

The room started spinning. A colourless kaleidoscope. He could feel himself falling. Jane reached out towards him, but he was slipping off the floor, slipping down, falling away, getting closer to the edge...

It took Dean a moment to remember where he was. In the darkness, he lay in a foetal position, his muscles aching. He rolled slowly onto his back and tried to guess the time, then decided he didn't care. The thought of switching on the light made him feel sick: light means life and anyway, electricity costs money. But then, for all he knew, he was probably being charged regardless. He imagined his debt as a row of numbers spinning on a meter, the figure getting higher and higher. The strange thing was that *right now* he felt OK. Despite everything, right now, something felt fine. He focused in on the feeling. Some part of him felt good. Jane would have called it self-pity. She used to say that playing the victim was just a neat way of avoiding responsibility. Maybe she was right. He didn't want to think about it. Too complicated. Hold onto the good feeling, at least until the hunger and thirst kick in and the debt unravels. He imagined himself back at Pete's Bar, looking for the old man. They'd have a drink together, have a moan about the system, tell everyone to go frack themselves.

Rolling over, he tried to find his way back to his dream, to Jane in the spinning kitchen...

* * *

He woke again, his heart jumping. Still darkness. He sat up in bed, the sweat-soaked sheet falling off his frame. He ran his hands through his hair – there was some comfort in motor action – and the panic started to subside. *That feeling of fear again.*

The night felt blacker than usual, the air more cloying. Dead silence. Was this a panic attack? Or maybe it was 'night terrors', but isn't that what happened to children? Children were afraid of everything, but adults were meant to be logical, in control of their emotions.

Laying back down, he tried thinking about something else. What would he do tomorrow? He'd have to be resourceful. Contact anyone and everyone he could think of. Ask around about work, about cheaper apartments, consider any option. Surely there would be cleaning work? He could move further downtown. It wasn't as if he needed a swanky address to impress anyone. He thought about Jane. If only he could talk to her, apologise. Things hadn't been so bad, had they? But why would she want him now? A penniless skeleton going downhill fast. Downhill, he thought, and he remembered being a child speeding downhill on the sledge his father had made that winter when the snow came up to his knees. His dad, in his big old coat with the woolly collar, had given him a push start. He'd crashed at the bottom of the hill. Lying in a ball of laughter, his father had brushed the snow off his anorak. Then they'd both collapsed into fits of laughter for no real reason. He had no words for it at the time, but he knew what it was now: he'd felt happy, he'd felt safe.

* * *

Despite having had a bad night, Dean woke early, as usual, his body clock warning him to be ready for the siren. He groaned and rubbed his eyes, then remembered he had no work to go to and briefly felt glad he could take it easy. Who the frack wanted to work anyway? Working hard to pay the bills, just to keep the show on the road… an endless cycle until you died. If that was all there was, then why not save yourself the hassle and give up on the whole damn thing? Of course, it wasn't that simple. Survival instincts tended to get in the way.

Untangling himself from his bedsheet, he sat up and swivelled round so his feet were touching the floor. He would collect the day's water and then, if he felt like it, go back to bed.

He stood up and shuffled to the sink. Looking in the mirror, he was shocked by his pale skin and the bags under his eyes. Then, picking up a cup, he steadied himself to collect the daily water ration. Something stirred in him. No, he thought, I won't give up hope! He decided he would go down to the bus stop and talk to whoever was there. Ask them to listen out for vacancies. Tell them he would return the next day. He would visit company headquarters and fill out forms, whatever it took to get his name on their files. If his timing was right, with a bit of luck, he could find something. It was going to be OK.

The taps spluttered into life. Three litres – a good sign! He looked back in the mirror and thought the bags under his eyes maybe didn't look so bad. In fact, if he was a French existentialist philosopher, or some such, people might say he had a look of romantic intensity. Maybe this time he could find a job that better suited him. All he needed was an opportunity for the chiefs to glimpse his skills and qualities and things would pick up.

Excited, he washed quickly. Automatically, he picked up his work overalls, then he paused: he didn't have to wear them. But what else did he have? Without enough water or detergent to clean anything other than essentials, all his other clothes had been packed away underneath the bed. Throwing down his overalls, he fell to the floor, reaching and rummaging under the bed for whatever he could find. He pulled out a small rucksack. In it he found a couple of T-shirts, an old favourite jumper and – to his delight – a formal black shirt, something he used to save for special occasions. This was what he'd wear today. In another bag he found a couple of pairs of trousers. He'd forgotten about these also, and they seemed clean enough.

He finished getting ready, treating himself to a morning glass of water and a Better Life Nutri-Bar. He stepped out into the corridor and shut the door – then stopped dead. In a flurry he plunged his hands into his pockets – thank frack, he had it! He pulled the ID-card out of his pocket and kissed it.

He walked quickly to the stairwell – too quickly. Why was he rushing? Slow down. Breathe.

Stepping out of his apartment block, the blazing sun hit him. Looking around, he could see a kind of industrial beauty in the sheer concrete walls and the grey metal window frames. The scarred grey dirt where grass had once grown looked like a Zen garden.

A handful of people were waiting at the bus stop. He slowed down, hesitating. There were a couple of people he recognised, though he'd never spoken to them. People didn't speak, so what would they think if he approached them? He imagined the situation reversed. If someone approached him he'd feel embarrassed, or something like pity. Or maybe, if someone was begging him for work, he'd assume they'd done something wrong or else they were an unemployable misfit or lazy or unreliable. After all, isn't unemployment the individual's fault? Wasn't that true in his case? He was irresponsible, *just like Jane had said.*

He stood still, self-conscious. Now he was a loiterer. He felt his face prickling, turning red. He was a cog without a machine. A spare part. 'Come on, Dean,' he whispered to himself. 'It's tough, but you can do it. Just walk up to the guy at the back, or even speak to them all at once while there's only four of them. What's the worst that can happen?' The worst that could happen was that all of his remaining pride would evaporate.

Dean turned and hid himself around the nearest corner. He would take a moment – gird his loins, so to speak – then approach them. But even now he could hear the bus in the distance. It was now or never. Crouching down against the wall of an apartment block, he closed his eyes. The bus engine revved as it drew nearer, closer and closer. He wiped his forehead, now dripping with sweat. He heard the bus pull up, heard its breaks go on, the electric whine of the engine quietened. He closed his eyes, felt his adrenalin racing, but couldn't move his legs. Then the bus engine fired up again as it moved on.

It took a long time until the sound of the engine had faded into silence. Maybe he could come back tomorrow, try again? He stood up, heart thumping, and started walking, not knowing where to go, not wanting to head home. The piercing sun was blinding. He needed to get indoors. He turned a corner and saw the sign for Pete's Bar. It was so early, but he remembered the sign on the door said '24 Hours'.

He lingered outside, checking up and down the street, not wanting anyone to see him go in. But, once inside, it was as if the morning had vanished. It felt like evening; the same mausoleum atmosphere as last time – the same emptiness.

The barman began uncapping a bottle of green as soon as he saw him, holding Dean's gaze for a moment, non-judgemental. He would make a good priest, thought Dean, administering the sacraments of beer and snacks. A smile threatened to break through his numbness.

He chose a bar stool and accepted the bottle placed in front of him. Before taking a drink, he surveyed the empty bar, hoping to see the old man. But there was no one. 'Just you and me!' He sighed.

'Seems so.'

Dean stared at the barman, shocked that he had responded, and looked away. There was a warmth in his voice he hadn't detected during his last visit. 'Big day for me today,' said Dean, taking a hit on his beer.

The barman nodded, picked up a cloth and gave the bar top a wipe.

It took a while before Dean realised it was silent in the bar. His eyes flicked up to the blank TV screen.

The barman must have noticed. 'Gets on your nerves after a while,' he said.

Dean shifted, uncomfortable in his seat, so rare was the experience of hearing a voice not simply issuing orders. 'Yes,' he said eventually. 'I suppose it must.'

'Drivel.'

'Drivel,' Dean agreed.

The barman busied himself re-arranging a small selection of bottles.

'That man,' said Dean, 'the old man who was in here the other night, will he be coming in?' He didn't even know his name.

The barman stopped and looked over to the empty table where the old man had been sitting. 'No, I don't think we'll be seeing him again.'

Dean couldn't stop himself asking the next inevitable

question. 'No? Why's that?' He didn't want to hear the answer.

The barman looked down for a little while. 'When someone can afford to drink here, it usually means they won't be around much longer.'

Just like that, the walls closed in and the panic re-surfaced. He swallowed hard, his head down, hoping the barman hadn't noticed. He imagined the old man returning to his lonely apartment, tipsy, maybe drunk, penniless, hopeless... but Dean stopped short of picturing the next scene. He realised he hadn't paid for his drink and reached into his pocket, looking for change.

'That one's on the house,' said the barman.

That did it. His body shaking, Dean's head dropped onto his forearms and he let the tears flow out.

* * *

Back in his apartment, Dean sat on the edge of his bed, his posture twisted, staring out of the window. The sun glowed chemical orange, the end of another blistering day. He watched the shifting patterns of the clouds. Behind it all, no matter what humans did, nature, the whole universe, remained indifferent. He shifted position and lay on his bed, eyes wide open. What was the use of a human brain – thinking all the time – more trouble than it's worth? When they first met, Jane used to like it when he talked like that. But, as the years went by, she started telling him to stop being 'maudlin'. She just got on with things.

'Oh, come on,' he remembered her saying one time, perhaps realising she'd upset him. 'Let's go out and do something. Cheer ourselves up!'

'We can't afford it.'

'We don't have to buy anything. We could just walk, talk. I don't know, look at things!'

'There's nothing to look at!'

Finally, she'd lost her patience. 'Forget it, then. Sit there in your misery. I'll go out by myself.'

Dean winced at the memory. Over time, the arguments had grown more heated, more hopeless, until the day she didn't come back. But was it his fault? Maybe no one was to blame? They just spoke different languages, saw the world differently. They were both shouting to be heard but neither could understand what the other was saying. He wondered what Jane was doing at this moment? Surely she had done the right thing, moving out? Right now, he wouldn't wish himself on anyone.

He closed his eyes and let the anaesthesia of sleep take over, pressing delete on the day.

* * *

Something moving. Unfamiliar sounds. Lying in the stillness, Dean strained his eyes to see into the murky grey light. He must have been asleep for hours. It was too early for the siren. A scratching – shuffling. Someone was outside his apartment. Adrenalin peaked. Time stopped.

DAT DAT DAT DAT!!!

His hand shaking, he fumbled to open the door. Two guards stood there, one to the fore – giant in his regulation body armour, the other behind him holding a laser.

'Yes?' asked Dean, head spinning.

'Dean Rogers?' The guard's voice deadpan, eyes hidden behind a brown visor.

'Yes.' Dean looked down the corridor. He thought about the Wall. He thought about Jane. He thought about the heat – the fracking relentless heat.

'Dean Rogers. Formerly of Harding's Emporium?'

'Yes.' He felt a rush of anger. Futile to express it. Patience needed. The guard at the back hid behind a visor too. He turned his head away when Dean glanced in his direction.

More silence. Why were they playing games?

'Look,' Dean tried to steady his voice. 'Could you please tell me what I've done?'

'What you've done?' said the guard, a thin smile below the visor. 'That's an interesting question. Have you done something we should know about?' He turned round to his partner, who shrugged his shoulders in response.

Dean imagined his neighbours, ears pressed to their doors, listening. 'I haven't done anything. I'm just trying to live my life.' Don't let them see your fear. Anything but that.

'That's what everyone says,' said the guard.

'So, what now? Come quietly? Don't resist?'

The guard looked at his partner again. Dean imagined he was rolling his eyes, but the visor made it impossible to tell. He turned back to Dean. 'If you say so.'

'Let me get some things.' He tried to shut the door, but it jammed. He looked down. The guard had put his boot in the way. Dean stared at the guard and noticed his reflection in the visor made him look tiny. He turned round and looked at his apartment. He couldn't think of anything that would have any practical use, nor had he any valuables. Some old clothes. A tin of tuna. What's the first thing you'd save if your house was on fire? He scrambled down onto the floor and reached under the bed, pulling everything out. A brief panic until he found what he was looking for: the photograph of him and Jane. He never liked the bulky frame – something Jane bought from a charity shop when she was going through a kitsch phase. He turned it over and pulled off the back, took out the photograph, folded it and put it into his shirt pocket. He gave his apartment one last look, his eyes now accustomed to the light.

* * *

The air outside had a thin texture, as though it had holes in it, as though there wasn't enough of it. The guards walked either side of him towards their armoured van. The first guard opened the rear door. Dean cowered as he stepped inside, expecting a whack on the back of his head, but nothing came. The door shut and, with a judder, the electric engine sparked into life. As the van moved off, he put his hand on his pocket, checking the photo was there. Then, blood draining from his face, he quickly checked his wrist then all his pockets... no watch and no ID-card. He'd left them behind. 'Frack.'

He looked through heavily tinted windows, watching his apartment block disappear from view. He couldn't say he'd ever loved the place, but it had been home. Jane would have been horrified to live somewhere like that. And he briefly felt glad his dad was not alive to see what had become of him. Not because he would have been disappointed, but because it would have broken his heart. When he was a boy, Dean loved to sit in the back of the family car and listen to his dad effusing over some new favourite topic. Sometimes Dean couldn't tell if his dad was angry – he would be saying something about the government or the television, using long words. Then Mum would laugh and Dean would know that everything was OK; he could relax. Outside the car the world was complicated and frustrating, but on the back seat, behind his father, he had felt safe.

From the van window, he could see the Better Life Complex coming into view. They were in a part of town he didn't recognise. But before he could get his bearings, the outside world disappeared from view. The sun went out. They were underground. Dean hadn't thought to ask where he was going. He simply assumed they wouldn't tell him. He told himself the shaking in his body was due to the vibration of the van.

Eventually they came to a halt. There was the sound of doors clunking open and shut, movement outside the van, then the rear door opened. Dean stepped outside to find himself in a dank underground terminus. The air carried the smell of disinfectant.

Other armoured vans stood in parking bays, some of them hooked up to electricity re-chargers.

'This way.'

The guards led him towards a metal hatch, one in front, one behind. The guard in front lifted up his visor to look into the eye-recognition monitor. 'Sebastian T316 Home Security.'

A computerised voice replied: 'Identity accepted.'

With his visor up, the guard's face was visible. A chubby, ordinary face, more like a plumber or a cleaner than a trooper. But then, what did troopers look like? They were only regular people, paid to do a job. It was the uniform that was frightening: the permission to do violence that it bestowed on the person wearing it. Even so, Dean doubted he could do that job.

They were inside the building now, walking down dimly lit corridors. Dingy, dusty underfoot. Less frequently used, he imagined, than the ones at the back of the Better Life Complex.

'Why am I here?' Dean asked the guard in front.

The guard didn't turn around. 'I wondered when you were going to ask that.'

'I mean, do I have to be here? Can I go?'

'Did we make you come with us?'

The question stunned Dean. Then it occurred to him – they hadn't used force. They hadn't arrested him. They hadn't even touched him. So why had he followed them so willingly, without protest? Fear of authority. He'd felt compelled to, as though obliged to play his role in an avant-garde play. Maybe he'd followed them because he had wanted to.

In silence, they continued, in an elevator, then down more corridors, until they arrived at a plain grey door. A small 3D sign read: 'Home Security Ops 107.'

The guard knocked. No eye recognition? No swipe cards?

'Come in,' came the reply. A man's voice.

The door slid open and Dean followed the guard inside. A middle-aged man in a light-blue suit sat behind a desk reading a book. It was the first time Dean had seen anyone with a book in years. Harding's Emporium sometimes stocked books as antique artefacts, but there was little demand.

The man closed his book, put it down and smiled. 'Take a seat, Dean.' He pointed at the empty chair facing him across the desk. Then he looked blankly at the guard. 'Thank you, T316. Good job. And your partner, there.' He flicked a hand in the direction of the other man, now out in the corridor. 'This will be noted for your appraisal.'

'Very good, chief.' The guard looked briefly at Dean, his expression empty, before turning to leave, shutting the door behind him.

Dean and the man were alone. The office couldn't have been more basic. A grey square with nothing on the walls, just a desk and two chairs.

'It's borrowed. Not my usual office. It's better this way. More discreet.'

Dean didn't know what to say. With the guards gone he tried to calibrate the level of threat. Perhaps this man carried a gun.

'Try and relax, Dean. We're just going to have a conversation.' The man studied him. 'Do you enjoy reading? Here...' He pushed his book towards Dean.

A simple white jacket. Dean's stomach turned when he read the title, written in stark black letters on a white background: The Machine Society by Erich Vinty. An illustration depicted a clockwork man with a key sticking out of his back.

'Know his work?'

Was this a trick question? 'I'm aware of it.'

'Only aware of it? Surely you've read it? It's a classic.'

'But it was banned. He was banned.'

'He certainly was. *"That which is not conducive to maintaining the status quo will be eliminated, silenced or, better still, co-opted as part of the system. The latter is preferable because, in this way, the Machine can retain an illusion of democracy."* I must have read it twenty times, maybe more. He was a genius. Still is for all I know.'

'Still is? I thought he was...' Dean was going to say 'murdered'. 'I thought he was dead. Or gone mad or something.'

'Yes. Something like that. But we still have this. His magnum opus. It's like a bible in my line of work.'

The room had a slight echo. The flat, plain surfaces gave nothing away. They sat in silence. With nothing in particular to look at, Dean returned his gaze to the book, then had a sudden feeling that he shouldn't give it too much attention, so he looked at the man and smiled weakly. The man's clothes were simple but expensive. He was clean shaven but for a three-stripe goatee. Clean living, Dean suspected. His face and skin suggested middle-age, while his hair had life, showing no signs of receding. Of course, with cosmetics...

'You don't say much,' said the man. 'You don't know why you're here, but you haven't asked me anything. You don't know my name. You don't know who I work for. Of course, I realise this must all be deeply unsettling.' He paused. 'The name's Ferry, by the way. Call me Ferry.'

These mind games were more unnerving than the guards. Brute force can wipe out a life, but this was different. Dean weighed his words. 'People don't talk much these days. I guess I've got used to listening. Can't be too careful.'

'Quite right!' Ferry stood up and straightened invisible creases out of his suit. As he moved it changed colour slightly, darkening with a hint of pin-stripe. 'You say people don't talk much, but some people talk a lot. Perhaps they're making up for the rest of us.'

'Maybe.'

Ferry stared impassively at Dean. 'That's a very non-committal response. You say "maybe", but I wonder what you're really thinking. Are you inscrutable or do you lack conviction? Maybe you lack confidence in yourself, is that it?'

He shifted in his chair. 'I don't like this psychoanalysis stuff.'

'No? Vinty was a psychoanalyst.'

'Was he?' Dean couldn't hide his surprise.

Ferry laughed. 'Now we're getting somewhere, an honest response!'

Perhaps Ferry suspected he was a Vintian. Maybe that's what all this was about.

'Look, let's move things along a bit. There's a lot at stake. I want you to tell me about yourself. Make sure our stories tally. Make sure you and I are on the same page.'

Dean wiped his hands on his trousers. 'I don't understand. Is this about what happened yesterday?'

Ferry sat back in his chair. 'Yesterday? What happened yesterday?'

'At work. The thing with the boy and the water pistol. I had a rash moment. I plan to get another job soon, then I can continue to pay my bills and the rent.'

'Nothing happened yesterday.' Ferry shrugged his shoulders.

Dean felt his fingers slip off the cliff edge. Free fall.

'Nothing happened yesterday,' repeated Ferry. 'Yesterday is history. Now tell me something more.'

'What about? Don't you know everything about me?'

'Start at the beginning.'

'The beginning?'

'Yes.' Ferry was a blank slate.

'OK,' he started tentatively. 'I grew up in the north of England. A rural suburb of Lancaster, sorry, Gap-caster as it's called now. Normal childhood. Me, my parents, my sister. Normal school. In the Great Recession my dad's business took a nosedive. He was a craftsman, of the old school. Handy work. Wicker furniture for the garden, bird tables, rabbit hutches. Those walls, with all the stones that fit together.'

Ferry rolled his eyes. 'Why so much detail?'

'Right, yes, so that was Dad. Mum was a teaching assistant at a starter school. She doubled up with secretarial work when Dad's business went under. She worked at my school, in fact.'

Dean paused and swallowed hard. This was a story he didn't often get to tell. He could picture his parents clearly. A happy family. He and his little sister Meg grew up shielded from everything that was going on: the wars around the world, the economic collapse, the diminishing resources, global warming, the water crisis. But around the age of ten, reality hit home. He heard his parents talking in their bedroom. There was something unsettling about the tone of their voices. He sat outside the door and listened. Something about having to sell the house and send Dean to live with Aunt Beth in London so he could continue with a decent education. Dad thought this was best, but Mum said the family should stick together. Dad said his sister was family and they could visit and even use the new technology to keep in touch.

'So, in my teens I moved to London to live with my aunt. I did well at school, West London Starbucks University. Got into the system, so to speak. In fact, after graduating I returned to Starbucks to teach design. Met my wife there, she worked in the office.'

Ferry sat as still as a stone.

The next part of the story was difficult. 'Then there was the London War. It was difficult. It wasn't a good time to be a northerner but Jane – erm, my wife – she's from London, so we had to make a choice. During the amnesty, my aunt left to go back to be with my parents, and I got a London passport so I could stay with Jane. We had a flat. I wanted us to have children.'

He checked himself. Too much information. Too much detail. Ferry stared, poker faced.

'So, they started putting up the Wall. Then communications went down.' He swallowed. 'I didn't hear again from my family but, obviously, I've seen the pictures. The scorched earth, the drought, the bomb sites.'

The worst thing was not being able to say goodbye to anyone. He'd had to choose between his family and his wife. Not just that. In London he had a job he liked and the prospect of a family of his own. And as much as he loved his family, why would he want to go back to the sticks?

'So I stayed in London, I mean, New London. I had to identify the bodies of my family by video link. Of course, it was impossible to tell.'

It was the most gruesome, horrible, painful experience. Bureaucratic nonsense. They couldn't organise the economy or stabilise food rations, but they still insisted on completing their forms, admin, number crunching, statistics. Perhaps that's what people do in a crisis, they can't do anything of practical use, but they have to keep busy, even if the work they're doing is futile.

'Bringing the story up to date. Jane and I...' Something told Dean he wasn't in trouble. Maybe he didn't need to give Ferry any of this information. Hadn't Ferry indicated this himself: talk little, leave out the detail? 'Jane and I decided to part company.'

What came next? Losing his job at Starbucks University? Losing his job at Harding's Emporium? According to Ferry nothing happened yesterday, so maybe nothing happened at Starbucks either. He decided to end his story there.

Ferry watched him. This time Dean could hold his gaze.

'Good,' said Ferry. 'So, according to what I've just heard, you moved to London, got married then separated, which means you still have a nice flat and a nice job. Let's forget the rest.'

Dean was desperate to ask about the Wall, his debts, Harding's, but he sensed something was going his way.

Opening a desk drawer, Ferry pulled out a glinting ID-card bearing a Better Life logo and pushed it across the desk top. 'Dean, you've no doubt heard many rumours about what life is like outside the Wall. But that needn't concern you because I'm giving you this golden opportunity.'

What did Ferry mean, mentioning the Wall like that? Was that a threat?

'This ID-card is your hope for a new life. You're a lucky man. Not many people are given this chance. You've been chosen. There are many like you who fall off the bottom of the ladder, but you managed to hold onto the bottom wrung. And I'm reaching out to pull you up. I've got a job for you, providing you can keep your eyes open and your mouth closed. You'll be working for me inside the Better Life Complex. If anyone asks about where you've come from, just tell them you're working for Starbucks University, let's say, doing a little research. You and Jane have just parted company. Let's end your story there. You're single and you've just upgraded to a nice new apartment, and you'll find some new clothes in there too.'

Dean knew he was being manipulated. There must be a catch, but for the life of him he couldn't work out what it was.

'The alternative is – how did you put it – scorched earth. I think that's how you described it out there. So what's it going to be?'

Dean thought about the screams in the middle of the night and the finger lying in that pool of blood outside the apartment. He remembered the old guy in Pete's Bar. Ferry's offer sounded good; it also sounded like a trap. An informant? Is that what was being asked of him? But not informing on people he knew, only on the rich elite in the Better Life Complex? Even if this was just a stay of execution, it sounded a hell of a lot more desirable than scorched earth. 'I'll do it.'

'Good to have you on board.' Ferry held out his hand. His handshake was firm. 'The first thing we need to do is tidy you up a bit. But, remember, keep this shut.' He indicated his mouth. 'The important thing to remember is that we'll come to you.'

'So I just wait in my apartment? I don't do anything?'

'Like I say, we'll come to you. Hopefully you won't have to wait too long. In the meantime, if you get bored, maybe do a little reading.' Ferry pointed at The Machine Society. 'That's a gift from me.'

'Thank you,' said Dean, picking up the book and turning it over in his hands.

Part II: The Better Life Complex

'Imagine a machine that can convince people they are awake when really they are asleep.'
Erich Vinty

Where's the catch? The question kept going through Dean's mind. Everything had a sense of unreality. That sense of falling, waiting to hit the ground.

He was collected by a thin man in a tight purple suit, who walked with quick, short steps. 'We can't have you arriving in tinsel town looking like a hobo,' the man said. 'Time for a scrub up! We're going to the Better Life Complex Aesthetic Technology Centre.'

'Where?' Dean asked. When the man repeated himself, Dean replied: 'Oh, you mean a beauty parlour?'

'It's a little more sophisticated than that.'

True. There were intensive treatments for the whole body. Hair removed or refolliclised. Teeth aligned and whitened. Nails manicured. Skin photo shopped, with colourant and blemishes removed. There were injections for facelifts – tightening the skin – no messy surgery. But Dean drew the line at his eyes; he didn't want anyone lasering or otherwise interfering with them.

At the end of it all, he looked in the mirror and saw a stranger staring back at him. The dark rings under his eyes had all but vanished. He thought he looked like a poster: spruced up, polished – handsome, even – but unreal: airbrushed and plastic. 'What's your persona?' the technician kept asking, 'you need to find it and live it.' This was what it must be like backstage at a TV talent show. It seemed with enough money anyone could be made to look half decent – and here was the proof. Looking into the mirror, he posed and puckered his lips like a model.

'That's a good look for you,' said the technician, his brow furrowed, stroking his chin.

Then a second assistant joined them, a man who specialised in couture. 'OK. So what do we have here?' He struck the same pose as the first technician, studying Dean as if he was a mathematical problem.

Looking Dean up and down, the first assistant offered a commentary on his own efforts so far. 'As you can see, we've gone for the basics – very pure, simple, classic look. Good work, so far. Now I'm looking for the twist. Who is he? The broody intelligent type or maybe the rebel?' He put a finger to his lips.

'I can see him as the rebel,' said the second technician. 'Definitely. The classic styling provides the foundation and, on top of that, I think we can give him a rebellious twist.'

'But nothing too serious,' said the first. 'Not like he's going to bring down the system!'

'No, of course not. I'm thinking something a little more satirical. Cheeky, even.' His face lit up. 'I've got it!' he exclaimed. 'I've absolutely got it.'

The first technician looked at him, head wobbling with excitement, hands cupped in prayer. 'Go on, I'm waiting – this is going to be genius, I know it.'

'Are you ready?'

'Go on.'

'A tartan tie!'

'I absolutely love it!' The first assistant clapped his hands. 'Simon, you're a genius!'

Dean said nothing.

There followed a thorough medical examination, after which Dean was handed a small imitation leather satchel containing pills and supplements. 'You need to be beautiful on the inside as well as the outside,' the nurse told him. There was a drug that claimed to reduce anxiety by lowering your IQ; the less you are able to cognate, the less you are able to formulate your worries, so the theory went.

One of the bottles contained red, star-shaped tablets. *NewDay-NewU: Deep Sleep Rejuvenation.* He remembered seeing the adverts on TV back when he was with Jane.

'What's going on?' he remembered saying. 'Does someone want the whole population addicted to drugs?'

'They're just for vain people,' Jane said. 'Probably nothing in them. Just expensive placebos.'

'I'm not so sure. They put stuff in them, I reckon. They're trying to control our minds.'

'You're so cynical.' Jane smiled. 'You always think the worst of people.'

'I tell you, they're controlling our minds!' Leaping up, he ran around the room holding his head. 'Help me, Jane! I'm losing my mind!'

After two days in the Aesthetic Technology Centre, he was given the all-clear for his new assignment. Detective work, in theory, going undercover.

Finally, he was escorted to his new home in the Better Life Complex, by a woman this time. These assistants all looked like movie stars, but, then, so did he now.

There were so many questions he wanted to ask, but Ferry's words kept replaying in his mind: *'I've got a job for you, providing you can keep your eyes open and your mouth shut.'* But what did that mean? He hadn't wanted to ask too many questions in case he didn't like the answers. Too anxious to get out of there. *'We'll come to you,'* Ferry had said. Be patient, Dean told himself, keep your head down and wait.

* * *

'We're entering through the rear,' said Dean's escort, standing close to him in the elevator. She wasn't tall but stood level with Dean due to incredibly high heels. 'We're here to service all Better Life residents,' she said. 'If you need me, you can contact me via your apartment info pad.'

'So maybe I'll be seeing more of you?'

'Only if you want to.' The escort winked. Then she reeled off the small print in a quick monotone. *'Service providers – cleaners and administration staff – can only access apartments via the owners' permission, but cannot otherwise gain access to the Complex interior. All staff have agreed to have implants under their skin. If a staff member attempts to leave an apartment and proceed into the Complex the implants will set off an alarm. Contact us for a range of attractive price plans.'* The escort paused and looked Dean in the eye. 'So if you need a bit of a scrub and a polish, you know who to call.' She raised an eyebrow.

It was difficult to hold her gaze. 'Thank you, I'll keep that in mind.'

The escort shrugged her shoulders and looked away obtrusively, giving Dean an opportunity to inspect her figure, with her flat stomach, deep cleavage and round hips. Oddly, nothing moved in that solid looking plastic dress. Were those curves her own or the work of the dress?

The elevator eased to a standstill, and the door slid open.

'And here it is!' she announced, walking ahead of him into the apartment. 'I don't know what you did to deserve this, but enjoy it. You are a very lucky boy,' she said, making doe eyes. 'This is a nice part of the Complex. I suggest you take some time to get to know your new place, then go out and start doing whatever you have to do.' She offered a theatrical smile. 'And if you ever want our extra special services, here is my personal card. Plug it in and use it to message me.' She handed him her holo-card.

The card displayed a series of holographic images depicting the woman, first in a ball gown on a beach at sunset, then a close up of her laughing, then a glimpse of her in a bikini dancing by a swimming pool. 'Thank you,' he said, feeling his face reddening.

'Well, mustn't fraternise on duty. Don't be a stranger!' The woman turned and sashayed back to the elevator. She struck a pose and waved as the door slid shut.

The apartment was huge, but basically a single empty room. It made his previous residence seem like a cupboard by comparison, but it was plain, as if half-built, and windowless. A shell. A touch-screen device lay on the L-shaped sofa in one corner, the only piece of furniture. The device looked similar to the old Internet tablets that were once the world's biggest craze;

Dean had scoffed at them until he had become addicted like everyone else. He remembered telling Jane: 'They're not iPads, they're Me-Me-Me-Pads.' When he picked up the tablet, it lit up. Images of a dozen faces stared up at him, blinking. A range of ages, colours and genders awaited his selection. Dean tapped on the face of a young brunette woman.

'Welcome to Better Life Complex Luxury Apartment 7910. This tablet is authorised only to function inside this apartment. Please say your name.' The woman paused, smiling, showing perfect white teeth.

'Dean.'

'Hello, Dean. It is my pleasure, Dean, to describe all the amazing features of your brand new apartment. Where would you like to begin, Dean?'

There were several options: Décor, Dining, Entertainment, Exercise, Relaxation. Dean tapped Décor.

'Thank you, Dean. Dean, let me talk you through the décor options for your new apartment. Dean, you can choose from a range of preset arrangements or customise your own.'

The woman's face zoomed into a small square in the corner of the screen, where she remained, watching. Now Dean was faced with a menu of patterns in a range of colour palettes: Edwardian Elegance; Victorian Sophistication; Minimalist Mood; Nature Abounds, and so on. Dean selected Edwardian Elegance. Immediately the walls of the apartment turned from plain cream into a formal but delicate floral pattern, and the sofa morphed into a three-seat leather Chesterfield. 'Whooah! Amazing!' Laughing, he started playing with the different options. The mood of the apartment changed each time. Nature Abounds turned the walls into a luscious countryside scene: impossibly beautiful. From the sub-menu he selected Autumn, and the leaves of the swaying trees on the far wall changed from bright greens into a patchwork of reds, golds and yellows. He dabbled some more until he felt happy with his selection: Late Spring. The plain apartment had been transformed. Dean sank down into the sofa – now bails of straw – and took it all in. 'Fracking hell! You've not done bad here, mate.'

It had been years since he'd seen actual trees, and now here were copses, rolling green hills, bubbling streams and cottages placed just so. It reminded him of his childhood home in the rural north. No doubt that had all turned to dust now. Picking up the tablet again, he quickly switched to a Minimalist Mood arrangement: gold and maroon rotating lines with tasteful under-lighting. Stretching out his legs, he selected the main menu on the tablet and chose Dining.

'Thank you, Dean. Dean, let me talk you through your dining options.'

A plan of the apartment appeared, with a figure indicating where Dean was sitting. If he raised an arm, so did his avatar on the screen. An arrow indicated where Dean should go, and he obeyed. When he arrived in what the screen labelled the kitchen area, the tablet displayed animated instructions for how everything worked: how he could find food, utensils, plates, and so on, behind touch sensitive panels in the walls.

'Your pre-stocked freezer will automatically replenish itself via the Better Life Nutrition System. Simply complete your order via this tablet, giving at least one hour's notice. Or, if you prefer, simply leave us to make your selections for you according to previous purchasing patterns.'

Was all of this included for free as part of his new life? No more bills? Was this possible?

He placed his hand on the part of the wall the tablet indicated would be the freezer. As soon as he did so, a panel slid aside to reveal fully stocked shelves. A blast of cold air hit him. He quickly chose a ready-meal: Asian Sunset. The animated 3D packaging showed a beautiful Indian woman, black hair falling onto a crisp white blouse. In front of her were a huge array of ingredients: peppers, tomatoes, chillies, garlic, aubergine, various herbs and spices, and exotic vegetables he couldn't even name. The box gave off a delicious scent. He tapped the 'Cook now' button. The Indian woman winked at him then silently began slicing and chopping ingredients, before throwing them into a large sizzling pan. It reminded him of cooking shows on TV when he was a boy. Homely. The woman finally tipped the contents of the pan onto a plate, stood back, tipped her head to one side and smiled.

'*Your meal is ready,*' the box declared.

Peeling off the lid, inside was a steaming lumpy red slush, with bloated rice in one corner. 'Bon appétit,' he muttered. Finding a disposable fork in the utensils hatch, he started eating as he walked back to the sofa. The meal may have been an anti-climax but at least it made a welcome change to dry Nutri-Bars.

So this was his new life. Minimalist today. Perhaps Edwardian or Victorian tomorrow. *If Jane could see him now!* He picked up the imitation-leather medical satchel and pulled out *The Machine Society*. Tucked inside the pages for safe-keeping, he found the photo of him and Jane. They looked so young and so happy together. He wondered whether she still worked for Krane Media, and whether she had also undergone 'aesthetic technology'. Would he even recognise her?

* * *

Dean slept badly. He dreamed he was balancing on top of the Wall, hurrying along, as though walking a tightrope, chased by a nameless force. Down one side, way below, was his brand new apartment, only it was made of plastic, shiny and pink; down the other side was his old apartment, brown and disgusting, sinking in a swamp of mildew. Ahead of him stood Ferry, smiling enigmatically, holding out a copy of a book: it was *The Machine Society*, but the author was Dean Rogers. He stood still, scrunched up his eyes, and waited for the force behind him to catch up… At this point, he woke up. The dream had been so vivid he felt relieved to find himself safe. He stretched out on his bed – a mattress located underneath a retractable section of flooring. Staring at the ceiling, he tried to focus on his breathing. This was an old Buddhist trick he'd once read about in one of Jane's self-help books. If he did this he found he could distract himself from some of the confusing thoughts, for a while at least.

He reached for the tablet, 9:36. With no water siren and no job to get up for, he could sleep all day if he wanted. There had been no messages from Ferry. Would Ferry visit personally, or send one of his underlings, or send a message perhaps? A waiting game.

The previous evening had been spent trying to make sense of his new apartment and looking up what the Better Life Complex had to offer – but it was all on the other side of his front door, and he didn't even know if he could leave. Why had Ferry chosen him and not someone else?

He'd discovered via the tablet that his apartment – not him – had a bank account that received a daily salary. Deductions had already been made for rent, food, lighting, even for adjusting the décor. The balance sheet looked complicated, but one thing he noted: he was in credit, perhaps for the first time in his life. Whatever was going on, money was no longer an issue.

With a sigh, he resigned himself to getting up. A bathroom lay behind one of the wall panels – it had one of the new multi-directional showers. Then he ate a Mediterranean Daybreak breakfast; the woman on the box assured him that the slightly fluorescent fruity yellow mash inside was 'filled with sunlight and packed with Vitassium^{TM} energy'. The flavour was not dissimilar to Asian Sunset, and the taste was growing on him. The tablet read 11:06. Still nothing from Ferry. He activated the TV – it filled one wall – and tried to concentrate on the news, thinking of it as research. More financial announcements, success stories.

...and there's more good news for the economy. A record day's

trading on the Better Life Trading Floor yesterday means prices on all your favourite consumables are going up once more, with a corresponding all-round increase in salaries. President Afini praised the hard work of his economics team for…

This was the first time he had sat down like this to watch TV in years. The dizzying bombardment of information caught him off guard. So many flashing images, and announcers so excitable they could be certified. It was difficult to work out where the news, adverts and mini-dramas started and ended. A drama resembling a remake of *Pride and Prejudice* consisted of the female characters largely comparing wardrobes and discussing the new styles announced by the Better Life Fashion Bureau. Did people watch this stuff for entertainment or information? But then, with no Internet and few alternatives, maybe they lapped it up.

As if on automatic pilot, Dean switched off the TV and went over to inspect his suits behind the wardrobe panel. He'd been given five suits, in various styles and colours, and nearly a dozen tartan ties. There were controls pads on the inside pockets to adjust the colour and pattern of the electronic cloth. He recognised the label – Suitability – from one of the TV adverts. It felt weird, but pleasingly so, to think he might now be in fashion for the first time in his life.

He paced the floor. What was Ferry doing to him? At least he could look out of the window in his old apartment, see the sky. In here there was just air-conditioning. And he may have hated his job but at least it gave him something to do and he got to see other human beings, even if he didn't converse with them. He thought about Clare arranging merchandise on the shop floor. At least those awkward glances and exchanges with her were *something*. Ferry had said he should wait. Dean couldn't recall him saying specifically that he shouldn't leave the apartment. Unless this was a trick? Maybe there wasn't anything on the other side of the door? Maybe there were still prisons and he was in one of them. What if there was a power failure, or some glitch in the system, or what if the air turned sour? He tried to remember precisely what Ferry had promised. Nothing specific. What had he hinted at or alluded to? Nothing really, just a vague sense of being given a mission.

Picking up *The Machine Society*, he took out the photo of him and Jane and slipped it into his inside pocket. He walked towards the apartment door. As he approached it, an illuminated outline of a hand lit up.

'Dean, please place your right hand on the detector,' said a woman's voice.

He obeyed.

'Apartment occupant identified. Dean, you may now exit.'

The door slid open. No alarms. No lasers. Just a compliant, obedient apartment. When he stepped out of the apartment, the door slid shut behind him.

'Dean, enjoy your day!'

He found himself on a balcony walkway situated half-way up a rectangular high-rise courtyard. Above and below him were maybe twenty levels of apartments – dozens of identical white balconies, hundreds of identical black doors. Overhead, the golden glass dome; below him a spacious foyer with a towering red tree in the middle. There were also people: a few here and there, walking along the balconies and, down below, a bustling crowd of people going about their lives. The tree morphed from red to green into yellow. An entertaining tree, thought Dean. One that stayed the same colour would be boring.

Running his hand along the balcony rail, he moved slowly, captivated by the scene. He'd seen this – or something very much like it – on the TV. Now he was inside it, actually living it. So if this wasn't a prison, maybe it was some kind of experiment? TV cameras on him. Or a test – an examination – an assignment he had to work out for himself? Whatever was going on, surely Ferry would have stopped him by now if he was meant to stay in his apartment?

The sound of a door sliding open made Dean jump.

'Oh, hello!' A woman emerged from her apartment. She looked surprised to see him, but quickly composed herself. 'I mean, Good day. *Every day is a good day with Nutri-Taste Breakfast Cereal!*' She had the garish appearance of the customers at Harding's Emporium.

'Erm, hi.' Dean realised it would be rude to dash back into his apartment.

'Just "Hi?"' she asked coyly. Her make-up and facial optimisation made her age impossible to guess. Her hair was gold and auburn, with lacquered ringlets piled high, and she wore one of those plastic dresses, purple with huge shoulder pads and a heavy cleavage on display – although whether it was her own cleavage wasn't clear and he didn't want to stare.

'No, what I meant to say was…' He thought quickly. Some sort of advertising slogan seemed appropriate. 'I wear Suitability suits. They're always, erm, suitable.'

'Oh, really! That's a new one.' She smiled that smile again. 'You're cute!'

They stared at each other. Dean had the feeling it was his turn to speak. Shiz! Ferry should have given him some lessons in Better Life etiquette. It's not enough to look the part, you have to speak the part too. 'So, you like Nutri-Taste cereal?' he offered.

The woman rolled her eyes. 'Sure, I love it! Why not order a dozen boxes and tell them I recommended you, then I'll get a nice commission.'

'OK.'

The woman looked stunned then suspicious. 'Are you kidding me?'

'Of course not! I mean, unless you want me to be kidding.' He felt himself blushing and looked down at his feet, until he realised that wouldn't convey confidence. Stand up, strike a pose!

'I take it you're new around here?'

'It's that obvious, is it?'

'That line about the suits. Did you make that up?'

'Yes.'

She laughed. 'That's funny! How original.' She moved closer. 'Someone like you, I wouldn't mind giving private lessons, but my old man never leaves the apartment. That said, here's lesson one: get yourself a real sponsor as soon as you can. And while I'd love to take a little commission, learn to be more careful about how you throw your money around.' She paused and sighed. 'You're different, but it won't stay that way. You'll learn all the tricks and then they've got you. There ain't no escape!' She put her hands up to her throat and mimed being strangled.

'Thank you,' he said, 'for all of that. You're different too. I mean, nice.'

The woman closed her eyes momentarily, savouring his compliment, then she ostentatiously adjusted her cleavage. 'I'll see you around,' she said, looking him in the eyes, then she turned and wiggled away, her plastic dress accentuating dramatic curves.

These plastic people were certainly weird, he thought, but they must be human underneath. He looked down into the foyer. The tree shifted from green to yellow. Finding one of these sponsors would be his first task.

At the end of the balcony walkway, he found the elevator. His handprint activated a sliding door. Inside, the elevator lit up with advertisements... *Do you want a higher salary? Vote Afini: place your handprint here... Nutri-Taste: Yesterday's Flavours, Today's Science...* It took a while to find the buttons among all the changing images. In a top corner of the elevator, an electronic eye pointed in his direction. Dean located a 'G' and pressed.

At ground level, he braced himself before stepping out into this new world he'd only glimpsed through the service hatch at Harding's; now he stood in its bustling centre. It reminded him of shopping malls from his youth, but multiplied in every aspect. Women in shapely plastic dresses, with hair piled high in multi-coloured ringlets, strode by confidently, carrying shopping bags that displayed short film clips of advertisements. Men in colour-shifting suits looked purposeful, carrying brief cases and electronic devices. He'd seen this dizzying display on TV and had assumed it was a constructed scene, but here it was unfolding before him. He felt like an extra in a commercial. It was so different to the world of low-paid work, where the uniforms made it difficult to distinguish between genders. He moved out, and was quickly surrounded by people. Stepping to one side, he found himself in the entrance of a clothing retailer, getting pushed by the customers coming in and going out. It was difficult to stand still. But one good thing, with his new look, he seemed to be invisible or rather, he blended in perfectly.

It was difficult to get a sense of the precise size of the Complex. The whole of the ground floor was apparently given over to shops, cafés and boutiques with brightly lit, animated fascias and signs: endless small frontages. When the Complex was built, maybe twenty years ago, at first it was just another new complex of luxury apartments – a gated community with its own shops and facilities. The marketing boasted you could 'Live like a Superstar' from cradle to grave, never having to set foot outside the safety of the building. Quickly it became the go-to-place if you wanted to escape rising crime in the Perimeter. Then the police were militarised and the utopianism of New London slipped into a two-tier society. The same old story: rich and poor. The haves in the Complex; the have-nots in the Perimeter.

An animated shop sign depicting delicious steaming coffee being poured into a cup caught his eye. He headed for it, dodging people en route, and dipped inside. He found an empty booth with a good view of the world outside. Sitting down, he felt he could finally breathe. The glass tabletop immediately started flashing.

Welcome to The Designer Frothaccino. Place your hand here.
Dean obeyed.

Hello, Dean. Previously you have had 0 drinks with us. As a new customer, you are entitled to 1 free drink. How would you like your Designer Frothaccino? Please choose from the following options: Hot or Cold?

He selected Hot.

Frothy or Extra Frothy?

Frothy.

Large or Super-Size?

Large.

Nutri-Caf or Nutri-Vit?

Nutri-Caf. Whatever that meant, presumably some caffeine derivative.

The options came so fast, he started making selections at random: Mineral-enhanced, Super-spice, Surprise-sprinkle, etcetera. Finally, a unit in the wall lit up and there was the sound of whirring and fizzing. After a couple of minutes, a panel slid aside to reveal his drink in a tall beaker. Pulling it out, he took a quick sip and winced.

'They take some getting used to.'

Dean looked up to see an older-looking man, with a two-stripe goatee, standing by his table.

'*Make a fresh start with the LiveLife^{TM} programme. Terms and conditions apply.* My apologies for the interruption, but I noticed you were going through the whole menu and guessed you're a first-timer here at The Designer Frothaccino?' The man pointed at the tabletop control panel. 'Do you mind if I...'

Dean did mind if the man joined him, but didn't want to seem rude and risk making himself conspicuous. 'Erm. *It's a good day every day with Nutri-Taste Breakfast Cereal.* No, please.'

The man sat down. 'Regulars here just tap in their usual order. That's how I knew you were a first-timer.'

'Yes.'

'The system remembers all your previous orders and you can either repeat that or try something that other people who bought your drink also liked. But going through the whole menu is such a bore!'

'I see. That makes sense. Do you work here?' said Dean, rather more sharply than he intended.

'Not exactly. I'm freelance. Here's my card.'

He took the man's holo-card and inspected it. It was the same style as the one he'd been given by the woman who'd escorted him to his apartment. Here was an image of the man in a formal suit standing on a beach, the same beach and scenery as the other card. Also like the other card, there was a close up of the man laughing. A cheap, generic product, he thought. It gave the man's name: Carlton Dexter: Bespoke Life Solutions Consultant.

'Hello, Carlton. I don't have a card at the moment.'

'And your name?'

Was it OK to reveal this information? Maybe he should have stayed in his apartment. He looked around to see if there were cameras in the café. Of course, there were – plenty of them. 'It's Dean. Dean Rogers.'

'Nice to meet you, Dean. I'm Carlton. Sorry, you already know that.' The man laughed and shook his head, just like on his holo-card. He composed himself, his hands folded in front of him on the table. 'So, Dean Rogers, are you new to the Better Life Complex? How are you finding it?' Carlton smiled, his eyes fixed on Dean.

'Er, well...' Dean felt the need to get into character, but he had never liked acting. One of his earliest memories was an infant school production of The Wizard of Oz. He was a munchkin, but he got stage fright and ended up sitting in his mother's lap for the duration of the play. It seemed the Better Life Complex was a stage production he could not get out of. He put on what he hoped looked like a sincere smile, trying to mirror Carlton. 'I'm loving it!' he said.

Carlton nodded his approval.

'Yes, loving it.' he repeated, remembering with unease Ferry's instructions to him: *Eyes open, mouth shut.* 'I'm just settling in.'

Carlton continued smiling, motionless. There was perspiration on his brow.

'So what about you?' asked Dean. 'I imagine all of this is very familiar to you?'

'Ah, yes!' said Carlton, springing into life. 'It's my business to know! *Got a question? I've got the answer! Discount rates for first-time clients.* If there's something you need I'd be happy to help. I've been in this game a long time.'

'Sounds interesting. Tell me more.' Asking questions was a trick Dean's dad had taught him: 'Son, everyone's favourite topic is themselves. They're more interested in themselves than anything you've got to say. So ask questions, show an interest, and you can get along with anyone.'

Carlton responded. 'If you're new here you'll be wanting to know the best places for food. Local eateries are my speciality. *Celebrating? Dine at Carlotti's Replica Diner for an authentic Italian experience. Discounts available.* Or clothes? *Forget retirement. Remember Attirement*^{TM}, *the fashion shop for men who like to take it easy.*' He paused and lowered his voice. 'Or if you're looking for *entertainment*, I'm your man.'

Dean noticed a couple of diners looking in their direction. He wondered if Carlton was a well-known face. 'Entertainment?'

'Ah, yes. *For the discerning customer, the recently refurbished Fantasorium is offering an experience so life-like that the phrase hyper-reality seems obsolete. More real than reality! So, whatever your inclination, the Fantasorium can take you there. Revisit great historical moments and meet the characters up close and personal. Rule the world: it will be at your beck and command, I mean, call. Travel in space and encounter wondrous new species. Meet women whose beauty is truly out of this world. We go beyond your imagination! Discounts available for new clients.*'

Dean had seen adverts for the Fantasorium. They tried to sell it as an educational product, but the implication was clear: 'up close and personal' meant you could frack any historical character you wanted as part of a hyper-real experience.

'Carlton, that's good to know. And thanks for your card. I'll look you up if I need anything.' Dean pocketed the holo-card with a flourish and sat back in the hope of concluding the meeting. He'd never liked salesmen.

Carlton looked startled. 'Right. OK.' He looked down at his hands, then back at Dean. 'Look, I don't often say this but, because I've enjoyed talking to you, I'd like to offer you some of my exclusive special discounts. Very attractive, but not for everyone.'

'Thank you, Carlton, that's very generous of you. I'll definitely keep you in mind.' Dean waited for the man to get up and go, but he remained seated. The inquisitive diners had looked away and were engrossed in their own animated discussions. One woman threw her head back and laughed loudly as if she was re-enacting her own holo-card. 'Carlton, are you OK?'

'I'll be honest with you, Dean. I'm in the market for new clients. A client of mine was unexpectedly obliged to cancel a significant contract this week, which has released me to offer some very special deals.'

So that's how it works, thought Dean. These exotic people might seem as free as birds, showing off their plumage, but, like real birds, they're not really free. They're pre-programmed to scavenge, always on the hunt for their next meal.

'There is one thing you could help me with, Carlton. I'm considering taking on a new sponsor. What would you suggest?'

Carlton lit up. 'Ah! You're asking exactly the right person. I can match you up with any number of suitable brands. What we need to consider is what direction you're going in? How do you see yourself right now? Let's work on that and then I can make a few suggestions. Give me three words to describe your brand.'

'My brand?' Dean wanted to laugh. 'You mean, my personal brand. My market persona, so to speak'

'Exactly.'

'OK. Then I'm going to say I'm inquisitive.' He looked around the café for inspiration. It was quite full now. He felt more anonymous. 'Quiet.'

Carlton shook his head a little. 'Rather than "quiet", might I suggest enigmatic or mysterious?'

'Yes, good. I like enigmatic. Thank you, Carlton. So, I'm inquisitive, enigmatic and, and...' He remembered how the woman on the balcony had described him earlier. 'Original.'

'Hmmm. I like it, but original is difficult to pull off. Novices – sorry – newcomers to the Complex need to learn the ropes before they know how to stand out as original. So, in your case I'm going to suggest creative. Good?'

'Sure. I can see you've done this before.'

'Dean, I'm an expert,' said Carlton, with no hint of irony. 'Let me show you a few things.' He pulled out a tablet from his inside pocket and started tapping. 'Inquisitive, enigmatic, creative. That's a good selection.' He looked at the little screen. It turned from red to blue. He scrolled through. 'So, I'm getting a couple of nice options. I'm getting hygiene, also spirituality, and media. How do they sound?'

'Tell me more.'

Carlton tapped the screen. 'So, for hygiene I can offer *Say Hello to 'Goodbye', the New Fragrance for Men.* And: *Sharp Attack: The Bath Gel for men at the cutting edge.* For spirituality I've got: *The Spirituality Workout: Improve your Karma in Five Easy Steps.* Also: *Welcome to The Shrine: The one-stop shop for enlightenment today.* Any of these appeal?'

Cosmetics or spirituality – vanity or navel-gazing? – neither of them appealed. 'Interesting,' said Dean.

'OK. Let's keep going.' More tapping. 'Aha! I've got a special offer from Krane Media – they always have lots of offers. This one is for *Wall to Wall Games: Extension Pack 14.*'

'Krane Media?' His heart beat faster. Jane was a creature of habit; she'd surely still be working for Krane. 'That sounds possible. What do you think of them?'

Carlton sat forward. 'They have a huge share of the market. Big players. A reputation for excellence. Consistent. Reliable. Perennial favourites. You can't go wrong, really. But then, I think all of these offers are excellent.'

'So, if I was to choose Krane Media, what happens next?'

'Simple. We agree terms. I take your handprint. Job done. You'll be an official sponsor.'

'How long is this offer available?'

Carlton made a pained expression, something all salesmen must practice for hours in front of the mirror. 'I'd like to say you can take your time, but I'm afraid a special offer like this could be withdrawn any minute.'

'Can you tell me more about the terms?'

'As I said, this is a special deal. On each confirmed handprint sale of this Krane product you will receive nine per cent from Krane, of which I am happy to settle for five.'

'Why should I go with you? Why not go direct to Krane?'

'Let's not be hasty. You could go direct, of course, but you're unlikely to get the same deal. I'm offering you two per cent more of the cake, plus, if you change sponsors through me, your percentage goes up each time.'

Krane Media. Jane started as a deputy assistant producer, so she said. Surely she must be higher up now. Perhaps a producer. Maybe there was a way being a sponsor could bring him closer to wherever she was.

Dean noticed Carlton getting fidgety.

'Dean. I'm really enjoying this. So much so that I'm going to improve on the deal. I can raise your percentage to thirteen and, at the same time, because I think we've got a connection, I'm going to reduce my commission to three. And, what's more, I'll throw in the extension pack for free. Have we got a deal?'

Dean thought about Ferry. Maybe he should have stayed in his apartment? Ferry hadn't said anything about mixing, let alone signing up for sponsorship deals. 'Does Krane offer any other perks?'

Carlton laughed. 'You drive a hard bargain. Look, sign up and I'll see what I can do. There are sponsor events, games launches, and so on that would give you privileged inside knowledge, giving you the edge on other sponsors.'

'Does that mean going to the Krane Media offices?'

'We'll see. Let's sort out the deal and I'll make some enquiries. And here's something else. Meet me here – in this café – in, say, three hours, and you can be my special guest at a sponsor party. Put your new sponsorship to the test.'

'OK. I'll do it.'

Carlton put his hand on his heart and exhaled audibly. 'Good choice!' he said after a moment. 'You won't regret it, I assure you!'

He offered Carlton his handprint.

'Good doing business,' said Carlton, already standing up. 'When you go back to your apartment, everything will be waiting for you: confirmation on your tablet, instructions for Krane sponsors, and the extension pack I promised. All yours to enjoy!' He was now walking away. 'See you later. Any problems, you can message me using my holo-card.'

Carlton had gone before Dean realised he didn't know how a holo-card works.

* * *

So much for keeping a low profile. Dean headed back to his apartment, anxious to check his tablet and assure himself there were no catches in the Krane deal. Taking a risk felt new. It felt good. Entering his apartment, he noticed his hand left a wet mark on the door.

Picking up the tablet, he could find no messages. He thought about it. If there was no internet, how else could a message get through? He thought about and had an idea. There was a slot in his table for the holo-card. He plugged his tablet into the re-charge console, waited for a few moments and – happily – a message came up saying this tablet had linked up to Complex-City, that must be the name of the Complex's computer network. And then it appeared: a message from Krane: *Welcome to the world of Krane Media – Your Life, Your Dream. We are delighted to have you on board as a sponsor of Wall to Wall Games: Extension Pack 14. The extension pack has been automatically installed for your apartment – and we know you will love it! Terms and conditions apply.*

He flopped backwards onto his sofa. 'Thank frack!'

So far so good. It all seemed above board. Maybe this sort of improvisation was exactly what Ferry would want. 'Good work, Dean,' he might say. 'You're integrating yourself well. And, what's more, you're doing it on your own initiative. The best undercover agents are those who need the least nannying.'

Picking up the tablet again, he started reading about Extension Pack 14 to get up to speed now he was a sponsor. Lots of waffle about living life on your own terms, life in the fast lane, living the dream, and so on. He'd never been into computer games but maybe this would be different. He selected a game called *Purgatory*. His apartment lights cut out and a tower of roaring holographic flames leapt up all four walls. The flames receded, leaving the room in pitch darkness. His eyes quickly adjusted and, on the far wall, he detected two white dots. They were blinking. Eyes! Someone was there, staring at him. A dim, red-tinged spotlight lit up a pensive-looking boy standing alone in a bleak wilderness. The tablet screen revealed four direction buttons – North, East, South and West – with a central red button. The boy looked imploringly in his direction. A low, ominous crunch echoed in the distance. The figure looked about franti-cally, then back at Dean; he cupped his hands in a gesture of prayer. Dean tentatively touched North; the character moved hesitantly, looking back at Dean as if seeking reassurance.

Suddenly, a deafening roar. An ogre's head reared up behind the boy. Yellow teeth glistening in 3D. The boy screamed. A grotesque splash of blood. Then silence. Dean's heart pounded. Pitch darkness again. But, on another wall, two white dots blinking. A second chance.

It didn't take long to get the hang of guiding the boy about the room. Were they escaping the ogre or searching for something? A way out? When grisly weapons appeared on the ground, Dean pressed the red button and the boy picked them up, ready to fight back. The next time the ogre appeared they would be ready. With a mace in his hands, the boy gestured thanks to Dean with a smile and a nod. They were in this together.

Moving about the room, from wall to wall, they negotiated swamps, cliff faces, trees which hid creatures. Dean wiped his forehead, death only a heartbeat away. The temperature in his apartment was rising and he could feel a thin breeze.

Some time later, Dean suddenly became aware of himself, as if waking up from a dream. He found himself crouching down in the opposite corner of the room from where he'd started. He had been so caught up in the game he'd lost any sense of time. You could lose yourself in this world for days on end, he thought,

Ending the game was a wrench. He gave a brief salute to say goodbye to his new friend, then swiped the tablet to exit the game. The room burned up in flames, the walls morphing back into minimalist décor and the lights reverting to their previous settings. Back in the real world, with no companion.

Regaining his bearings took some time. Checking the time on the tablet, he realised he'd been playing the game for over an hour, though it felt like minutes. When he was a teenager, his friends had been obsessed with computer games. He'd tried to join in, but he couldn't see the appeal. But those games were feeble in comparison with *Purgatory*. Sponsoring this would be easy.

Fetching a glass of water, Dean's thoughts kept returning to his new friend – lost and alone in that loveless world. 'It's only a game,' he told himself. Even so, slumping back onto the sofa, he picked up the tablet; he wanted to check his friend was doing OK.

* * *

A sponsor party sounded important. Worth dressing to impress. In the bathroom, Dean found a cologne called *Exuberance* and blasted himself liberally, but it smelled so awful he had to take another shower.

This time the short journey to The Designer Frothaccino was less fraught. The mall looked different from before. He didn't remember there being so many restaurants. It took him a while to realise the shops had changed. They must do this, he thought, turn into something different in the evenings. The Designer Frothaccino, however, remained unaltered.

Going inside, he found a seat. Then he felt a hand on his shoulder.

'Dean, you're early!' Carlton wore a red suit with wide shoulder pads. 'Good to see you, my friend.'

'Good to see you!' Dean was surprised by his own show of conviviality. Maybe he could learn to play the part.

'So, a little heads up. Take it easy tonight. This is a sponsor party so remember to work your new line in. Find your own style. Smile, nod, you'll get the hang of it. Who knows, you may even get a couple of deals, my friend. Let's work it!'

'I'm ready. Let's do it!'

'Just don't forget me when you're rich!' said Carlton. 'Now, the party is just over there.'

He followed Carlton across the mall to a restaurant called Barbarella. Inside, he was struck by how busy it was, until he realised the venue was small and the walls were displaying an actual-size holographic film of people drinking, circulating, laughing. In fact, the venue was almost empty. A few people stood at a bar along the far wall.

Carlton gestured towards a tall empty table. 'I've been putting word out all week, so hopefully we'll have a good turn out. Who knows what will happen? Networking is what it's all about. Take a seat, I'll get us a couple of drinks.'

Dean sat in the tall designer chair. He noticed two women walk in, one young, one older, but both in shapely plastic dresses, with high-ringlet hairstyles. The young woman had her arms uncovered; her friend wore plastic sleeves that flowed out of the most pointed shoulder pads he'd seen so far.

When Carlton returned with cocktails, he called over to the women. 'Ladies, we're just getting started! Come and join us.'

The women obliged.

'Dean, allow me to introduce Portia,' Carlton indicated the older woman, 'and this is Melitia. And, ladies, this is Dean, a new friend of mine. Can I get you two beautiful ladies a drink?'

'Thank you.' Portia smiled. 'I'll have a Paradise Pick-me-up. *I love the taste!'*

'I'll have a Sundown Satisfaction, thank you,' said Melitia, touching her hair, and struggling to make eye contact. *'It soothes and revives.'*

'Coming right up!' Carlton set off again to the bar while the women took their seats.

'So, Dean, pleasure to meet you. I'm Portia. I always feel so good after a Paradise Pick-me-up. It's just what I need at the end of a hard day. Have you tried it yet?'

'Er, no,' he mumbled. 'But it sounds nice. Maybe I will.'

'Really?' Portia sounded delighted. 'I could take an order. I even have a special offer on right now, where your fifth drink is free if all five drinks are enjoyed within four days at the same venue. *Let paradise pick you up.'*

'That's a tempting offer.' He felt himself wriggling on the end of a fishing line.

Portia lowered her voice and leaned forward so that her

cleavage bulged. 'If I can tempt you then I'll have succeeded.' She emphasised the syllable 'suck', and pushed forward a holo-card.

'Wonderful!' Dean could hear himself mimicking Carlton's style of speech. 'Let me think about it. I'm currently enjoying...' He examined his drink, a sparkling red fluid in a V-shaped glass with a green straw. 'This red drink with a green straw.'

Melitia laughed, then stopped herself and looked away.

Portia looked briefly flustered but continued. 'I can order a taster for you. A sample size. Then you can see what you think.' She paused for effect. 'If it's not big enough, I'm happy to make it bigger for you.'

Dean coughed and decided on a different tack. 'So, Melitia. Tell me more about the Sunrise, er, drink?'

Melitia looked startled. 'Sundown Satisfaction! Really? You want to know more?'

'Yes, sure. Why not?'

'Well, it soothes and revives. It's made from a concentrate of fragrant fruit substitutes that offer a vitamin-rich boost in... in...' Melitia screwed up her face. 'Frack, I've forgotten.'

Portia nudged her. 'Go on.'

Melitia looked down at the table. 'Sorry.'

'Vitamin-rich boost in a flavoursome smoothie,' Portia concluded, then smiled, although less enthusiastically than before.

Carlton arrived with the women's drinks. 'Everyone getting to know each other, I hope. Dean, have you told everyone a little bit about yourself?'

'No. We've been talking about drinks.' He took a sip of his red drink and grimaced. It was sour and syrupy. 'I'm quite new here. I mean, in this part of town, erm, Complex. But I met Carlton today and we've been talking business.'

'Dean's very sharp,' said Carlton.

'But not as sharp as this guy,' Dean responded, feeling obliged to repay the compliment.

An awkward silence. Portia started looking around. More people were arriving.

'Dean,' said Carlton. 'What was that thing you were telling me about before?'

It took a moment for him to catch on. 'Ah, yes. That new games pack. I played it. It's actually very good. Have you heard of *Purgatory*? It's powerful. It takes you out of yourself. My apartment actually got hotter, and the tension is incredible. This guy on the screen, it's like he's a real person – really there – like you're in it together, like he's your best friend and his life is on the line.' Dean suddenly felt he was sharing too much.

'Sounds amazing,' said Carlton. 'And what's it called?'

'*Wall to Wall Games: Extension Pack 14. Krane Media: Your Life, Your Dream.*'

Portia raised an eyebrow. 'It sounds wonderful,' she said in a flat voice. 'I'd love to hear more but I've seen someone I need to speak to.' She turned to Melitia. 'Would you like to join me?' The question sounded like an order.

'Sure.'

The two women hopped off their chairs and ventured into the gathering throng.

Pushing his drink away, Dean put his elbows on the table. 'I think it's going to take a while for me to get the hang of this. Sales has never been my strong point.'

'I must say, your sponsorship pitch was certainly different.' Carlton frowned as though struggling to find the right words. 'Highly personalised. That's good, in a way, but also kind of weird. It was like you were trying to tell the truth or something. So, if sales aren't your strong point, what exactly is your thing, if you don't mind me asking?'

'I'm a researcher with Starbucks University.'

'Nice job. So I guess that explains why you can afford to be quirky.' Carlton smoothed down his sleeves and glanced at each shoulder pad in turn, perhaps checking they hadn't become detached. Then he climbed off his chair. 'I'm going to circulate. Sell ice to the Eskimos.' The salesman smile was back, and he was gone.

This would take a while to figure out. In the Better Life Complex, it seemed the knack was knowing how to talk without really saying anything – unlike in the Perimeter, where you try and keep your mouth shut. He took another sip of his red drink and immediately regretted it. He scanned the room looking for Melitia. Everyone blended into each other – the men looked alike; the women looked alike. But Melitia seemed different. Not so slick or rehearsed. A quality of innocence, he decided. He spotted her in the middle of the room, now busy with people talking. She was a pair of blinking eyes in the fires of purgatory. But it was annoying that she and Portia were joined at the hip.

'Seen something you like?' A man in a pulsating suit appeared at the side of his table.

'Something I like?'

'Why not? Take a picture and the Fantasorium can replicate it. What I mean is, if there's someone here you'd like to get to know better, that can happen at the Fantasorium. *More real than reality!* My card.'

Accepting the holo-card, Dean read out loud: 'Dr Dylan Fairfax, Business Executive.'

'At your service!'

'I'm Dean. Er, no card. Did you know that *Wall to Wall Games* has released *Extension Pack 14*? It's new from *Krane Media: Your Life, Your Dream.*'

'Dean, I'll be honest with you, I did know that. But if you try out the latest applications at the Fantasorium you'll realise you can get a lot more realistic than *Wall to Wall.*'

'Are you sure? Have you tried *Purgatory*? It's pretty engrossing.'

Dr Dylan gave him a pat on the arm. 'I used to think like you. But after you've been to the Fantasorium you'll find that games like *Purgatory* no longer have the same impact. Keep at it, my good man. Need to circulate.' The man got up to leave.

'Wait. You said something about a picture? Any picture?'

'That's right. The science is very complex but, basically, we feed the photograph – or movie clip, it can be anything – into the computer. There's some very advanced simulation programming in there. The computer fleshes out the details. The subject of your photograph, or whatever it is, literally comes alive. As far as your brain is concerned, there's no difference between the photograph and reality.'

'Even an old paper photograph.'

'Of course! Old sweetheart, eh?'

'I was just asking. Curious.'

'Don't worry.' Dr Dylan laughed. 'Very discreet service.' He pointed at his card in Dean's hands. *'More real than reality.* You could read that as *better* than reality. Take care.' Dr Dylan moved off and immediately found someone new to sell to.

Slipping the card into his pocket, Dean re-scanned the room. He spied Melitia on her own, with Portia nowhere to be seen, and made his way towards her.

'That drink you were telling me about, I'll take one.'

Melitia's face lit up. 'You will? Wonderful!' Pulling her tablet out of her bag, she tapped at it quickly then held it out to Dean. 'I just need your handprint, then your drink will be ready to collect from the bar. Is it one drink or a Saver Seven: buy seven get two free, terms and conditions apply.'

'Just the one, I think.'

'Handprint, please.'

'Sure, it's just you're being so business-like.'

'Sorry?'

'Before. When you forgot your words?'

'Oh that!' she laughed. 'Good double act, aren't we?'

'Double act?'

'Portia is my mother. She's the tart and I'm the damsel in

distress. If you don't go for one, you'll go for the other. Men are so predictable.' She handed him her holo-card.

'Oh, right.' He offered his handprint, kicking himself for not seeing through the whole thing. Clearly, in the Complex, strangers were not friends you hadn't met yet, but customers.

* * *

Back in his apartment, Dean flopped on the sofa and found *Purgatory* on his tablet. The flames flared up around him, then darkness. First, the blinking eyes, then his friend's face came into view – looking a little older, a teenager, perhaps – and briefly he looked delighted to see Dean. But Dean sensed peril. He could see it in his friend's face. Nodding at Dean, the young man pointed to indicate which way they should go. This was new, the young man taking charge. They crept forward, together, carefully picking their way through rubble, around girders, under broken, wire fences: the remnants of a collapsed building, perhaps a collapsed civilisation. A distant howl. They stopped dead. Footsteps? Someone or something getting nearer. Finding a hiding place, they crouched down behind a pile of cracked bathroom fittings. Footsteps on gravel approaching from behind. The ground shaking. Dean crouched low. Looking up, he could make out a shadowy figure through the mist and his friend's eyes blinking next to him. A broken light flickered overhead. Dean looked at his friend, put his finger to his lips and held his breath. The ogre roared in the shadows. Flying creatures rose up, flapping, squawking into the air. A hot blast of air – stinking. Now almost doubled up, with his head on his knees, Dean hid himself with his arms. Another roar – the creature was close. Then stillness. The sound of guttural breathing. Keep quiet. Don't move. Footsteps. The ogre leaving? Peeking out from behind the debris, Dean checked on his friend, who was peering back at him. They both smiled and put their thumbs up, relaxed now. Then

SMASH! A huge club landed on his friend's head with a bloody crack. 'No! No!' Dean leaped up, fists flailing. In front of him, the ogre's face filled the wall, cackling through broken teeth, as the screen faded into flames.

Crawling back onto the sofa, Dean stared into blank space. He held up his hands and saw how much they were shaking. 'Shiz.'

The flames receded and the apartment's settings returned to normal.

Staggering towards the kitchen zone, he tapped the fridge panel and a screen lit up. An icon in the corner flashed in orange with the word 'New'. He tapped on it. *Dean, you ordered one Sundown Satisfaction at Barbarella and did not collect. Would you like your drink now?* He tapped 'Yes' and waited, listening to the smooth hum of machine parts in motion. Then a small panel slid to one side to reveal a white and yellow swirling liquid in a triangular glass. He took a sip. Creamy. A little sickly, but soothing. Not alcoholic, by the smell of it, but something was having an instant calming effect.

Putting *Purgatory* out of his mind was difficult. He didn't want to think about it... about anything. Taking another sip of his drink, his eyelids drooped a little. In his mind he saw his old apartment swirling around, morphing into his new apartment; he saw Portia's breasts and heard Melitia's laugh, then the ogre's cracked teeth. Then this image faded and with it all of his confusion and frustration. Peaceful now. Taking another drink, he recalled lying in bed with Jane, back when they were first together, comfortable. Finding his way to the sofa, he curled up. His head touched something. It was his copy of *The Machine Society*. He pulled out the photo of him and Jane. Jane looking her best; she rarely wore make-up, he preferred her that way, natural. She looked good in jeans and a T-shirt. What would she look like in a plastic dress? Sexy? That thought brought some pain – a reminder of what he didn't have. He drank another mouthful and the image faded. A sensation of warmth filled him: the warmth of bare skin next to his and the faint hint of Jane's perfume. *What is reality?* The question struck him with force. Didn't Vinty write something about that? He sat up, took another hit on his drink, and opened *The Machine Society*. He ran a finger down the list of contents until he found 'Manufacturing Reality in the Age of the Machine, page 67.'

It is common sense to assume that there are two states of being: we are either asleep or awake. But we would say otherwise. The mystics spoke about many levels of wakefulness, and psychologists have shown that much of what we label as objective reality is in fact a projection of our world view – a world view given to us by our parents, our experiences, our education. Our world view is an inevitable consequence of developmental processes. Perhaps we should conclude that reality is elusive and cannot be fully known. Maybe it doesn't really matter, as long as we are happy. But in the Age of the Machine we must add another piece to the jigsaw. The Machine is subtle and evasive. It tampers with, and even creates, our memories, our fantasies, even our biology. Imagine a machine that can convince someone they are awake when really they are asleep. Hooked up, that person might feel happier, but he has little sense of choice, of responsibility, of having a will. Imagine now that the whole of society is just such a Machine...

He could barely keep his eyes open. Putting the book down, he finished off his drink. The glass slipped out of his hand. He felt good. He could feel Jane wrapped around him, and he knew that when his friend in *Purgatory* had died he had gone to a better place.

* * *

With no water siren, and no job to punctuate the day, it was getting difficult to keep a handle on the time. Outside the Complex, the sun blazed in the sky, night followed day, the seasons changed. Time went round in circles. But in the windowless Complex, there was no sight of the sun. No day or night. Any timepiece Dean had seen displayed a 12-hour clock. Instead of the changing seasons, there was the changing of the shops, different seasons of commerce; the glowing fascias morphed from boutique to café to restaurant, with no apparent fixed pattern, always open for business. God created day and night, but humankind had decided they were superfluous.

So why do anything today? He could shower; he could feed himself; he could play his game; those Sundown Satisfactions were pretty good. As far as he could tell, he hadn't done anything to disobey Ferry, no breach of contract. He might have met a few people, but so what? Without clear instructions, what else could he do? Turning over, he let his body sink deeper into the sofa. Maybe if he spent a couple more hours like this he'd come up with a plan.

Grandma's house. The bottom of the garden, the gate open and the wood lying beyond it. Dean turned cautiously to look behind him. His grandma sat in a deckchair, her eyes closed, sound asleep. And behind her, in the house, everyone was content. He could take his time. He stopped to look in the stream – so clear! The water was alive. Everything was alive! The stones, the grass, the sky, the trees. Perhaps more alive than he was. They held a secret – something pure. He could learn this secret too, but he had to keep going. He looked up. The wood lay ahead of him – too dark. He looked again at the gurgling stream. He wanted to sit down for a long time, to stay here, but the wood beckoned, calling him, now surrounding him. But he couldn't surrender. Surrounded, but he refused to surrender. Surrounded, the trees morphed into the Wall...

Snapping awake and sitting up abruptly, Dean could feel his heart thumping in his chest. *Breathe. Focus.* What did the dream mean? He wanted to believe that dreams were just a jumble of memories. But what if they contained messages? And why did they hurt so much? His head in his hands, a good memory came to mind: lying in bed with Jane, in the early days of their relationship, holding her close. Out of the window he could see treetops, blue sky, clouds, and, briefly, he had a feeling of deep peace. He thought it was to do with Jane – but maybe it was something bigger than that: something about feeling free.

Time to venture out again into this strange new world. He showered, got dressed, and found himself something to eat – preparing himself for another expedition into the Complex.

Opening his apartment door, he saw his neighbour. He felt an impulse to step back inside, but she seemed different today. She was fishing around inside a bright pink, plastic shoulder bag, frantic. Then she noticed him, and looked at him with tired eyes; the vamp had gone. 'Can you help me? My eyesight's atrocious. I'm trying to find my medi-card. Can you look?'

'Sure.'

She handed him the pink bag.

'What does it look like?'

She smiled warmly. 'You really are new to all this. Now you're telling me you don't even have a medi-card? It's white with a red cross on it.'

'Oh! Of course.' He rummaged in the bag. It was surprisingly light considering there was so much stuff in it: cosmetics, electronic devices, electro-paper documents, pill boxes.

'Here!' he said, pulling out the medi-card, feeling like a boy scout who'd completed his Good Neighbour badge. He handed the woman her things.

'Thanks, doll.'

Yesterday she was a tiger, today she was a kitten.

She hesitated, then gave him the story. Frowning, she pointed inside her apartment. 'He used up the last of my *Trank-ease*. I'm a mess without those babies. You can tell, can't you?'

'I…'

'You're sweet. Very polite. I don't know if I'm coming or going.' She smiled weakly. 'Listen, if I didn't need to rush I'd ask you inside.' The tiger had peeked out.

'Sure. Another time.' He felt relieved, but also intrigued by the prospect of seeing into her world, not just his neighbour's world, the Better Life world. Research. And anyway, he was warming to her. 'Another time. I'm Dean, by the way.' He offered his hand.

'Cherilea,' said the woman, taking his hand hesitantly.

Her touch was surprisingly soft. Perhaps he was expecting her to feel like plastic. He realised this was the first flesh-to-flesh contact he'd had with anyone for months. There was a time when people used to hug or kiss their friends. Then it became taboo. Too much fear of transmitting bacteria, or some such. He blushed. Maybe he'd crossed some line.

'So, I need to get going,' she said.

She turned, but he remembered something. 'By the way, you can now buy *Extension Pack 14* from *Wall to Wall Games*. It's new from *Krane Media: Your Life, Your Dream.*'

Cherilea tipped her head back and laughed. A real laugh. 'I see you're one of us now. And, don't forget, every day is a good day with Nutri-Taste Breakfast Cereal!' She winked at him, back to her old self it seemed, and headed off.

He watched her perfect figure and imagined what it would be like having someone like that in his life. He leaned on the balcony and looked down at the colour-changing tree: green, yellow, orange, red. Of course, the colours represented the changing seasons, nature on fast forward. *Nature, the edited highlights.* When he was a boy, his grandmother had a fibre optic Christmas tree that changed colours. He memorised the sequence and tried to impress his family by announcing each colour in advance. The only family he knew now was Jane. He needed to know more about Krane Media and where she might be. Carlton could probably help, but could he trust him? However, there was someone else he felt sure he could trust; maybe Clare could help him?

Locating Harding's Emporium wasn't going to be difficult. There was a smart-nav built into the sleeve of his jacket. He tapped in the name of the shop. A hidden voice – the same voice as on his tablet – spoke to him from somewhere inside his collar:

'*Dean. Turn left and proceed to elevator. Then descend.*' He did as he was told.

Out in the courtyard, people hovered, darted, moved on, bees in a hive. He wondered how many others had been put here by Ferry. Many of the shop frontages looked new. The Designer Frothaccino was still there, albeit in a different colour scheme.

'*Continue straight ahead, Dean. Feeling thirsty, Dean? Why not try a delicious pot of Cashew-lite Tea, the new super-drink and pick-me-up from The Designer Frothaccino? Terms and conditions apply. Does not contain nuts.*'

Dean shook his head. What sort of idiot would instantly obey such an advert and interrupt their journey – maybe by 15 minutes or more – to enjoy a cup of tea? He remembered how much he used to hate the endless advertising on TV, on the Internet, on billboards. These adverts triggered something in him: frustration, even anger. Surely language wasn't invented for this? Were the first written words those of an entrepreneurial Neanderthal, scratched onto the walls of a dark cave: *Og's flints – be the sharpest tool in the box*?

'*Continue straight ahead, Dean. Feeling peckish? Mexi-can is the burrito-style snack with the can-do attitude. They're sizzling ahead in just 20 metres, Dean. Terms and conditions apply.*'

He examined the smart-nav, looked at the screen to get a rough idea of the direction to Harding's – it didn't seem far – then switched it off.

Catching sight of the store's distinctive retro-neon sign, he started to have second thoughts. That smarmy Coleman would no doubt be there, but he reckoned he could endure that if it meant seeing Clare.

Harding's shop window still contained a lot of the shiz from when he was last there. He'd never imagined he could feel nostalgic about Harding's, but so much had changed in his life that the shop now felt reassuringly familiar. Looking at Clare's display of New Deco wall clocks, strangely he could now see the appeal. In a world in which the passing of time had become taboo, he could see how buying a timepiece had a sense of rebelliousness. Passing something off as an 'antique' was a good trick; it appeared to be a novelty throw-back to the past, but it was actually about trying to reclaim a part of what life was like before the plastic people took over.

Through the window, over the clocks, he could see customers moving among the plastic treasures. Suddenly Coleman was standing in front of him, his big stupid face on the other side of the window. Instinctively, Dean turned away and retreated. His heart was beating. He remembered the cruelty in Coleman's eyes that day he got sacked. From a discreet distance he looked back. He had panicked needlessly. Coleman was retrieving a clock from the window – he hadn't even seen him. He tried to calm himself: what could Coleman do to him now? He'd have Ferry to argue with.

Approaching the shop again, this time he went in. Standing there, the shop seemed smaller than it looked from the other side of the storeroom hatch.

'Greetings, sir. Could I be of assistance?'

It was Coleman, dipping, fawning, an appalling smile across his face. Dean thought it must be sarcasm.

'Erm, the clocks,' said Dean.

'The clocks? New Deco? I think I noticed you browsing from outside. A discerning choice.'

Not sarcasm, Dean realised. This was not Coleman the manager, but Coleman the obsequious shop assistant. Coleman hadn't recognised him. Dean knew he looked different due to his make-over, but there was something else in his favour: how could Coleman have imagined a mere storeroom assistant could become a resident of the Better Life Complex? Coleman's brain simply could not allow him to see that possibility.

'That's right,' Dean said, feeling calmer. 'New Deco. That's exactly the thing I had my discerning eye upon!'

'Then, allow me.' Coleman gestured towards the New Deco display, bidding Dean to lead the way. 'As I say, these are a discerning choice. Made of solid 100 per cent plastic. Not artificial plastic. These are authentic reproductions of original facsimiles.'

'Wonderful.' Dean stared at the in-store display, not knowing what to say. Coleman hung by his side like an obedient pet. 'The plastic really...' he made a meal of searching for the right word, 'shines.'

'Good observation, sir. This particular range employs double carat plastic.'

That was a new one. Double carat plastic. Next they'd have 'plastic leaf' and bars of plastic bullion.

'I'll just browse for a while, thank you.' Dean felt he could play with this if he wanted. 'I'd like to meditate upon this potential investment.'

A flicker of something crossed Coleman's eyes. Was that anger? Surely, the man couldn't enjoy toadying to self-important customers all day long? Why had Dean never seen how pitiful Coleman really was? Give a weak man a little power and he will try and transform himself into lord and master.

'Now, please leave me to my ruminations.' With a flick of his hand, Dean swatted Coleman away. Coleman nodded obligingly and reversed out of sight.

Dean scrutinised the clocks for a while, playing his part, even contemplating that he might buy one, then he started to scan the shop. There was a lot of browsing and not much purchasing going on. The assistants all looked desperate. He supposed they must be on commission. Maybe that was how it worked: no wages, just commission? Not the easy job he had imagined it to be.

Then he saw her, standing with her back to him. He recognised her hair, tied up in ribbons in that distinctive style. From what he now knew of life in the Complex, this act of self-decoration – ribbons instead of plastic lacquer, hair natural instead of in ringlets – was a mark of individuality. Turning round, she headed in his direction.

'Excuse me,' he said.

She looked a little frustrated, a little bored. He liked her for that too, the fact she was an assistant who didn't bow and scrape.

'Could you tell me more about these clocks?'

She sighed. 'Yes, certainly.' She was thinking hard. 'They're Art Deco clocks.'

'Clocks, yes?' He nodded, furrowing his brow to feign seriousness. 'Do you mean like timepieces?'

'Yes, that's right.'

He remembered her innocent quality.

'They're original replicas. Vintage. Antique copies. Plastic. One hundred per cent.'

Coleman walked up. 'Sir, you require more assistance?'

'That's all right,' said Dean. 'I had a few more questions which this young lady is helping with.' He swatted Coleman away, but realised he shouldn't tease him too much. Shouldn't draw attention to himself.

Coleman scuttled away, no doubt fearing a lost commission.

'Is he your boss?' asked Dean.

'Who?' She looked startled. 'Oh, him? I mean, yes. He's the manager. He likes,' she paused, no doubt searching for a diplomatic phrase, 'being the manager!'

Dean lowered his voice. 'Well, I wish he'd tone it down a bit.'

Clare lowered her voice, 'I'm not saying anything!'

Briefly, they smiled. And now he couldn't resist it any longer. In a hushed voice he asked, 'Clare, don't you recognise me?'

She looked shocked. 'How do you know my name?'

'Shhh! It's OK,' he said hurriedly. 'It's me. Dean Rogers. I know I look different in these clothes and with this face! Surely you remember me? From the storeroom? I got sacked about two weeks ago.'

She frowned, and he thought about leaving the shop immediately. She reverted to her shop voice: 'They're collectable. If there's one you like, I'd buy it today because we will not be able to re-stock.' Then she lowered her voice again. 'You squirted a water gun at that annoying little runt. It was brilliant!'

Now it was Dean's turn to laugh.

'But what happened to you? You look so…'

'Weird? I know. It's a long story.' He looked across the shop floor and briefly caught Coleman's eye. He turned back to Clare. 'I don't feel comfortable talking here. You're meant to be working and I know what your boss is like. Can I meet you somewhere?'

She screwed up her face.

'I'm not trying to trick you or sell you anything,' he said quickly. 'I just want to talk about this strange place. I'm trying to make sense of it.'

'Sure, why not. It's just that nothing's straight forward. I can't explain now.'

'Do you know The Designer Frothaccino, the one by the big tree?'

'Yes.'

'Meet me there tonight at seven?'

'I'll try. Make it six – straight after work. It's easier for me.'

'OK.' He raised his voice again. 'Thank you for your assistance. I will not buy on this occasion, but I will think on it. Goodbye.'

'Goodbye, sir. Thank you for visiting us.'

Hastily leaving the shop, on his way out, he caught Coleman's eye again: the man was speaking quietly into an antique novelty phone in the shape of a large ear. Maybe he had recognised him but hadn't let on. Or maybe Coleman was undercover too, another agent recruited by Ferry? Anything seemed possible.

Outside the shop, people hurried about their business like wind-up toys. Plastic people playing games. He thought of Portia and Melitia and licked his lips – a Sundown Satisfaction would go down nicely. But not now, he convinced himself, that drink had knocked him out cold.

It felt late, though he hadn't been up long. Nothing in this place helped to give a sense of time. He noticed the sign for Allday Breakfast morph into Dusk 'til Dawn Dining. He looked up at the golden glass dome. Was it daylight or night-time outside? He thought about his old job at Harding's, which was a daytime job, and Harding's was open, so it must be daytime. He was meeting Clare at six. That was evening, surely? Come to think of it, he didn't know Clare's shift patterns. His tablet told the time, but he didn't have it with him. Any timepiece he'd seen told only the 12-hour clock. He felt dizzy, like he'd already had that Sundown Satisfaction.

Back in his apartment, his tablet told him it was 1:00. Morning or afternoon? Afternoon, surely? This tablet was a lifeline. He needed to get to grips with communication; there were no phones, so he'd need to get one of those holo-cards. He had so many questions. Hopefully it would all start to make sense soon. Be patient. Now he felt hungry. It's all this worry, he thought. There were plenty of options in the freezer: Taste of Africa, Asian Sunrise, Fasta Pasta. When he opened the freezer it spoke to him. 'Dean, people who enjoyed Asian Sunrise and Mediterranean Daybreak also enjoyed Flavours of China.' He hadn't tasted Chinese food for years. Growing up, his family had always gone to their favourite Chinese restaurant on special occasions. The last time must have been when he got his grades for university in London – not yet New London. His mother had tried to hide her tears when they toasted him. He'd wanted to reassure her, say he'd be back to visit often, but he knew that would be wishful thinking. Though he didn't know much about politics back then, he knew enough to realise the mood of the country was changing. There was an idea that London was getting everything: first Scotland went independent, then Wales, then Cornwall. The government drew the line at independence for the North and implemented military rule. Opportunities in the North were dwindling and its infrastructure was at breaking point. Maybe his parents thought he could find stability in London. Maybe they thought he would be safer. They were right about that. No one could have imagined how quickly the country would change, with the Internet breaking down; the Solar Summer, when the temperature didn't drop below 34 for nearly four months; then the London War and the construction of the Wall. These changes had been so quick and huge he wondered if everyone was still in shock, in denial, suffering post-traumatic stress. There had been the Ice Age. Were they now living in the Sun Age? Depressing thoughts. But some food would help. Inspecting the freezer again, he pulled out Flavours of China, activated the box and watched the Chinese chef merrily throw ingredients into a sizzling wok. A burst of steam filled the screen on the lid, then cleared to reveal a bowl of delicious-looking noodles and vegetables, chopsticks balanced on the edge, sitting on a pristine white table cloth. Removing the lid revealed the now familiar fluorescent mush, yellow in colour, only this time his mouth watered. It was an acquired taste that he had acquired. Clearly, he had been won over by the revitalising power of 'Vitassium^{TM} energy'.

* * *

Eating lifted his mood. Bouncing onto the sofa, he reached for his tablet and activated *Purgatory*. The apartment darkened in an instant, taking him by surprise once again, flames lighting up the walls, then burning out to reveal a dark, apocalyptic landscape. Despite scanning the walls and ceiling, he could not locate his friend. A deep rumble broke the silence. A growl – something alive, prowling. A crack of lightning briefly lit up a swamp, fumes rising from putrid waters. A dank smell made him gag. Crouching down by the wall, he felt damp, sticky, unclean.

'Hey.'

The hushed voice made Dean jump. There, next to him, crouched his friend. 'Hey,' he replied. 'What's happening?'

'Shhh!' said the young man, a little older than before. Putting a finger to his lips, he pointed over Dean's shoulder.

On the opposite wall, Dean could see a light flickering in a derelict shack in the middle of the swamp. A sickening stench. He turned back to his friend, but he had gone. 'Hello?'

'Over here,' came his friend's voice, his eyes blinking on the far side of the room. Dean wanted to be near him. For his friend's protection or for his own? But trying to move, his feet started sinking. The illusion was unsettling. He knew he was in his apartment, but it felt real. Signalling to his friend, he whispered, 'Stuck'. Then, a light flashed on. A spotlight on Dean from above. Across the swamp, something was moving in the shed. He heard heavy, monstrous breathing. Where was his friend? Panic. The spotlight went off. But the thing in the shed had woken up. It let out a shattering howl.

'Frack, frack.' Heart pounding, Dean looked around. Darkness. The stench getting unbearable. 'Where are you?' he hissed, angry, alone. Then, two blinking eyes, a flash of lightning, his friend beckoning – but behind him, the ogre, rising up on tree trunk legs, mottled reptilian skin, blazing eyes, salivating yellow fangs, a club raised. 'No!' screamed Dean, torn between scrambling for safety and rescuing his friend. The lights went out. A terrifying crunch. Silence. Flames. Game over. The apartment decor came back on.

The rank smell abated, the sinking feeling subsided, but Dean felt nauseous. He wanted fresh air, even the hot air outside the Complex would bring relief. His friend had spoken to him this time. The game was changing. With the sense of panic abating, Dean felt a need for something real. Human touch, maybe. He remembered Cherilea, and the handshake from before, and wondered if she might be at home.

Running water over his face, he tried to compose himself. He could go next door and just say hello, check she was feeling OK, very innocent. 'Just research,' he told himself as he headed out of his apartment.

There was a small holo-screen on his neighbour's door. When he wiped his finger across it, the smiling face of Cherilea appeared, the sea and palm trees incongruously behind her. 'Hi! *Every day is a good day with Nutri-Taste Breakfast Cereal.* I'm not at home right now. Please leave a message and I'll be in touch as soon as I can.' The Cherilea on the screen tipped her head to one side and winked. Then the screen went dark and a computerised voice announced: 'Please begin your message.'

'Oh, hi. This is Dean, your neighbour. I just wanted to check you were...'

The door slid partially open, letting out a waft of perfume. 'Do you want to come in?'

The perfume smelled good. 'Yes, sure.'

The door opened fully. Cherilea stood there in a silk robe, her face and hair free of its usual lavish styling and adornments, but her face still taut and her hair set rigid, like an undressed mannequin. The apartment was low-lit. A holographic coal fire burned on the far wall. It was a single room, like his own apartment, but strewn with clothes, boxes, gadgets, random stuff. In the corner of the room, lying on the sofa, buried under blankets, someone wheezed and coughed horribly, then turned over. Dean looked at Cherilea, her eyes blank, and realised she was showing him everything.

'Is that...?' He pointed at the person in the corner.

'Yes. My husband. He's barely awake, though he has moments of lucidity. Half-alive since he flipped out a couple of years ago.'

'Flipped out?'

'Flipped out. Spaced out. Never the same after his trip to the Fantasorium. I told him not to go – we couldn't afford it.' Cherilea touched the collar on Dean's suit. 'I forgot. You probably haven't seen anyone in this state before. You'd be surprised how common this is. It's in the food, it's in the drinks. They're probably pumping it into the air too.'

'What? Chemicals?'

'Who knows?' She drew closer, placing her hands flat on his chest. 'A rule of thumb: the more nutritious it claims to be, the more artificial it probably is. But it's no guarantee. The trick is to pay close attention to your body, how it reacts. If what you put in leaves you dazed or desperate for more, try something else. Or at least mix it up. Sometimes one chemical counteracts the effects of another. And pills, like Trank-ease, they help. But you have to keep fighting. Some people have more willpower or a stronger constitution. While others,' she nodded towards her husband, 'they give in and, in time, there's nothing left of them.'

Her touch felt good, but he was trying to make sense of what she was saying. 'You make it sound like we're all drug addicts or fighting not to become addicts.'

'Why not? Getting people addicted is a simple way to guarantee repeat custom.'

Her hands slipped inside Dean's jacket, ran across his chest and down his sides. Taking hold of her hands, he said, 'I'm sorry. I feel uneasy.'

She raised an eyebrow. 'You're quite the saint, aren't you? It's cute, but it's not necessary.' Taking a couple of steps back, she let the robe slip off her shoulders. Underneath the porcelain mannequin head was the naked sagging body of a sixty- or seventy-year-old. Dean felt sick. She cupped her breasts in her hands and licked her lips. At that moment, the man in the corner sat up and stared at him.

'Frack! He's awake!' said Dean, edging backwards towards the door. 'I'm sorry. I'm not into this.'

'Not getting shy on me, are you? Don't worry about him. He's in la-la land. He doesn't even know where he is.'

As if on cue, the man lay back down.

His back to the door, Dean spoke quickly. 'I remembered the thing with the medi-card and wanted to check you were OK.'

She cocked her head to one side and made a pouting sad face. 'Don't go.'

'Sorry. I can't,' he said, turning and fumbling with the door controls.

* * *

Back in his apartment, Dean paced the floor trying to comprehend what had just happened. He ordered up a glass of water, but didn't drink it. Holding up the glass, he moved around the apartment, inspecting it from different angles. It looked clear enough, but who knew what it contained. Taking a sip, he imagined all the poisons Cherilea had spoken about slipping down his oesophagus. They get inside you, he thought, into your bloodstream, into your brain. Drinking a little more of the water, he found the Vinty book.

Beware! Watch and listen! In the Machine Society, we are further removed from the truth than at any other stage in human evolution. Perhaps we will discover that the dystopia I am describing is a necessary stage, but only if we are able to live through it and come out the other side – and that is not guaranteed. Evolution is only possible if humans remember that we are animals; that we are human beings, not electronic beings. But it is becoming harder to distinguish between our innate animal needs and the manufactured needs programmed into us. This programming begins when we are born. For those of us who are fortunate, life starts with warm human interaction and our instinct for what is natural is allowed to flourish. But the earlier the programming begins, the more quickly our children lose touch with natural instinctual feeling. In the future, there will be people who operate like robots, animated corpses going through the motions of a life, simply responding to stimuli with no original thought or feeling of their own. We have seen the warning signs already. Come the day I am speaking of

— the day of the Machine Society — we will see a generation of people who have become machines.

Vinty certainly wrote with conviction. His claims were unsettling – it was easy to see how he might be mistaken for a madman – but he also made sense. To Dean, at least. Cherilea had advocated using Trank-ease, but maybe Vinty's words could also counteract the effects of the Better Life Complex.

* * *

Welcome to The Designer Frothaccino. Place your hand here.

Logging in, Dean half heartedly scrolled through the menu, with nothing appealing to him.

'Spoiled for choice?'

Clare stood next to his table, smiling and looking fantastic. He couldn't tell what she'd done to look so good, but he liked that her dress wasn't made of plastic.

'Hi,' he smiled. 'I was plucking up the courage to order one of these drinks.'

She wrinkled her nose. 'Not great, are they?'

'They're certainly an acquired taste.'

'Want to try somewhere else?'

'Sure!'

'OK. Follow me. We're going to the less fashionable end of the Complex. I hope you don't mind.'

She said this with a tone of irony that he liked. 'I didn't realise there was a fashionable and a non-fashionable part. I just assumed it was all...'

'Weird?'

'Yeah. Exactly.'

He followed her out of The Designer Frothaccino.

'So, that was a surprise, seeing you today,' she said. 'Can you tell me what's going on? And why me?' She sounded guarded.

Here came the crunch. Could he trust Clare? She had always

seemed different and now here she was: straightforward, plain-speaking, natural. Unless this was her game? Oh, frack it! 'I've been recruited,' he said, not too loudly, 'at least, I think I have.'

She surveyed him briefly, her expression inscrutable.

'I think I might still be in shock,' he said. 'Life has become very strange. Before it was horrible; now it's just strange. I don't really know what's going on.'

'Does anyone?'

'That day I got sacked.'

'Which was both horrible and great, by the way. Sad for you, but well done on getting that kid.'

'Thank you,' he smiled, encouraged. 'Well, maybe it was great, in a way, but I felt like I'd committed suicide or something. I mean, no job, no way to pay the rent. For someone living out on the Perimeter – well, you know what comes next.'

She nodded.

'So, there I am, panicking, waiting for the end. I get this knock on the door. The heavies have come to get me. I remembered the finger outside the apartment door...'

'Finger?'

'Oh, yeah. A severed finger. They come to get you in the night. And if you put up a fight.'

'I see. Snip.'

'Yeah, well, more like whoosh, with a laser.' They were walking in a part of the Complex that was new to him. Less frantic. Fewer holographic adverts. 'So these heavies take me. I'm sure it's the end, but then I'm taken to see this guy and he gives me an assignment. Kind of. A second chance. Instead of chucking me over the Wall, he gives me a make-over and an apartment here. Now I'm waiting to find out why.'

'He didn't tell you? He just gave you an apartment?'

'Basically, yes.'

'Here we are!'

The café was called Retro-respect and the decoration made

Dean stop in amazement. 'Woah!' The walls were covered with vintage posters dating back to when he was a boy, and earlier. There were even books and magazines displayed in glass cases on the walls. Instead of electronic screens and holographic displays there was real metal and paint and original plastic mouldings. Dean's eye was drawn to a poster of the Jump-step group, Straight Talkin'. 'I loved that band, Straight Talkin'. They were my teen idols. I had a poster of Gerd Torme playing his guitar with his teeth.'

'Glad you like it. There are still a few of us into this stuff.'

'I can now see why you work at Harding's. You're into the retro stuff.'

'Mmm. Kind of. Come on.'

'Is there something you're not telling me?'

'We'll come to that. One story at a time. I've got some questions for you. But let's get a drink first.'

There was an old-fashioned service counter, the first one he'd seen inside the Complex. Clare picked up a menu made of synthetic paper.

'Do they serve retro drinks as well?'

'Of course,' she said, handing Dean a menu. 'The good thing is they're still using the original-additives – all the old e-numbers – so that makes this one of the healthiest places to eat in the Complex.'

He inspected the menu. 'Incredible. To think that a Fizzyade Supershake is now a health food. Do you think anyone still grows food in the ground anymore?'

She shrugged her shoulders. 'How could they? The rain is full of poison and there are no fields in New London; just miles of greenhouses and GM crops.'

'Yeah.' He nodded. 'Listen, this is my treat. What are you having?'

'Well, because you're so excited about it,' she laughed, 'I'll have a Fizzyade Supershake. Purple flavour.'

The man at the counter didn't say a word. As he made up the drinks, Dean felt he was being given the evil eye.

They picked up their Supershakes and carried them over to an empty table in the corner.

'Don't think he liked me much,' said Dean.

'Oh, don't worry about Giovanni, he's lovely. Though he doesn't suffer fools gladly.'

'Maybe he was trying to work out if I was a fool or not?'

'And are you?' Clare teased.

'Not all the time! Anyway, cheers!'

They clinked glasses and had a drink.

'Wow! That brings back memories.' Sitting back, Dean realised he was enjoying himself for the first time since he'd arrived at the Complex. No, longer than that, for the first time in months. 'Thanks, by the way,' he said. 'I mean, we haven't really spoken before, but I feel like we sort-of know each other. I literally know nobody in this place. I mean, I've bumped into one or two people, but essentially I'm alone.'

Clare raised an eyebrow.

'Oh, hey, this isn't a pity story. I'm used to being alone. Maybe I prefer it.' He sipped at his drink. 'I suppose what I'm trying to say is, it's good to have someone to talk to. Someone normal.'

'Thanks!' She fidgeted with her glass, moving it around on the table top. 'I know we didn't speak at the shop – not the done thing – but you seem like an OK guy.'

He took another drink. 'Strange how I used to fantasise about becoming an acclaimed writer or academic. Famous, even. But now I'm just glad to have my life and my sanity. At least...' Maybe he was being too open, but he couldn't help himself.

'At least?'

'At least I hope I'm holding on to my sanity. This world is so confusing. So much game-playing. All this stuff about chemicals. It's hard to keep level-headed. Does that sound mad?'

'No, not at all. The truth is, sometimes I used to envy you

because you didn't live in the Complex. I know it's tough out there on the Perimeter, but at least you could escape all the bright lights and the junk. And you get fresh air, however hot it might be.'

'I was thinking the same thing. What wouldn't I give to open a window? But is that the grass is always greener thing? It's awful out there; I just don't want it to be awful in here as well.' He wondered whether to tell her about the Vinty book, but something told him to tread carefully. 'So what's your story? How long have you lived here?'

She looked around the café. 'I virtually grew up here. My family was one of the first to move into the Complex. I was only little, but as I recall it wasn't quite so extreme in the beginning. My parents were level-headed. Good at keeping their heads down.'

'Were?'

'Yeah. They got into some trouble. I didn't hear the full story, but I have my suspicions.'

He thought it best not to ask. Not yet.

'So my brother brought me up. Kind of. He was old enough to be my guardian, but we pretty much did our own thing. I went to school, then hung out right here in this café. My friends were the regular customers. I liked it. My brother was the one with aspirations. I guess I learned to enjoy my own company.'

'You have a nice style.' The words slipped out. Frack!

She laughed. 'You mean I'm one of the few people who haven't been dipped in plastic then had a smile etched into my face! Yeah, I do the minimum so I fit in and don't embarrass my brother too much.'

'You still live with him?'

Now she looked embarrassed. 'Don't feel awkward about this but you actually know my brother. And, don't worry, he is a bit of an idiot.'

He frowned. 'I don't understand.' Then a sickening feeling:

did she mean Ferry? 'Who?'

'Coleman.'

'No! You're kidding? He's your brother?'

'Yes. Like I said, he's got ambitions. Hopes for promotion. It makes sense. He's my big brother. He wants to look after me. We've found a way to get along OK.'

Shaking his head, he wondered what it would be like if he and Clare became friends; he'd have to interact with Coleman socially. But that was running ahead of himself. 'Sorry for shizzing him.'

'Don't worry about it.'

They sat in silence; he looked around the café. The posters took him back to the days before the Great Recession. 'I don't know if all this nostalgia is a good thing or not. I mean, it's great, but it makes me sad. Do you know what I mean?'

'Yes. I wonder about that too. Sometimes, I close my eyes and imagine it's fifteen or twenty years ago, or maybe even longer ago – before I was born – and everything's perfect. I think that's OK. Other people fantasise about the future, about being billionaires or something. At least I'm not kidding myself that my fantasy will come true.'

'I suppose getting lost in the past isn't much different to getting lost in a computer game or watching one of the old films. They're just different ways of escaping.'

She thought about it. 'Yes, I think so. Except, when it's my own fantasies, I'm in charge. I'm not giving myself over to someone else's idea of a better world; I'm creating my own. Maybe that's why I like it; I'm creating my own fantasy.'

'I like that. You're in control,' he said. 'Trouble with me is I go over things in my mind. I have regrets. Why do you think the past has such a hold on us? Is it because the future seems so hopeless?'

'Is that how you feel? It might not turn out so bad.'

'Maybe.'

'I mean, this is OK, isn't it?'

'This café?'

'This café. You getting a second chance. Having a drink with me!'

'Hmm, let me think.'

'Don't think too hard!' She laughed. 'How do you feel right now?'

The question caught him off guard. He was used to feeling bad, but now, to his surprise, he felt different. 'Well, doctor, I'm not used to talking about my feelings, but I suppose I'm feeling happy to be here. I feel OK!'

'Yeah. Me too. Good, isn't it?'

They smiled, but he couldn't hold her gaze. He looked down at his hands.

'Listen,' she said, 'I'm glad we got to chat. I'd like to stay longer, but I told my brother I'd get some groceries. I shouldn't stay out too late.'

'Yeah, sure. It's been nice.' He wanted to say more, then he thought how she must be nearly ten years younger than him.

'Yeah. Very nice.'

He checked Clare's expression for irony. She seemed genuine. 'OK. Well, I know where you are,' he said.

'Except, my brother'll see us.'

'Yeah, shiz. This is all a bit cloak and dagger.'

'That's OK.' She leaned forward, a mischievous look on her face. 'Maybe I can be undercover like you?'

That sounded good. Then an image of Jane popped into his mind, but, frack it, he wasn't married to her; she'd run off. 'We could meet here sometime?'

'That'd be good.'

'When?'

'Tomorrow, at seven. I'll find a reason to be out.'

'Tomorrow at seven. Providing I can get the hang of telling the time.'

'You'll get used to it. It's disorientating when you first get here. Trust your body clock. But if that doesn't work, here.' She fished something out of her bag and handed it to Dean: a watch, Roman numerals on a white face, silver metal casing, a green and yellow striped strap.

'Wow! It's so...'

'Old-fashioned? It's from the shop. Perk of the job. Only, it's clockwork, so keep winding.'

'It's wonderful. Thank you.'

'My pleasure.' Standing up, she waved, then turned to go.

'Oh, Clare, one more thing.'

She turned back, curious.

Striking the pose of a TV newscaster, he pointed at her and intoned: 'You can now buy Extension Pack 14 from Wall to Wall Games. It's new from Krane Media: Your Life, Your Dream.'

She giggled. 'Come to Harding's Emporium: antiques, facsimiles and replicas. Beautiful objects to make your home special.'

Laughing, he watched her go. He wondered what it would be like to start a new relationship. But what about Jane? Jane! He still wanted to see her, didn't he? Even if it was just to say hello.

* * *

Back at his apartment, Dean inserted Carlton's holo-card into his tablet, plugged in his tablet, and sent him a message: 'Carlton, I love Krane Media. As I've mentioned, Purgatory is the most amazing game I've ever played.' He added a smiley emoticon, then worried it might look unprofessional, so he deleted it. 'I want to take it to the next level. Can you get me inside Krane Media?'

Carlton replied immediately, his message arriving with a bleep. 'Great news. To put it simply, yes, I can definitely sort you out.' He looked tired. 'But this needs thinking through. We must discuss face to face.'

This was excellent. 'Carlton, there's no time like the present.

Can you meet now?'

A pause. Then Carlton's reply, 'Not now. Tomorrow. Designer Frothaccino.'

'What time?'

'Twelve.'

'OK. Tomorrow at twelve.'

This was good. Things were happening. But he needed to stay alert. Keep an eye on Carlton, and anyone else for that matter. Make sure he didn't get drawn in too deep. The trouble with getting attached to people is that when things go wrong, getting un-attached is so painful. This time he needed to rely on himself. Inspired, he got down on the floor to do press ups. It felt painful, but good. He couldn't remember the last time he'd done exercise. Sometimes the body just needed stretching and pulling into shape. Squats. Sit-ups. He'd never been into fitness, but maybe he should start running; there must be a gym in the Complex. He could feel his heart rate picking up – he was sweating – it felt good. He'd sleep well tonight.

* * *

Sitting in The Designer Frothaccino, Dean brushed a fleck of dust off what he reckoned was the sharpest suit in his clothes cabinet. Yellow and blue checks. He was getting the hang of the fashion codes. Bright and colourful was in. This week, at least. And he'd finally got the hang of the café menu, ordering what he hoped was the healthiest option: a *Nutri-ccino – contains only the purest laboratory-tested additives*. But what did that mean? And why were there additives that *hadn't* been tested in a laboratory? It tasted strangely similar to the Asian Sunrise freezer meal he'd become fond of and he suspected that was not a good thing.

'Dean!' Carlton announced in a sparky voice as he took the seat opposite and, like a machine, tapped out his order on the table top. He ordered a Triple-Strength Special.

Bizarrely, there was no indication of what the drink contained in 'triple-strength'. It seemed the content was irrelevant; all that mattered were the adjectives and superlatives.

'Dean, I'm delighted you want to explore new options. I think this is a very good move for you. I can see you're a man with talent.' Carlton's eyes dropped down. 'Hey! Nice suit.'

'Thank you.' He'd obviously chosen well.

'Nice cloth,' said Carlton, stroking Dean's sleeve. 'I mean, that is cloth, isn't it? Not one of those new reinforced paper suits? No, it feels real. I believe these suits contain extracts of reprocessed polyester. Sweet.' Carlton eyed Dean. 'Where did you get it?'

He felt an urge to tell Carlton the truth, but that wasn't the game plan. 'Aha! That would be telling!' He laughed.

Carlton took a slug of his triple-strength mystery drink. 'Well, it's a nice suit. Anyway, down to business. Tell me straight: what are you looking for?'

Something in Carlton's attitude had shifted. He was more respectful, almost deferential. Having the right clothes, the right presentation, the right attitude, that's what did it. People were impressed by the froth on top of the Frothaccino, not what was underneath.

'So, my ideal,' Dean began, embodying his persona as fully as he could muster, 'is to get inside Krane Media. To discover their essence. To feel their passion. To really understand what they are offering. What's behind the hype? I want to get to the heart of Krane Media.' Sitting back, he took a sip of his Nutri-ccino.

'Nice. I like your style.' Carlton leaned in. 'Look, I've taken the liberty of sending some messages, calling in some favours, and I might be able to get you to a sponsors' gathering at Krane Media.'

This sounded perfect, but he kept his expression blank. 'I'm not sure, Carlton. Do you mean like that sponsorship gig you organised here. It's not really…'

'No, no, no!' Carlton shook his head vigorously. 'That was small time. This would be at Krane Media, organised by Krane

Media themselves. Only specially selected guests will be there, people with ideas, people with ambition, people who can make things happen. People like you.'

He had to hand it to Carlton, his rhetoric was top notch. 'I'm still not sure. Who will be there from Krane?'

Carlton's forehead glistened. 'I don't like to mention names,' he said, leaning forward, 'and it's never 100 per cent guaranteed, but I'm confident there'll be some of Krane's executive innovators and opportunists there. Believe me, you won't be disappointed.'

Dean narrowed his eyes and took a dramatic moment to pretend to consider the offer. 'Carlton, what time should I be there?'

Talking to Carlton was as tiring as a game of chess.

'All I need is your handprint here.' Carlton proffered his tablet.

After Dean had placed his handprint on the screen, Carlton stood up with a flourish and they shook hands. He had a tight grip.

'Must be on my way. Good to do business, Dean.'

'Likewise.'

Watching Carlton leave, he wondered which of them had just played checkmate. He couldn't tell if Carlton was desperate for business or if his acting was of an altogether higher calibre. There was a sense of competition, but it wasn't clear what they were trying to win.

A few moments later, Dean realised no concrete plans had been made. He had no idea where, when or even if the sponsorship gathering would take place, yet he'd given his handprint.

* * *

To-ing and fro-ing, back and forth between his apartment and the shopping mall, it was like having a job. Maybe this was how people lived in the Complex? Networking. Making deals. This was hard work, thought Dean. He remembered when he was very young, how he would often feel agitated and pace up and down the living room.

'You're going to wear a hole in that carpet,' his mum would say.

'But I'm bored. I don't know what to do!'

His mother would smile kindly. 'Well, I know plenty of things you could do. You could clean the kitchen floor, vacuum the carpet, go to the shops...'

'No, I don't want to do things like that. I want to do something interesting.'

'I'd like to do something interesting as well, but life's not like that.'

'It's not fair,' he might say, then stare out of the window or slump down on the sofa. 'Life is boring.'

It might have felt that way then, but he would give anything right now to go back and be staring out of that window again.

He looked at the shops selling their trinkets and treats, and the scurrying people in their multi-coloured garb, empty expressions on their faces. What a strange world people had created. No one really knew what they were doing but, rather than admit it, they invented all manner of distractions. However, the distractions only worked for a short time.

Arriving at his apartment, he heard a woman's voice. 'Dean, do you have a minute?' Cherilea's front door was open a few centimetres. 'I'm sorry, Dean. Can you help?'

He sighed. What now?

'Dean, please, it's not what you think. My husband's ill.'

'OK,' he said. Strange how, back in his old flat, in that desolate concrete tower, he'd never spoken to any of his neighbours.

The door slid open wider and Cherilea stood there in her dressing gown, buttoned up.

'OK, I'll come in.'

'I'm sorry about earlier,' she said. 'I think I shocked you.'

'It's OK,' he said, walking in. 'You took me by surprise. I didn't know what to say.' The door slid shut behind him.

'I know you're a good man. You're not like other people in the Complex. I don't know why you're here, but I'm thinking you must know things.'

It seemed in Cherilea's eyes he'd graduated from being the naïve newcomer into some sort of sage. Sometimes you only need to stand still and the whole world changes around you. 'I'm not anything, really.' He was struck by his own words: they weren't true, not any more. He was something, he just didn't know what yet.

Cherilea walked over to where her husband lay, inert, silent, and put her hand on his chest. 'It's OK. He's not dead,' she said quickly, pointing at wires and tubes dangling down. 'He's hooked up. He had another turn. I couldn't afford it but I called Home Medical. They've attached him to the Life Extension System.'

Like a Krane Media extension pack, he thought. 'I see. Will he get better?'

'I doubt it. But I can't afford to lose him.'

'I'm not surprised. You must be very close. I was married once and…'

'No. I mean, literally, I can't afford to lose him. It's purely financial now. He'll never be like he was, but I need him alive to keep my apartment.'

'Oh. I see,' he said, but his expression suggested otherwise.

'My account's taken a massive hit,' she explained. 'Sales of Nutri-Taste Breakfast Cereal aren't going well. There's something new on the market. A tastier, more nutritional meal.'

Choosing his words carefully, he ventured, 'So if sales aren't going well, and your husband's in a bad way, is there a less expensive way of treating him?'

She looked surprised. 'You must be joking.' She was pacing

the floor.

The dim light in the apartment failed to conceal clothes strewn about, piles of boxes containing who knows what, and more furniture than necessary.

'Could you sell some of your stuff?'

She snorted. 'I wish.'

He put his hands in his pockets. 'Cherilea, I'm sorry about your situation but I don't know how I can help.'

She stopped pacing and looked at him blankly. 'You're a strange one. I mean, you're nice. But I don't get this act. I know you're new around here, but do you know nothing?'

'Maybe I should go.'

'No!' Rushing over to him, she grabbed his lapels, then thought better of it and took a step back, her hands by her side like a small child. 'I can see there's no hinting with you. I just want to buy that Krane Media extension pack and for you to buy my Nutri-Taste Breakfast Cereal. I haven't got the energy or the time to negotiate. As you can see, I'm desperate.'

'OK. No problem. Sure.'

'Really? Thank you!' She clapped her hands.

'But do you need it? You don't strike me as a games sort of person and if you don't have the money...'

Her shoulders dropped and she stared. 'Are you shizzing me? Of course I'm not a games sort of person. I'm not an anything sort of person, but my account activity has dropped badly. I've not been selling, so I've had to buy more than I can afford, just to keep my rating up. It's a bad time.'

'I'm sorry, I still don't understand. Why buy if...?'

'Do I really need to spell it out? You may be as snug as a bug in a rug, but not me. If he dies I lose this apartment. I'll get a single person apartment, and that's just the beginning of the end. I just need more account activity, incoming, outgoing, that's all, without breaking the bank.' A tear trickled down her plastic cheek. 'I can't bare to think about it.'

'Sorry.' He could see his questions weren't helping either of them. 'So do you want my handprint?'

'No, I'm the one who should be sorry.' Gathering herself, she found her tablet. 'I panic easily. Every day, I panic. The thought of losing this apartment, then the next apartment, then, pretty soon, it's the end.'

'The end?'

'Yeah. Over the Wall for me.'

'The Wall?' He couldn't hide his surprise. 'You live in the Complex and you're scared of the Wall?'

'Sure. Isn't everyone?' She held out her tablet and waited, her patience finally exhausted.

He placed his handprint on the screen. Evidently, he'd lost his sage-like status.

'Thank you.'

* * *

Inside his apartment, Dean thought again about Ferry and why he had put him in this place with so little information. He felt like a character in a computer game or a play – maybe a play being written by Ferry. Maybe that was the point: everyone he had met was an actor, testing him, monitoring his reactions. Carlton, Cherilea, Cherilea's husband, they might all be brilliant actors. Perhaps unlikely. At least he had Clare, who he could trust. Unless? No, he refused to believe that.

He picked up his tablet, but before he could press a button, the lights went out. Instinctively, he fell to the floor, then he darted to the side of the sofa and crouched down by some bushes, watching, listening. Flashes of lightning on the horizon, lighting up a dense copse at the top of a hill. Wind blowing into his face made him shiver. No sign of life. Tentatively, bending low, he started to explore the area. The ground sloped. He heard the ripple of a stream and headed towards it, walking uphill. A fence stood in the way and beyond that, the copse loomed larger. Something told him his friend had sought refuge in the copse, but the copse looked more like a trap than a refuge. Reaching out, he felt the rough wood of the fence. Should he climb over and make his way up towards the copse? Maybe his friend lived there, scavenging, struggling for survival each day. As he climbed over the fence, a thunder crack startled him and he lost his footing and stepped into the stream. Scrambling through it, his shoes and trousers getting soaked in the freezing water, he was now in open fields, but he sensed a presence behind him, following. His heart beat faster, his body cold, sweat on his forehead. The copse was close. Gnarled bark made faces at him, thick foliage overhead – and now he was among the trees. Looking behind him, he could see no one.

'Hey!'

The voice startled him. Turning, he found himself face to face with his friend.

'You made it! You came for me.'

They both grinned.

Amid the confusion and the danger, their bond gave Dean strength. 'Is this where you live? Is it safe?'

'Sometimes it feels safe. Sometimes it feels like a trap. Like I'm a sitting target.'

'Yeah, that's what I was thinking: a trap. But a sitting target for what?'

'The beast.'

'What is the beast?'

'You've seen the beast.'

'But where does it come from?'

Then: branches breaking somewhere behind his friend. Pounding footsteps. A deafening roar. Dean's friend turned to stare at him – fear and dismay on his face. 'You brought it here!' he yelled.

'Run!' screamed Dean. As he turned to flee, the grotesque face of the ogre appeared, jaws open, sharp yellow teeth bearing down on his friend. Stumbling, almost falling down the hill, Dean could hear screams behind him and the sound of bones breaking.

Lying on his back, with the room settings returning to normal, Dean could feel his heart thumping in his chest. Slowly he re-acclimatised to the real world. But something haunted him: his friend's accusation of betrayal. Nothing could be further from the truth, but he felt tried and found guilty. Did he do wrong to venture towards the copse? And if the beast had followed him, was that his fault? What else could he have done? *Purgatory* no longer felt like a game. Slapping the floor of his apartment, he said out loud: 'This floor is real. This apartment is real. The game is not real.' Each time he had played *Purgatory*, it had taken him longer to return to reality.

* * *

Maybe he had passed out, because he felt dazed when an alert on his tablet woke him, telling him a message had arrived. It was from Carlton – urgent – giving details for the sponsors event at Krane Media. It brought some comfort to know he would finally be getting inside Krane Media, one step closer to Jane. Then he remembered his date with Clare. One thing at a time. He was meeting Clare first. Perhaps he could ask her about Krane. Surely she must be curious about them too?

The fog in his head was starting to clear. He couldn't afford to lose focus. He thought about Cherilea's husband: there were things in this place that ate into you.

* * *

In his flashy suit, Dean felt out of place in Retro-respect. The clothes in his wardrobe seemed a little conspicuous in the café's bohemian atmosphere. Wherever you go there are tribes and hierarchies, even here in the Complex. For the first time, he started to regret the surgery to his face, though at least the face-lift injections would wear off – so he was told.

'Hey! Someone's looking stylish!' Clare slipped into the seat opposite him.

She looked even better than before. It was those little touches that set her apart from the Complex's production line beauties, the unlacquered hair, the bows and bangles. 'Thank you,' he said. 'But do I detect a little sarcasm?'

'Maybe a little. Is this what they gave you to make you fit in?' she asked. 'You look OK, I suppose.'

'I'm going to take that as a compliment! I've never been into clothes or fashion. Now I've had the whole make-over, though I didn't exactly have a choice.' He thought for a moment. 'Hey, what is it with fashion in here? Out in the Perimeter, men and women mostly wear uniforms, you know, overalls, and they look pretty much the same. We're like, I dunno, an army of workers, united, but for the fact that everyone's too afraid to communicate, of course. But in here there are very different dress codes for men and women.'

'I know. Not much room for feminism in the Complex. My theory is that people are so anonymous in here that at least they can express themselves as a man or a woman. They can be an anonymous man or an anonymous woman, but at least that's something compared to being an anonymous person.'

'What a choice! A stereotype or anonymity. But you don't seem to be either of those.'

'Well, I don't want to be a clone, but then I don't want to stand out too much, either. Getting noticed isn't helpful. I just want to be Clare.'

'Out in the Perimeter, it's as if gender's been blotted out. But in some ways I prefer that. Before the war, in the old days, there was this big pressure on men to be macho, without fear, strong, a fighter. All that bullshiz. Gender is a complicated business.'

'It certainly is.'

They sat in silence for a moment. Unable to think of something to say, Dean pretended to study the menu. Maybe, more accurately, he knew what he wanted to say, but he didn't feel comfortable saying it; he wanted to say: 'I think I'm falling in love with you.'

'Not very chatty, are you?' she said. 'I'm not either.'

'Sorry,' he said, putting down the menu. 'I've spent too much time on my own. I've forgotten what it's like to spend time with someone I actually like.' He laughed to hide his awkwardness for being so honest.

'I know. It's not easy to be open and honest these days. Maybe it never was.'

'Yes.' He picked up the menu again and propped it upright, something to hide his vulnerability behind. 'It's funny. My wife used to say I talked too much, but I think she meant she didn't like what I talked about.'

'Your wife?' She said this casually, but he could tell she was surprised.

'Yeah.' He bent over the corner of the menu and pressed hard. He always found it amazing that silicon paper couldn't crease. 'I haven't seen her for years. I mean, I don't know if we're technically still married. She left me.'

'I see. A married man.'

Why did he feel like he'd been caught out? 'So how about you? Are you married?'

She cocked her head to one side. 'You think I'd be living with my brother if I was married?'

'No. I suppose not.'

'How long were you together?'

'About eight years.'

'Is she still out there in the Perimeter?'

Now Clare was reminding him of Jane, putting him on the

spot with no wriggle room.

'No. She got a job with Krane Media. I told her it was selling out, but she got a job with them anyway. I had these principles about living with integrity, but maybe I was being idealistic or naïve.'

'So you were the idealistic one and she was the pragmatic one?'

'Frack, you're putting me under the spotlight.' He didn't mean to sound angry.

She held up her hands. 'Hey! Pardon me! Excuse me for taking an interest.'

'I'm sorry. It's just, I've never talked about this. I suddenly feel a bit stupid.'

'Why? This is called getting-to-know-you. It's what people do. Or, at least, what they used to do. They're just questions. For example, do you have kids?'

Sighing, he realised it would be difficult to hide anything from Clare, and he didn't know if he wanted to. 'No. No kids. I didn't think we'd be having a conversation like this?'

'Like what?' She looked surprised.

'Frack, Clare, I…'

'Look, Dean, let's cut the crap. What's going on here? What do you want?'

'OK, OK, fine!' He put his hands flat on the table. This felt like a lover's tiff. He lowered his voice. 'I'll be honest, I'm confused. I like you. I feel like I can trust you. You seem to have your feet on the ground. You understand things. I'm lost here. I'm trying to work out what's going on.'

'So you're looking for your wife and I might be helpful to you?' She said this with her poker face firmly in place. Frack, she was sharp – like a mind-reader.

'Maybe.' This was the most out of control he had felt since arriving in the Complex. 'Maybe it was like that. But not entirely, and certainly not now.' He stared at his hands. 'When I said I like you, I mean I'd like to be your friend. A proper friend.'

Clare put her hands on the table and slid them forward so their fingers tips were touching. 'I like you too, Dean.' Her voice was softer now. 'I'm confused too. I live every day with confusion. And I hate it. Have you any idea how much I might be putting myself at risk even meeting you here in public? I'm not meaning to give you a hard time. It's my choice to be here, but I don't want to be messed around. I want you to think about that.'

He lifted up his hands to put them on top of Clare's, but she drew her hands away.

'So what's your plan?' Her voice was matter-of-fact.

'Right. OK. So,' he began, folding his arms. 'Here's my plan. I'm going to Krane Media this evening. My idea is partly to see if I can see Jane.'

'Jane?'

'My ex. I don't know why. Unfinished business, I suppose. Wanting answers. Not just about me and her, about everything. What she knows. There's something weird going on. You mentioned the additives. My neighbour: her husband is on some sort of life-support system. He's drugged out. She's destitute but she wants to keep buying stuff even though she can't afford it. And she's afraid of the Wall. Why would anyone in the Complex be afraid of the Wall? And then there's Vinty.'

'Shhh!' Clare leaned forward. 'So, first of all, thank you for being honest. Secondly, those are good questions. But, thirdly, please don't mention Vinty in public. People talk about little listening devices planted everywhere, I'm not so sure. Either way, best to keep quiet. How long have you got?'

He looked at his watch – the watch Clare gave him, and he realised she had given him so much more. 'I need to be there soon. I don't really know what I'm doing. What I do know is that this place is nothing like I imagined when I was on the outside. And now I'm in here, I'm not sure I want to be.'

'Dean, I'm going to leave you to it. You're getting the hang of it. The additives? There are drugs in everything – they don't want us to think – but we do our best to keep healthy. Buying too much stuff is just how the economy works. It's all about account activity. We're all in debt. I guess your neighbour thinks she knows what she's doing. About the Wall, I need to think about that.'

'What do you mean "Leave me to it"? Will I see you again?'

She smiled. 'I hope so.' Reaching into a metallic-look satchel draped over her shoulder, she pulled out an envelope. 'A little gift,' she said, then she quickly got up and left the café.

Taking the envelope, he watched her go. He noticed the man behind the counter staring at him. He hadn't even ordered anything and now he had to go. Slipping the envelope into the inside pocket of his suit, he stared at the table top. It was perfectly clean. With Clare he felt brave – ready for anything – but now she'd gone he felt even more confused than before. They hadn't made an arrangement to meet again, but she had smiled and said 'I hope so'. Shiz.

* * *

'Dean, turn left at the next intersection. Stuck for gift ideas for someone you love? At The Gift Station you will find an impressive selection of beautiful and creative objects and ornaments. New this week: flowering artificial plants – they flower and un-flower fives times a day or at the touch of a button. Terms and conditions apply. Warning: may not function as advertised.'

This was a new part of the Complex. Dean spotted a Designer Frothaccino and some other familiar names, plus some new names: Cyber Pet Vet, Hair Surgery Centre and what appeared to be a sex shop called Into-Me-See.

'Dean, relationships are messy, but there's one person who will always love you: Yourself! At Into-Me-See we offer intimacy with yourself: interactive self-love programmes and devices to help you to *become more intimate with the lover in you that loves you.'*

It seemed someone had had the bright idea of marketing masturbation as a self-help programme. But, with the Internet no longer working, he reckoned *self-lovers* had to get their kicks somewhere. Is that what relationships had become: an orgasm with a virtual lover? He remembered the Fantasorium and the card Dylan Fairfax had given him: *More real than reality!*

'Dean, Krane Media is straight ahead. Why not take time out of your hectic schedule to...'

Switching off his smart-nav, he stared at the biggest shop he had seen in the Complex, stretching several times the height and width of any other shop front: *Krane Media: Your Life, Your Dream.*

The Krane Media shop floor was open plan. People streamed in and out. Dozens of centre staff were stationed at pods where they demonstrated games and devices to customers, their arms flailing about them like octopi, activating touch-sensitive screens to bring holographic dramas to life. At one pod, he caught a glimpse of his friend in *Purgatory*, and he wondered whether he should go home and speak to him, explain that he hadn't betrayed him. But it's only a game, he reminded himself.

Dodging his way through the melee of shoppers and sales activity, he headed for the back of the shop, hoping to find someone official to speak to.

'Dean!'

Feeling a hand on his shoulder, he turned to see Carlton.

'Good to see you! I saw you come in. Lucky for me it's a quiet spell at the moment, this place is usually packed.'

'Really? Seems busy to me.'

'Ah, of course, I forgot. You probably haven't been here before. Well, welcome to my world!'

He flung an arm around Dean's shoulders, which made Dean flinch, though he hoped it hadn't shown.

'Come with me. Let's get to where the real business is happening.'

Following Carlton to the rear of the store, they came to a large holographic door flanked by two security guards, dressed in video-suits displaying security camera footage of lawbreakers being violently manhandled. Carlton indicated for Dean to stay where he was, then approached one of the guards to explain about the sponsors' event. The guard barely acknowledged Carlton's presence, but deigned to put a handprint on Carlton's tablet. A relieved-looking Carlton turned around to beckon forward Dean, who tried to avoid the glare the guard was giving him.

'We're in,' said Carlton as they emerged into a huge open plan office, filled with staff operating glowing screens and devices. 'Let's make the most of it. I'll introduce you to a few people. I think about an hour should be enough.'

They were in a large area, similar to the shop front, but with sharper lighting and staff in snazzier clothes, listening with bored expressions to gesticulating visitors. Some of the staff wore suits displaying moving images of the people they were talking to. Other staff sat on seats that slid back and forth between screens and holographic interfaces, busily executing unfathomable procedures that involved using both hands at once to activate gaudy displays. Their busyness felt hypnotic.

'Come on,' said Carlton, heading for one of the officious looking Krane staff who was alone but deeply focused on the tablet in her hands.

'Carlton Dexter: Bespoke Life Solutions Consultant.'

The staff member – with the apparently natural beauty of a model – took a moment to finish what she was doing before looking up and staring expressionless at her visitor.

'I'm here for the Executive Opportunities function.'

The woman slowly offered her tablet for Carlton's handprint. Clearly bored, the woman checked the screen, swiped it a few times, then pointed at a set of holographic doors. As they headed towards it, the woman gave Dean a quick smile.

Even if Carlton was making it up as he went along, at least something was happening. Dean sensed he was getting closer, though closer to what he didn't know.

On the other side of the doorway, the atmosphere changed entirely. They were in something like a cocktail lounge, dimly lit, plush carpets, fabric-lined walls, low ceiling, a murmur of piano music, people mingling or seated around tables in convivial exchange, hushed voices.

'We're here! This is it, Dean, we can do a lot of business if we play our cards right.' Carlton rubbed his hands together.

'We?'

'Sure. You. Me. We.' He looked about the room.

Dean remembered what Clare had said about not messing her around. She was talking about integrity. Sometimes you have to put your cards on the table. 'Carlton, be straight with me, have you ever been here before? Because you seem a little overwhelmed. I thought this was all for my benefit?'

Carlton fiddled with his sleeve. 'OK, I admit it, this may surprise you but I might not be as successful as I come across.'

Dean said nothing.

'The fact is, business hasn't been brilliant of late. But you've inspired me. I want to make deals, too, make contacts. I thought we could help each other. We could be a good double act.'

'Double act?'

'You know, share leads. You're a natural, Dean, you just don't know it yet. And I've got a few moves up my sleeve. Let's play to each other's strengths.'

At least Carlton was being honest. It was difficult not to like him, though Dean felt sorry for him, too. At times he felt sorry for almost everyone in this place, although the Krane staff seemed to be doing all right for themselves. 'OK, Carlton. So how does it work?'

'To be honest, I've no idea. Just keep up the energy, make contacts, and maximise!'

With that, Carlton made a beeline for a waiter carrying a tray of elaborate cocktails. So it was another meet and greet, not unlike the one at The Designer Frothaccino, but more upmarket, closer to the source. At least Dean was not a novice this time. And anyway, what he really wanted was information, not sales. He wondered if Jane had kept his surname. Unlikely.

He scanned the room, suddenly nervous. Carlton might be an oddball, but he did at least give him some confidence: maybe they were a double act. Carlton was difficult to fathom, but at least he was starting to prove reliable. The guy had already struck up a conversation at the bar with a woman who seemed to be competing with him to see who could make the most elaborate gestures. Around the room, elegantly dressed people were animated, energetic, which was exactly how Dean didn't feel. Then he noticed a man, on his own, at a table in the far corner. He could have been asleep, but then he took a drink from the glass in his hand. Dean ambled towards him via an indirect route, so as not to appear to be pouncing upon him.

'Hi, my name's Dean Rogers. *Wall to Wall Games: Extension Pack 14. Krane Media: Your Life, Your Dream.*'

The man briefly looked up with an expression of horror. 'Oh, shiz,' he said, hurriedly taking a drink.

'Mind if I take a seat?'

'Do what you want,' said the man, not making eye contact, 'it's *your life, your dream.*'

He was clean-shaven, with a long nose and surprisingly unkempt long hair, which must surely be some radical style statement and not as scruffy as it looked. He wore a plain brown suit. In Dean's opinion, he looked pretty cool, but what did he know.

'I'll be honest,' said Dean, 'this is my first time at one of these gatherings.'

'Lucky you.'

'I came with...' He paused while deciding what to call

Carlton, '…my colleague. He's an old hand at this. Actually, he got me into Krane Media.'

'So you said. *Wall to Wall Games: Extension Pack 14.*'

If this guy was always this difficult, no wonder he was sitting on his own. 'Yes. Very powerful stuff. I'll be honest, I hadn't played many virtual reality games before but I put on *Purgatory* and – wow…' He could see his friend now, in the copse at the top of the hill, accusing him of betrayal. He didn't even know his name.

'Sounds like it made quite an impression.'

'Yeah, definitely. I put the game on, not expecting much, but it kind of took over. It's a cliché, but I felt I was really there. So powerful. The feelings were real. My friend – the guy in the game – the last time I saw him, there was a misunderstanding. He thought I'd betrayed him, but I hadn't.' He realised this was more detail than was necessary, but at least he had the man's attention.

'So what will you do about it?'

The question took him by surprise: this was exactly what he had been trying to work out. 'What I don't understand is the reason for the game. Initially I thought it was about avoiding or killing this monster. But it's become something else. It's about friendship and compassion.' His own words surprised him.

'Go on,' said the man, 'tell me more.'

'OK, so bear with me on this, I'm thinking out loud. It seems that what's being put to the test is not my military strategy or my firepower – although that could come into it – but my decision making. This might sound weird, but it's like I'm on trial. Or maybe I'm testing myself – I'm the defendant, judge and jury; I've only just realised that.'

The man finished his drink and sat back in his chair, staring up at the ceiling, his long, thin legs stretched out, hands resting on his belly, fingers entwined. Dean watched him, respecting his space, not knowing whether the guy was thinking or zoning out.

Finally, still staring upwards, he asked, 'Why did you choose to speak to me?'

'You want the truth?'

'Why not?' The man fixed his gaze on Dean. His eyes were bright green. 'Tell me the truth.'

Dean laughed, wondering if this was a joke. 'Really? The truth?'

'Say whatever you want.'

'OK, the truth is I saw you were alone, which meant I wouldn't be interrupting a conversation. And there was no one nearby, so I thought I could test out my patter without anyone listening in.'

'Any more?'

Dean felt uncomfortable, but he was in it now. 'OK, how about this. I imagined you might be a loner or shy. You didn't seem threatening. But now I can see I got you wrong.' To his surprise, he was shaking.

The man sat up. 'What are you feeling now?'

'I'm confused. I don't know why I'm telling you all this.'

'Why are you?'

'I don't know.' He shifted in his seat. 'I feel like you're judging me.'

'But all I've done is ask some questions. You don't have to reply. You don't even have to stay here. You can walk away. I'm not judging you.'

These comments took Dean by surprise. 'I hadn't thought of it that way.' He paused to think it through. 'I suppose I should take responsibility for this. For being here, for talking to you, even for my own feelings. Maybe I'm judging myself?'

'Exactly! See what we do to ourselves! And all those things you imagined about me – a loner, unthreatening, shy – where did that come from? I'm just sitting here minding my own business. Your ideas about me are your own issues projected onto me. That's what people do; they look at other people and imagine they're the same as they are. You look at me and you see a loner, but that's not me, that's you.'

Dean didn't know where to put himself. He felt stripped bare, like the man could see right to the core of him.

'Dean Rogers, you said?'

'Yes.'

'I'm guessing you feel a bit dizzy now. I can recommend you get yourself a drink. Just plain water. They'll have it at the bar.'

'Yes, right. Good idea.' He didn't know if the man was dismissing him or offering advice, but he did feel thirsty. 'Can I get you anything?'

'I'm fine, thanks.' Smiling, the man closed his eyes and stretched out.

The volume in the room seemed to have doubled, voices doing vocal acrobatics, words tumbling through the air. Reaching the bar, he said: 'Water. Just plain water.'

'Coming up,' said the barman.

'Dean! Incredible!' Carlton slapped Dean on the back.

'Hi, Carlton.' Dean wanted the drink, then he wanted to go.

'You're a smooth operator. More than that, you've got balls! What happened?'

'What do you mean?'

'Did you get a deal? Are you moving up in the world? Don't forget me when you're rich and famous!'

'Your water, sir.' The waiter presented a glass which had its own glass straw attached as part of the design.

He took a long drink and felt better.

Carlton was frowning. 'You don't know, do you?'

'Know what?'

'Who you were talking to?

'I don't want to talk about it.'

'Dean, just tell me: Do you know who you were speaking to?'

'Some bloke.'

'Yeah, I'll say. That was Charles Krane. Ring a bell? Krane Media!'

'I've got to go.'

'I'm coming with you,' said Carlton.

'No.' There was anger in his voice. He patted Carlton on the shoulder and spoke softly. 'I mean, please, I'm fine. I need some rest.'

'Sure, no problem.' Carlton stepped back. 'Take care of yourself and keep in touch.'

Finishing his water, Dean looked over to the table in the corner. Charles Krane had gone.

* * *

Back in the mall, Dean walked slowly past the flickering, kitsch shop frontages. Before they had all blended into one collage of light and colour, but now he noticed details. The sign for a shop called *SuperGym* had a squished up 'm' – as if the sign maker had run out of space and squeezed it in as best he could. How was that mistake even possible in a world of computer precision? Yet there it was. He noticed the bored expressions. These people were in such a hurry, did they even notice how bored they were? We make ourselves busy, he thought, because if we were to stop and think, we'd realise how difficult life really is. Then he remembered Krane's unusual words: perhaps it was Dean himself who was bored and seeing it in others.

He took in the cavernous avenues and the sheer size of the Complex. Mostly it comprised of empty space. More of a monument than a practical building. He wondered how many people lived and worked here. All of this information used to be available freely on the Internet – at least in the form of conjecture if not fact. Now society was a mystery to itself. Who was at the heart of all of this? He thought about those dizzying news reports describing the public's appreciation for the government's latest successes. Who were these people and who was making all these TV bulletins?

He was back on familiar territory, close to Harding's Emporium. He knew he wasn't supposed to visit Clare at work, so he would glance in, hope to get a glimpse of her, then walk on quickly. As he got nearer, he could see someone adjusting the shop window display – a young man, someone he didn't recognise. Probably he was Clare's age; a much better match than he was. Why had he blurted out all that stuff about Jane? Stopping in the doorway, he looked inside but couldn't see her.

'Can I help you, sir?'

Shiz! Coleman.

'I'm not even in the shop!'

'I beg your pardon, sir? I merely wondered if something had caught your eye or if you were looking for something or someone specific?'

What did he mean 'someone'? Had Clare told him? Surely not. 'I'm OK, thank you. I'm busy.'

At that moment, Clare walked up from behind without noticing them. She must have been on an errand in the mall. When she saw them she looked shocked, but composed herself and, without a word, side-stepped them into the shop.

'Clare,' said Coleman.

She turned to face him, anxious.

'We have a new consignment of clocks in the storeroom. Would you mind selecting a few for shop display?'

'Certainly,' she said.

'Oh, wait!' said Coleman, turning to Dean. 'Do I recall you visited our shop the other day enquiring about such clocks? Perhaps you'd like to see our new shipment? Wonderful quality.'

'No. I'm fine, thank you. Perhaps another time. I must go.' He made a short bow, bizarrely, as if it was the nineteenth century, and regretted it immediately. Then he shot off, not daring to look back. Frack.

Hurrying back to his apartment, he kept going over his exchange with Coleman, analysing everything. What if Coleman had worked out who he was? Maybe he should have stayed indoors and waited for Ferry to contact him? Maybe Ferry kept trying but he was always out.

Stepping out of the elevator at his balcony level, he saw two men in helmets standing by his apartment. Police or security of some kind. One of the men turned and saw him. *Panic. Don't show it. Keep walking.* The man kept staring and when Dean got closer, he could see Cherilea's apartment door was open. The security man turned back to his colleague as Dean walked past. Cherilea's apartment was brightly lit and bare.

He walked around for a good half hour before returning home. The security men had gone. So Cherilea's fears had come true, it seemed.

Slumping onto his sofa, the phrase 'out of the frying pan, into the fire' came to mind.

Taking off his jacket, he remembered the envelope Clare had given him. It felt lumpy. He unzipped the poly-paper and was hit by a long forgotten smell. Inside, was a slice of brown bread – real bread! The first he'd seen in years. He held the envelope carefully so as not to spill any crumbs, and broke off a chunk. It tasted wonderful. He closed his eyes. Childhood memories came to him of savouring thickly buttered slices of bread. He'd ask his mum for sweets, but she'd say: 'If you're hungry, you can have a slice of bread.' This was his trick; he preferred bread. But he'd reckoned if he asked for bread, his mother would tell him to eat something else – something less appealing. For some reason, it was always wrong to ask for what you wanted. Fresh bread with thick crusts, there was nothing like it! What a gift! It must have cost a fortune – but Clare didn't seem wealthy. Maybe she had made it – or someone she knew had made it – so the question was; where did the ingredients come from and what was she trying to tell him?

Carefully putting aside the envelope, he picked up the Vinty book and ran a finger down the contents list: 'Chapter 5: What is truth?'

'We have to think about something. That's what the brain does. Imagine a newborn thrust into the world. What is she to make of it? The brain tries to make meaning out of the chaos. The newborn begins the project of constructing an internal mental representation of the world. Once this world view is established, that is what the world looks like. But it might not reflect what is really out there. Consider how different that world view must be depending where in the world one is born or in which century. Or, to take this further, imagine being born as a different type of creature: as a cat or a bird or an insect. Clearly, our personal world view is not the only way of seeing things; the world – and ourselves – can be thought of quite differently. This is a good start. So let us accept that there is not one truth. Rather, there are many. Or perhaps there are none. What is truth? Whether there exists an ultimate truth is not our immediate topic. For now, we must discern – or, rather, dismantle – the notion that whatever we believe right now is the truth. To sum up: whatever you believe, it is not the truth.'

Putting his head back, he closed his eyes. He'd read these words before – a long time ago – but this time they meant something. The truth is elusive, perhaps beyond our reach, which is scary in one way, unsettling, but also liberating because it frees us from the pressure of needing to understand. Picking up the envelope, he ate the rest of the bread. It tasted substantial – something he could be sure of.

* * *

It took Dean a moment to work out where the sound was coming from. Emitting an alarm, his tablet screen flashed blue-yellow, blue-yellow. 'Message from Krane Media,' the screen read. 'Dean Rogers. I enjoyed our conversation. Come and see me. Let's chat some more. Charles Krane.'

The plot thickens, as his dad used to say.

All Dean could remember about his conversation with Krane

was tripping over his words and feeling uncomfortable. Maybe Krane liked what he'd said about *Purgatory*. The next time they met he would be more guarded, that was for sure. Fetching a beaker of water – hopefully free from additives – he fired up *Purgatory*. Not dark this time, but dawn. Sitting on the sofa, the holographs transported him to a small wooden cabin on the edge of a forest. The sun lingered on the horizon, an orange glow filled the room and a gentle breeze carried an earthy fragrance. He knocked on the door. A short pause, then the door opened and his friend stood in silhouette.

'Oh, it's you,' he said.

'I came to see you.'

'Come in. Take a seat.'

An open fire flickered in the hearth, an iron pot hanging over it. Pots and pans hung from nails on the wall. It reminded him of the one time he'd visited his great-grandmother's house. He must have been only five or six years old. A pile of rugs in one corner suggested the sleeping arrangements.

'I don't even know your name,' said Dean.

'Not important.' His friend sat on a wooden chest. Lying next to him was a pair of shears that looked familiar. In the flickering light the young man's face kept changing so Dean couldn't get a fix on it.

'Have I done something wrong?' asked Dean. 'The other night, with that thing, the creature, I didn't mean to draw it towards you.'

'Is that why you came? For forgiveness?'

'No. I mean, maybe. I don't know.'

'You need nothing from me. What you do to me, you do to yourself. If you want forgiveness, forgive yourself.'

'Frack. Why is everything in riddles? I just want some straight answers.'

His friend laughed. 'Then ask straight questions.'

'OK, so tell me, who are you exactly?'

'I think you'll find out soon enough.'

'Oh, shiz, that's not fair! You said I should ask some straight questions.'

'I know. But I didn't say I'd answer them!'

'Then how about this,' said Dean. 'Can you tell me why that monster's after you?'

'Who says it's after me?'

'Frack! This is a waste of time!' Dean flopped back in his chair. 'Riddles again.'

'Not a riddle. Think about it: was it a monster or just a living creature that's different to you and me?'

'But it was horrible, the eyes, the teeth, the...' He closed his eyes. 'I was terrified. And you died.'

'Thanks to you! Maybe I was doing fine. You're the one talking about monsters. Perhaps that's the better question. Why did you create the monster?'

'I created the monster? What does that mean?'

A distant grumble, a low growl. Reducing his voice to a whisper, Dean leaned forward. 'Are you saying I'm making the monster up, inventing it?'

'Well, are you?'

'Frack, you're as bad as Charles Krane.'

His friend smiled. 'Is Charles Krane bad?'

He stared at him. 'Is that a clue? What are you telling me? Are you Charles Krane?'

Laughing, the young man said, 'Not quite, but a good guess. He helped to create *Purgatory*. But you're helping to create *Purgatory* too. That's what purgatory is: a place of our own creation, somewhere between our own personal heaven and hell.'

Dean felt his stomach turn over. 'You're saying that I'm inventing this game as I go along? All this darkness. It's from me?'

'You see, ask some straight questions and you'll start to get some straight answers. You're answering this puzzle yourself.

Clever game, hey?'

Folding his arms, Dean looked around the cabin. He noticed a wooden plaque on the wall, with burned-on lettering: 'Dun Roamin.' He remembered his father putting that plaque up next to the front door at home. Other parts of the cabin looked familiar too, from the picture books he used to spend hours gazing at when he was little: *Aesop's Fables*, *Grimm's Fairy Tales*. And the shears with the red handles, they were the ones his grandfather used for pruning the rose bushes.

A deep growl outside the door. Alarmed, Dean stared at his friend.

'You know what to do,' he said.

Sitting forward, feeling his heart race, Dean closed his eyes.

'Breathe,' said his friend.

Dean took a deep breath, and then another.

'Focus on your breathing, not on your fear.'

Dean knew he had read these instructions somewhere before, in that self-help book Jane had bought.

'Feel the weight of your body in the chair. Feel your feet on the floor. Relax your shoulders. Focus on the breath going in and out of your nostrils.'

Doing as he was told, a sense of calmness flooded his body. The growling faded into silence.

Eventually his friend spoke. 'See, you did it.'

They smiled.

'Thank you.'

'Ha! Don't thank me, thank yourself. The instructions were in you, deep in your memory. A book you read. And, in fact, you already have thanked yourself.'

It took a little while to work this one out. 'OK. I think I get it now. You're me, aren't you?'

His friend laughed. 'We got there in the end.'

The cabin faded from view and the lights in the apartment returned to their normal settings. There was a noise outside the front door. Movement. He remembered the security guards standing outside Cherilea's apartment earlier. Maybe they had come back, whoever *they* were: the authorities, the people in charge.

Activating the screen viewer in his door, outside he could see a tall man dressed meticulously in black, with a quiff hairstyle and black eye-liner, standing outside Cherilea's door. Then the man turned suddenly and stared straight at him. It took Dean a moment to realise the man couldn't see him. Then the man activated Dean's door panel.

Now what should he do? Resting his head against the door, he tried to breathe. If he did nothing, the man would no doubt go away. Or he could open the door, but then what would he be letting himself in for? For an anxious person, Dean realised he was strangely impulsive. Jane had called it foolhardy, like he invited trouble. He opened the door.

'Ah! How wonderful! Somebody at home!' said the man, his hand extended. 'I'm Vince Style, Customer Satisfaction Executive, *Fantasorium. More real than reality!*'

'How can I help?'

'Nothing too onerous.' He beamed, revealing pure white teeth. 'I'm merely on a routine expedition, in pursuit of the best interests of our loyal customers. Sadly your good neighbour, Mr Nutri-Taste, doesn't appear to be at home and I thought opportunistically to seek further information from a source that may be able to shed light on the scenario, namely your good self.'

'You have a nice turn of phrase.'

'Thank you, sir. Good diction and erudition hurts no one.'

'Routine call, you say? For Mr Nutri-Taste?'

'That's right. We like to ensure our customers are fully satisfied.'

'Nutri-Taste is an unusual name, isn't it?'

'You'd be surprised. We have a number of Nutri-Tastes on our books. It all helps to clock up the credit.'

'Yes, I suppose.' He decided to play dumb. 'The thing is, my neighbours never mentioned the Fantasorium. Are you sure you've got the right address?'

'If it's on my list,' said Vince, wiggling his tablet in the air, 'it'll be accurate. We pride ourselves on attention to detail.'

'But if he was a happy customer, why wouldn't he want to tell me about it?'

Frowning, Vince considered these words. Then something twigged. Smiling again, he said, 'Well, perhaps this might help. I'm specifically tasked with what we call long-term follow-up. If someone is on my list, they perhaps haven't visited the Fantasorium for two years at least. This is why Mr Nutri-Taste might not have mentioned our establishment of late.'

'A couple of years.' Dean remembered seeing his neighbour lying in his bed, as if in a coma, and how he had suddenly sat up and stared at him, zombie-like. 'Is it possible that something happened to him and he didn't want to talk about it?'

Vince looked shocked. 'With my hand on my heart,' he said, putting his hand on his heart, 'I'm not aware of any customer who has not experienced total satisfaction at the Fantasorium. The mystery, for me, is why they do not return.' He narrowed his eyes while a new thought occurred to him. 'I'm guessing, sir, you have not yet experienced the Fantasorium for yourself?' Vince paused to let this incredible idea sink in. Then, in an expression approaching disbelief, he exclaimed, 'Might this actually be possible?'

Dean wanted to laugh at Vince's cartoon persona, but attempted to frown instead – creating what must have been an odd expression. 'I'm more of a Krane Media man.'

'Well,' said Vince, shaking his head, 'all I can say is: you're missing out. Virtual games are watery in comparison to the Fantasorium. Here is my card. If you want a first-hand experience, I can offer a generous discount.'

Vince handed over his holo-card. His blinking image stared

out, dark grey and purple clouds swirling in the background.

'I've heard the Fantasorium is dangerous,' said Dean. 'I've heard it can do things to your brain.'

'Ha! Quite untrue. Lies. The Fantasorium makes your fantasies come alive in the safety of your imagination. Even the most wild and exotic of fantasies can be enacted in safety. As we like to say: better in than out. So, you see, the Fantasorium is the *opposite* of dangerous. All I can suggest is that you put my word to the test and try it out for yourself.'

'Have you tried it?'

Vince looked down at his shoes: black boots with ornate silver snakes winding around them. 'Rule number one: we don't talk about our own experiences. Everyone's fantasies are strictly private and confidential. Our fantasies are unique, so no two people experience the Fantasorium in the same way. At this point, professional ethics oblige me to inform you that the Fantasorium cannot be held liable for any accident or illness that occurs directly or indirectly due to participation at the Fantasorium. However, I also want to assure you that the Fantasorium is risk-free. See terms and conditions for our definition of risk.'

'OK, but, small print aside, given that you don't talk about each other's experiences, how would you know whether what people are experiencing is dangerous or not?'

Vince looked about him, checking they were alone. The golden dome of the Complex had a darker hue today. He tapped at the small screen on his sleeve – something similar to the sat-nav in Dean's suit. A blinking blue light on Vince's collar stopped flashing. 'Off the record,' he said, speaking quickly and without the ingratiating smile. 'Everyone's heard the rumours, but if something goes wrong then I can assure you it's because the participant is unstable in the first place. We try to screen people, but no test is 100 per cent effective, and some people are good at hiding their deep issues. But, let's face it, a few oddballs might have a mishap, but most people just want a quick frack with

Cleopatra or whoever, no questions asked. Get in touch, and I'll give you a good deal.' He re-activated the device he had switched off earlier and his salesman persona returned. 'It's been wonderful talking to you, sir. Please get in touch before my special offer expires.'

They shook hands, and Vince winked as he turned to go.

* * *

'I'm here to see Charles Krane. My name is Dean Rogers.'

'Thank you for your enquiry, Mr Rogers. I will do all I can to fulfil your request. Terms and conditions apply.' The young shop assistant in the Krane Media centre spoke brightly.

Dean could feel the sweat under his arms. Playing around with Carlton and Coleman was one thing – low risk – but somehow he'd managed to leapfrog several stages in the food chain. Out of earshot, the young Krane assistant was talking to a stern looking colleague, who nodded grimly. All around him, shop staff with windmill arms demonstrated the latest toys to wide-eyed customers: Krane Media was the dealer, the shoppers were the addicts.

'Mr Rogers, thank you again for your enquiry.' The young assistant spoke as brightly as before, but with a new circumspection in her voice. 'Is there a particular product you're looking for? Or perhaps you have a comment you would like to make about a recent purchase? Our Customer Satisfaction Team is happy to help. We operate a no refunds policy. Ask in store for our latest special offers.'

'Actually, I'd just like to see Charles Krane. I received a message from him to come and visit. So here I am!'

'But I've never... Just one moment, please.' The assistant once more sought out her grumpy colleague, who looked over at Dean with disdain, then headed in his direction.

'Hello, sir, I'm the manager,' she announced through a gritted smile. 'I understand there has been a misunderstanding. I'm obliged to tell you that we operate a zero tolerance policy. All customers are security screened...'

'Hey, I'm not a terrorist! There's no misunderstanding on my part. Just a simple question...'

'...and any attempt to interfere with Krane property, including staff, will trigger an immediate response. *While stocks last, get your free Krane Indexing System with any game costing over 3,000 credits.*'

'I'm here in response to an invitation from Charles Krane to come and visit him. The message arrived on my tablet earlier, so here I am. I met him the other day.'

The manager sighed. 'I don't want to call security.'

'It's OK. I'll handle this,' a man's voice interrupted.

It took Dean a moment to realise the man was Charles Krane, looking very different from before, wearing a peach suit, with his hair slicked back into a pony tail that curved round to form a near-circle. If it wasn't for his long, thin nose, Dean might not have recognised him.

'Certainly, Mr Krane,' the manager said nervously. 'I was merely following protocol. My colleague was concerned...'

'Glad you could make it, Dean. Let's go to my office,' said Krane, putting a hand on Dean's shoulder.

Walking through to the back of the shop, staff members looked at their boss with reverence. As they approached the holographic doors, both security guards made an extravagant show of ensuring the area was clear of any danger. Passing through the doorway, they walked into a busy office area. A hush fell on the proceedings, the staff parting before their visitors like the Red Sea before Moses.

'Did you happen to be in the shop?' asked Dean.

'My screening system alerted me you were here. You came up on my tablet.' Krane looked at Dean. Raising an eyebrow, he added: 'Sorry about the fuss out there. I generally try to avoid interacting with my staff as much as possible.'

As they approached a glass elevator, three members of Krane staff waiting there quickly stepped aside. Krane proceeded, oblivious. He pressed a combination of buttons and the elevator took off immediately, travelling upwards then sideways, changing directions several times.

'How big is Krane Media?' asked Dean, uncomfortable with the silence.

'Big. Too big. That's the downside of success.'

Having lambasted Jane about Krane Media, Dean felt a little hypocritical being there, let alone in the company of the man himself. He reminded himself that his interest in Krane was different from Jane's. Jane was career minded, she wanted security, she wanted the system to cradle her. All he wanted was answers.

Out of the elevator, they stepped into a large, plain, dimly-lit room that slowly started to change shape holographically, the walls becoming contoured, the floors re-shaping to create organic undulations. The resulting effect was disorientating but homely, like a coral reef built out of cushions. In the centre of the room, two sofas faced each other at some distance. Sitting down, Krane pressed a button on his sofa and a holographic window appeared in the wall. Through it, a beautiful lake sat at the bottom of a wooded valley; simultaneously, a pine-scented breeze wafted across the room. Closing his eyes, Krane sank into the sofa, exhaling as if he had been holding his breath for a long time.

'Nice view,' said Dean, sitting down in the sofa opposite.

'According to our files, you signed up to Krane Media very recently.' Krane raised an eyebrow in a manner that suggested he'd turned his statement into a question.

'New to Krane, yes. Exploring my options.' Saying as little as possible was less likely to get him into trouble.

'Exploring?'

Shiz! This guy picked up on every single word! 'I mean, I'm

trying out Krane Media to see what I think of it.'

'Well, I have to say, you intrigue me. Not many people speak like you. You're new to Krane, and I'm guessing you're new to the Complex.' Again, the raised eyebrow.

Ferry had told Dean to tell people he was doing research for Starbucks University. Carlton had bought it, but surely Krane would make mincemeat of that story. 'Yes, new,' said Dean. Turning his head to look at the view out of the window, he wished he could go walking in that forest. Tent in his backpack, he would go fishing. He could get lost for days. Peaceful. Alone. Then he remembered it was all fake. Just a hologram.

'Anything else you'd like to tell me?' asked Krane.

'Nothing comes to mind. I suppose I'm just curious regarding why you asked me here.'

Krane smiled. 'How would you like to work for me?'

'Really?' Jane would laugh her head off, he thought.

'Yes, as a researcher. Have you done much in the way of research work?'

'Er, yes.'

'Starbucks University, am I right?'

'Yes, how did you know?'

'Are you surprised? Don't be. We're Krane Media. We're every-where.'

'What kind of research would I be doing?'

'Checking out the competitors. We need to know what we're up against so we can stay ahead of the pack.'

'I didn't think Krane had any competitors. From what I can tell, you've got the games market sewn up.'

'Not quite.'

Dean thought for a while. 'The Fantasorium?'

'Exactly.'

'Strange, I met a guy from the Fantasorium just recently. Do you know Vince Style?'

'The name doesn't ring a bell.'

'OK, right. So, the thing is, I don't think the Fantasorium is quite my thing. What would you want me to do?'

'Nothing much. Just pay a visit with some recording equipment.'

'Spying?'

'That's a loaded word. Why shouldn't you record your visit?'

Dean folded his arms.

'Defensive gesture,' said Krane.

He unfolded his arms, then regretted doing so. Krane would probably pick on that as a sign of anxiety or something.

'It's OK to call it spying if you prefer,' said Krane, putting his hands behind his head. 'Or you could call it customer research. Does it really matter? There are no goodies and baddies in this. It's just business. Think of it as a game. Isn't all of life a sort of game?'

That sounded like something Vinty might say. 'Is it safe?'

'Is anything safe? A person can lock themselves up in their apartment all day long, but would that make them safe?'

'I don't know.'

Krane sat forward and pointed a finger in the air. 'OK, OK, complete honesty. We'll make it as safe for you as we can. There's always a risk, but you'll be a part of the Krane team. We didn't get this far by making mistakes.'

'That's a good argument. You're persuading me.'

'Good. And here's the clincher,' said Krane. 'I'll appoint Jane as your liaison.'

'Jane!'

'Yes, why so surprised? Isn't she what you're really interested in? Finding your ex.'

Dean supposed there wasn't much he could hide from Krane Media; they were spies after all. 'So you know Jane Rogers?'

'Of course we know her. She's works for us. Although, she's not Jane Rogers now. She's Jane Tanner.'

'Tanner was her maiden name.'

'Have we got a deal?'

'Sure.'

Krane's lips were moving but the words weren't sinking in. He thought he heard Krane say, 'No time like the present' and he nodded in reply, turning to look at the lake.

'Dean.'

The voice sounded familiar, but Dean couldn't locate it within the room, it seemed to belong to another space entirely. He continued staring at the holographic lake. There were ripples on the surface. A large bird swooped down low and snatched something out of the water, then rose up quickly and disappeared into the trees.

'Dean? It's me!'

A figure stood between him and the lake. He tried to focus but his mind and his eyes were operating independently. Then he remembered where he was: in Charles Krane's office. And the woman standing before him used to be his wife. In fact, by law – that is, according to the old conventions of the law – she still was his wife.

'Jane! Wow!'

'Dean, you look... really well.'

He tried to stand, but his legs felt like jelly. Krane said something like, 'I'll leave you to it,' then got up and went away. Jane's face was recognisable despite cosmetic procedures. Her green and red plastic clothes were like the outfits he'd seen in the shopping malls, not as exaggerated as the dresses Cherilea wore, but in that style. Her face, her make-up, her extravagant blonde curls all conveyed youth, but her eyes contained sadness.

'I see you've had the full make-over,' he said, quickly adding, 'I mean, you look great.'

'Thank you. You look good, too,' she said, sitting opposite him. 'I can't believe this is happening.'

'Me neither. I didn't think I'd ever see you again.'

Jane's eyes flicked downwards. 'No. Neither did I.'

'Amazing what life throws up. The twists and turns.' He remembered how he'd felt when he was head over heels in love with her. He'd never felt happier.

'Are you glad to see me?' Her expression didn't change much, perhaps because of the make-over.

'Of course! Why wouldn't I be?'

'We didn't exactly part on the best of terms.'

'No. I suppose not. I remember being a bit of an idiot. Full of ideals and dreams. Always ranting about something.'

Shaking her head and laughing, she said, 'I'm amazed to hear you say that. I thought I was the nag. Always getting at you for something. I didn't know what you were going to do next. I used to worry.'

'I should have talked to you more. Kept you in the loop. I was headstrong, I suppose.'

'And now?' She put her head to one side, coquettishly, a gesture he didn't recognise from before.

'And now? Well, it's a long story.' He straightened his posture. 'I imagine Charles Krane has filled you in.'

'Oh, is it time to get down to business?' There was an edge in her voice.

'I'm sorry. I'm not being awkward.' This was familiar: part of him feeling like he'd done something wrong, part of him wanting to go right over and kiss her. 'I'm trying to take this all in. I'm still new to the Complex. Still learning its ways. I've got so many questions.'

'Yes, but at least you're here. I heard you've been doing some research for Starbucks University. So you did well after I left you! I can see I was holding you back.' That coquettish gesture and a salesperson's smile. 'Don't you love it in the Complex? The activity. The opportunity. Everything you need at your finger tips.'

She'd really bought into it then – the Complex lifestyle. He couldn't disagree more.

He got up and walked over to the window. Up close the holographic lake looked blurred, pixellated. When he tapped at the hologram, his finger went through it, causing the light waves to wobble: the whole picture rippled, not just the lake.

'I'm still getting used to this new world,' he said, turning to face Jane. 'I'll be honest, not all of it is to my taste. But there are some great things here. Some really good people. I'm learning the ropes. I'm a business man now.' Striking the pose of a salesman in a TV advert, he announced: '*Wall to Wall Games: Extension Pack 14. Krane Media: Your Life, Your Dream.*'

'Oh, Dean, you can do so much better than that!'

There it was again, that familiar sting. 'Yeah, well, not much call for pottery graduates in the Complex.' She had always referred to his ceramics degree as 'pottery' – initially in jest, but later in mockery.

'What I mean is,' she blustered, 'it's lower league stuff. Charles has got great hopes for you. If this investigation into the Fantasorium goes well, you could be earning serious credit.'

He sat on the sofa, less than a metre from her. If he reached out he could touch her. 'So now it's your turn to talk business,' he said.

'Krane Media is a wonderful organisation. I genuinely believe Charles is a genius. He's not making games. This is art. It's deep philosophy with a practical application – entertainment and life-coaching rolled into one.'

He laughed, but she looked offended.

'Oh, sorry,' he said, smiling awkwardly. 'I thought you were doing one of those advertising slogans.'

This didn't feel good. This is what happened more and more towards the end of their relationship, missing each other's point or not getting each other's jokes.

'Never mind.' She folded her arms. 'So, shall we discuss the procedure? I understand you're ready to go.'

'I'm sorry. Let's not argue.'

'We're not arguing. We're working. With respect to what we're asking you to do, it doesn't matter whether you believe in Krane or not. You still get paid. Isn't that what businessmen want?'

So here it was: reality slapping him in the face. The Jane he'd been pining for, the Jane of his fantasies, no longer existed. He didn't recognise this woman. 'OK,' he said, 'down to business. What's the plan?'

She started talking organic software that was able to identify an individual's unconscious mental and emotional patterns. Initially, Dean would be tested to determine the chemical make-up of the additives in his system. Krane's theory was that the Fantasorium had found a way to stimulate the additives in your body to trick the brain into thinking that the person's fantasies were actually happening. She spoke matter-of-factly about the additives: like they were a simple fact of life. The one thing Krane and the Fantasorium had in common was the simple formula: Additives + Virtual Reality = Addictive Pleasure. 'The main difference between us and the Fantasorium is that we retain ethical boundaries. We produce games that people can switch on or off, but the Fantasorium wants people to hand over their psyche to an unpredictable computer system, lock, stock and barrel.'

'This is a lot to take in. These additives, you're talking as if they're normal, acceptable?'

'They're neither good nor bad. They're just a part of life. The fact is, the additives have changed human biology. We simply recognise that and build software that makes use of that fact. There's an echo effect, in which the software and human physiology reflect and co-create each other. A mutual pliability.'

'So are these additives being put into people on purpose?'

Pausing, she scrutinised Dean.

'It's just a question,' he said. 'Not a criticism.'

'The fact is, the chemicals are there whether we like it or not. It's been discovered that when a person is in an agitated state –

for example when playing computer games – certain frequencies of light combine with the additives to create something resembling a transcendent state, an experience of deep fulfilment. It works by tapping into the unconscious and accessing the emotional charge of our fondest memories. The trick is to locate the happy memories without triggering the monsters under the bed. We're getting better at it. The Holy Grail is knowing how to trigger the maximum pleasure without risking the well-being of the customer. That's why we need intelligence on the Fantasorium, it helps to inform our research.'

It sounded like *1984*. He couldn't believe this stuff was pouring out of her. 'So where do I fit in?'

'We test you before and after your visit to the Fantasorium, simple as that.'

'Really?'

'And, for extra credit, we could put some additional chemicals into your bloodstream beforehand to see what difference that makes.'

'I see.' He stood up and walked over to the holographic window. A large bird swooped down and captured a fish out of the water: the same bird as before. The scenery was playing in a loop. 'And if you're paying me extra then I'm thinking it's because there are some dangers?'

'Not dangers. Different potential challenges.'

'Like I said, dangers.'

'Dean, I wouldn't let them do this to you if I thought it was dangerous.' She gave him that coquettish look again.

'Would you do it?'

'Don't be silly.' She laughed. 'They'd spot me a mile off! I've won awards. I'm one of Charles' chief assistants.'

'Ah, one of his chief assistants. And what exactly is the job description of a chief assistant?' He couldn't stop himself. She was his wife, after all.

'Dean, let's keep this strictly business.'

'OK. How long have I got to decide?'

'Let's put it this way: it's an open offer, but don't leave it too long. I'd say you've got a couple of days, and that's because Charles likes you.'

'OK, I'll let you know.' They say opposites attract. But not always, thought Dean. 'So what does all this science mean? What are these mysterious chemicals?'

'We don't know exactly, but the main theory we're working with is that the human body has started to produce an enzyme called hydro-tetrachloroside as a sort of antidote to the additives and preservatives that we're imbibing every day. It's evolution. The amazing thing is that this enzyme responds specifically to electronic media. It's as though our biology has started treating the virtual environment as if it was real. The trouble is, the genius who discovered all this had a breakdown before we knew what we were dealing with. So we're still experimenting.'

'A mad genius? It sounds like a movie plot.'

'All I know is this guy disappeared long before I came to Krane because he wrote a controversial book and got himself banned. I haven't read it. Anarchic stuff, apparently.'

Dean felt a lurching feeling in his stomach. 'This man. Was he called Vinty? Erich Vinty?'

'Yes. That's right. Although we're not supposed to mention his name. He's taboo.'

'OK,' he said, scratching his head. 'I'm in. I'll do the assignment.'

* * *

Almost everything in the Krane Media medical centre was brilliant white. A few men sat in the waiting room, perched on leather and chrome chairs. Dean wondered if, like him, they were all there for AP: Assignment Preparation. Two of them were engrossed in their tablets, playing games, intense emotions showing on their faces, from joy to devastation. When you were inside the game, in the flow of it, you barely noticed what was happening to you. But watching from the outside, the power of the games was shocking: a rectangle of plastic – pixels, drama and auto-suggestion – a lethal cocktail. It looked fun, but was it real life? Well, yes, it seemed our biology had decided it was. Another man, sitting with his head in his hands, looked up and caught Dean staring at him.

'All right?' he said, folding his arms, his legs bobbing up and down. 'You a guinea pig too?'

'How do you mean?' asked Dean.

'Taking the pills and that. Questionnaires. Wiring you up while you play the games?'

'I'm just getting some tests done. A bit private.'

The man nodded conspiratorially. 'Fair enough. Got the message.'

Dean didn't know what message the man had got, but if it meant him not asking any more questions, that was good. The men in the waiting room looked frayed around the edges. Desperate for a few extra credits. He thought of a sperm bank. Or those experiments where people volunteer to take an untested drug. Charles Krane had spoken as if this was a special assignment, an honour to be a part of it, but now the glamour was fading. Or maybe this was another test? Maybe the other guys in the waiting room were in on it? Fracking good actors if they were.

But the thing really bugging him was Vinty. Maybe Jane had dropped the name into the conversation deliberately; another test? According to her, Vinty was a chemist who saw where his experiments were leading. He glimpsed Armageddon on the horizon, so he tried to warn people. He wrote a book, but then he was silenced. Was that his story?

'Dean Rogers?' A young man in what looked like a pinstriped surgeon's gown appeared through a holographic door and smiled kindly as he looked around.

'Yes,' said Dean, getting to his feet.

'I'm Doctor Hulek. Please step this way.'

'Good luck,' said the agitated man.

Dr Hulek led Dean into another brilliant white room, with cabinets and machinery on all four walls and something like a dentist's chair in the middle.

'Just whip off your shirt, pop yourself down on the recliner, and I'll run a few tests. Nothing to worry about.'

Dean did as he was told. Jane had assured him the procedures were harmless. She'd given him a holo-pass for the Fantasorium, told him she'd see him after his visit and wished him well. And then she'd escorted him here. They didn't kiss or embrace when she said goodbye; they shook hands. He wondered what she had felt when their hands touched. Whatever had happened to her, whatever their differences, her touch still felt electric. Perhaps that was the secret of their relationship, they hadn't seen eye to eye, but they somehow clicked physiologically, two odd shapes that managed to tessellate.

He liked the doctor, despite his strange attire. He'd always enjoyed going to the doctor's, a legacy perhaps of younger days when his mum had gone to great trouble to reassure him whenever he was poorly. Whatever the problem – water on the knee, an in-growing toenail, ears blocked with wax – a trip to the clinic became a treat. He felt like he was being cared for, and he always got better.

'Are we all here for the same thing?'

'Oh, I couldn't say,' said the doctor, already busy with an electronic instrument that he was pressing against different areas on Dean's chest, arms and stomach. 'I mean, I couldn't say for confidentiality reasons, but I can't say anyway because I don't know. I just carry out the tests.'

'Sorry, I didn't mean to pry.'

'Oh, don't apologise. There's no law against curiosity.'

'You seem like a man who enjoys his job.'

'Mustn't complain! Not like the old days when surgery was all blood and guts. I mean, you need that sometimes, but now it's more like playing a computer game. You stick in the cameras and the wires and it's micro-this and micro-that. They thought we were all wasting our time playing games. But, these days, the best gamers make the best doctors!'

'I'd never thought of it that way. Maybe I should have spent more time playing games when I was younger?'

'So. We're all done,' said the doctor.

'Already? That was quick.'

'Yep. I've got your readings. Let me just feed in the figures.' The doctor inserted the electronic device into something that looked like a vending machine. A few seconds later, a batch of pills poured into a receptacle that the doctor duly picked up, sealed and handed to Dean.

The efficiency had to be admired. It struck Dean how lucky he was. Since leaving Jane, he hadn't been to the doctor once. He'd had the occasional stomach bugs and colds, but they always passed. Good job because of the medical bills.

'Take them regularly until they've all gone. These pills have a self-regulating mechanism which means they'll only dissolve when your body's ready for the next infusion. I take it you know what they're for?'

'Yes, sort of. Something to do with hydro-tetrachloroside…'

The doctor held up his hands and made a 'hup, hup' sound. 'I don't need to know. That's between you and whoever sent you here. I'm just the sweetie shop. I assume you've been a good boy, so I give you the sweeties. Please take this in the best possible sense, but the whys and wherefores are none of my business. So I'll wish you well.' The doctor extended a hand.

'Doctor, could I just ask one thing? You must have studied all about the chemicals and so on. Do you know about Erich Vinty?'

'Vinty is year one at college. If you work at Krane Media, you're working with Vinty's bio-technology. Except, we don't mention his name. Strictly taboo. You must know he lost his mind – psychosis – he became obsessed with conspiracy theories about the government being faked. Good thing he did so much of his pioneering work before he lost his marbles.' The doctor folded his arms. 'Now, come along, Dean. Can't chit-chat all day. I'm sure you've got things to do.'

* * *

Back home, Dean held up the container of pills: a small, plain white cylinder with the date stamped on it – no instructions, no sign of it having been produced by Krane Media. He put it down on the sofa next to his holo-card for the Fantasorium. So he finally had his assignment, except it hadn't come from Ferry. 'Take the pills, then go and have fun,' is what Jane had told him. Simple as that.

He remembered Dylan Fairfax, the sales rep for the Fantasorium at that first meet and greet in The Designer Frothaccino. Fairfax said people take in photos to help them create their fantasies, maybe of an old sweetheart or some famous person from history. He had his photo of Jane, but that wouldn't work. First, things were too complicated with Jane. What she meant to him was changing every day. And, second, he could hardly report back that he'd enjoyed a pornographic romp with her. Which led to another question: after he'd been to the Fantasorium and Krane did their tests, how much would they be able to see of his fantasy? And what else would they find in him? Guinea pig was the right phrase for it: a small powerless creature at the mercy of others.

He switched on *Purgatory*. The colours shifted and the lighting grew dim, but otherwise the room remained the same. Someone coughed. Startled, he looked over and, on the wall to his right, his young friend reclined on a sofa. For a moment, it looked like his friend was not a hologram at all, but real. Then he noticed how his friend's face kept changing, like many different faces projected consecutively onto a screen.

'Hi, Dean.'

'This is different! What's going on? Why are you in my apartment? I hope you're not going to tell me that you're the one playing the game and I'm a figment of your imagination.'

'Well, you'd better get used to it, Dean. You see, you don't actually exist.'

'Frack off!' Dean stood up, angry.

'Hey!' His friend laughed. 'I'm only kidding! Don't have a heart attack. Calm down.'

'Shiz! Fair play. You had me there.' Sinking back into the sofa, he let out a deep breath and put his hand on his beating chest.

'Sorry. It was too good to resist. Remember, I've got your sense of humour. I've known you long enough now to be able to reconstruct pretty accurately your world view. People don't realise it but their histories and beliefs can be seen in their facial expressions, their words, the choices they make. A person simply replays their history over and over, each day. Every small action is a microcosm of the whole. With the right key you can delve deep into the unconscious and unlock anyone's secrets. Take a word like car; to you it might evoke a happy childhood memory, maybe a time of closeness to your father. To someone else it means car crash, a horrifying moment. Bit by bit, I detect and process the emotional charge of the words you choose. I simply observe you, then give it back to you in interesting ways: either in a way that you like, which is comforting, or in a way that challenges you just enough to keep things interesting. That's how these games work. It's not rocket science, but it's just as complex.'

'Your face,' said Dean. 'It's always twisting. It doesn't settle.'

'I'm mirroring your thoughts. I don't just respond to what you do or say, but to what you think and feel. I'm an extension of you – a mirror image of your inner world, learning from you, growing – designed also to challenge, intrigue and comfort you in optimal ways. Good, aren't I?'

'At the start, you looked like a boy, then you were older, but I could see your face. Now you're something else.'

'I evolved, keeping pace with your level of engagement, your mental and emotional investment. When you first switched on *Purgatory* you were like a child taking baby steps. But you grew up, so I grew up. Now you're hard to pigeon hole.'

'You mean I'm all over the place!'

Dean's reflection laughed. 'Those are your words, not mine.'

'If what you're saying is true, that's pretty amazing. I mean, I didn't know computer games could do this.'

'Not many people do.'

'So, why are you telling me?'

'You've reached the next level. Very few people reach this level.'

'So what happens next?'

'That depends on you. I evolve. I follow your thinking and reasoning. This isn't pre-programmed. You're creating it.'

'But there are parameters, surely? We all hit limits eventually. The walls of this room, for example.'

'Maybe. Who knows? Maybe the game hasn't been tested to its ultimate capacity. After all, every player's unique. No one's played the game like you. Most people just shoot things because they're full of anger: they're trying to kill their own demons. It gives them what they need. It gives them an outlet for their unconscious rage. But you're not like that. You have different questions, different needs. Maybe the game can extend outside of this room and into your whole life.'

'Frack! This is too much.' He stared at the opposite wall. The wallpaper design was based on a drawing by Escher. He remembered it from an art book he had as a child: monks walking on never-ending staircases. The staircases were the games, and the monks were the gamers, unable to escape. Then another thought occurred to Dean: if Krane sent people to test the Fantasorium, then presumably the Fantasorium used people to test Krane Media: each checking out the opposition.

'I know what you're thinking,' said his friend.

'What? Are you a mind reader too?'

'Of course I'm a mind reader, that's what I'm telling you. Everything you utter, every facial expression, every gesture, I see it and deduce from it where your mind will go next. That's the whole point. You're asking – or are about to ask – whether you might be a guinea pig being used by the Fantasorium to test Krane Media games.'

'This is a mind frack!'

'It certainly is.'

'But if that's the case, who recruited me? Ferry?'

'You haven't told me about Ferry, but I'm guessing he's the person who brought you to the Complex. Am I right?'

'Spot on. This is like having a psychoanalyst.'

His friend laughed. 'You've got a good sense of humour.'

Dean laughed too. 'I keep forgetting this is a game. It feels more real than being out there in the Complex. I mean, I'm trying to work out what's true, what's really going on, and I'm learning as much with you as I am out there.'

'The game feels more real because you can drop your defences. When you're playing you don't need to act or put on a persona; it's the real you. Or, at least, as real as you dare. Ultimately, when we put up defences we're only hiding from ourselves.'

'This is too much. You're playing with reality.'

'What is truth?'

'You're sounding like Charles Krane now.' As he said this, he noticed his young friend's face flicker and he thought he caught a glimpse of Charles Krane's profile, his long, thin nose. He remembered how Krane said he knew when Dean had entered his shop because of his screening device. Well, what if these games were screening him, too?

'I'm not Charles Krane,' said his friend.

'So what do you think I should do next?'

'You'll need to tell me more. Tell me what your options are?'

'I thought you could read my mind?'

'Up to a point. But if you're after specific advice, then…'

He switched off the game. It was no fun anymore. The room reverted abruptly to its previous settings. The Escher wallpaper gone. Machines are alluring, he thought. They draw you in. They give you a taste of danger. But, ultimately, they just pass the time. Or, worse, they mess with your head. What he wanted was an experience of something that felt real.

He thought about the bread Clare had given him. It was a clue, he was sure of it. His mouth salivated at the memory. And now he had an idea: he knew what he wanted to investigate in the Fantasorium. Taking the container of pills, he got up and made his way into the kitchen area. 'Goodbye,' he said as he poured the pills down the garbage chute.

* * *

The Fantasorium was in another part of the Complex. In contrast to the blazing bright lights of the Krane Media centre, the Fantasorium had a more theatrical appearance. The shop front was a sheer wall of purples and black, a kaleidoscope of dark seething colours, shifting like storm clouds, with the words Fantasorium fading in and out of vision in blood red. Walking towards it, he remembered queuing to see the Tyrannosaurus Rex at the Holographic History Museum – it was the first hologram he'd seen. Standing in line, gripping his father's hand tightly, he could hear the growls of the T-Rex ahead of him.

A steady trickle of men were slipping through the small entranceway into the Fantasorium. He thought of New Soho, New London's red light district, and the men that went there, though he'd never been.

Through the entrance, down a twisting dark corridor, in the pulsating purple light he could see only a few metres in front of him. Taking cautious steps, eventually he emerged into a large waiting area, again dimly-lit, with all the furniture in black, and about a dozen men, seated randomly about the room. There was a console for registering holo-cards, and a large central screen displaying information. He slotted his holo-card into the console, waited for the display to indicate it had been accepted, then took a seat.

Next to the display screen, short films played depicting the sorts of fantasies visitors might like to choose: a man struggled up an ice-capped mountain, reached the top and proudly admired the vista, then, in the next scene, a beautiful woman journalist was asking him questions at a press conference; a woman competed in a series of Olympic events, then stood on a podium to receive a gold medal from a handsome man in a suit who gave her a suggestive wink; a man slammed his fist down on the table in a board room, the other besuited men and women looked upon him with admiration and, in the next scene, he was in a sophisticated bar, laughing with self-congratulation, while his colleagues toasted him. These were presumably the dreams that people wanted to experience as reality. Yet they were not the dreams that Dylan Fairfax or Vince Style had alluded to 'off the record', thought Dean, but the hints were there. In each scenario, the lead character had the attentions of a handsome or beautiful admirer. Sex, love and power: what else did people want?

On the central display, he could see his number, FAN2043, slowly making its way up the list as people ahead of him left the waiting area to take their turn.

Finally his number reached the top. BOOTH 8, the screen instructed him.

'Welcome to the Fantasorium,' intoned a young woman, sitting at a metal desk, not even looking up from her holographic computer which, surprisingly – perhaps for novelty effect – had the exact appearance of an old desktop computer. She looked glamorous, with blazing red hair and a skin-tight black dress. She held out her hand.

He gave her his card.

Quickly, she swiped the card and handed it back, then continued typing while reeling off the small print in a bored monotone: *'The Fantasorium – copyrighted trademark More real than reality! – cannot be held responsible for anything that transpires while you are on the premises. By proceeding with this transaction you are assuming all responsibility for any risk or harm or loss of possessions, body functionality or mental capacity, including any definitions of the above.* Would you like to proceed?'

He had already decided to go ahead, no matter how ominous it sounded. And Jane had offered him assurances for his safety. 'Yes. Please proceed.'

'Hmmm. Not many details coming up for you. Is it your first time, sir?'

'Yes, first time. Am I in for a treat?' A silly thing to ask. That was nerves speaking.

'We certainly hope so, sir,' said the woman without looking up. 'How long have you been in the Complex?'

'Good question. I'd say about two weeks.'

'I need to have your answer in months. The computer only accepts months.'

'Really? Well, then I'd have to say one month.'

'You've been here one month?' She looked at him, deadpan expression, eyelids half-closed.

'No, I've been here two weeks.'

'Two weeks isn't one month, is it, sir?'

'No. Two weeks isn't one month. Two weeks is two weeks.'

'So how many months are there in two weeks, sir?'

'No months,' he said, clenching his fists. 'There are no months in two weeks.'

'So, how many months have you been in the Complex, sir?'

'No months.'

'Finally, we got there,' she said to herself. 'Length of residence in Complex: zero.' She tapped away at the holographic buttons. Now she looked him dead in the eye: 'And what is the nature of your fantasy?'

He looked around to check no one could hear. 'I'd like to meet Erich Vinty.'

She turned back to her screen. 'Gay, then.'

'Pardon?'

'Well, Erich sounds like a man's name. And you're a man. So, two men, that would classify as gay.'

'I don't understand?'

The woman fixed him with another deadpan stare. 'You don't understand what, sir?'

He stared back blankly, until the penny dropped. 'Oh! I see!' He made a noise that was half-way between a laugh and a cough. 'I don't want to meet Erich Vinty in a gay sex scenario. I want to have a conversation with him.'

'A conversation?'

'Yes.'

'And would you like this conversation to involve any sex?'

'No.'

'Or any discussion of sex?'

'What do you mean?'

'I mean discussion of sex that leads to sexual climax.'

'No. Just a conversation and no sex.'

'OK. So, just talking? You say something, he says something?' The woman raised her eyebrows as if he had broken some sordid taboo. 'Fine, if that's what turns you on.'

'It doesn't turn me on!' he snapped. 'I just want a conversation.'

'Let's not lose our temper, shall we? All I'm saying is, you're the first person today who only wanted a conversation. So, it's a bit unusual. No offence, sir.' She returned to her keyboard. After a few moments of typing, she looked up. 'He's not in the system. Is this man a real or a fictional character?'

'Real.'

'Well, he's not real enough to be in our system. Do you have a photo or holo-card?'

'Why do I need that?'

'So we can construct him for you.'

'I don't have a photo.'

'Then how are we going to construct him for you, sir?'

'Do you remember how this is my first time here. I've no idea how this works.'

'Is there another fantasy you would like instead, sir?'

'Look, is there nothing you can do? I thought this Fantasorium was supposed to be...'

'Do you have anything else, sir?' the woman interrupted. 'An old email, a lock of hair, an unwashed sock... anything at all?'

'Yes. I do. I have his book.'

'His book?'

Checking again that no one was watching, he pulled out *The Machine Society* from his satchel. 'Will this do?'

'What is it?'

'A book.'

The woman looked at him, her eyebrows twitching, communicating her disapproval. Speaking seemed to have become too much effort for her.

'It's a book written by Erich Vinty. Perhaps you could scan this in, or whatever it is you do.'

Taking the book, she took her time opening it one page at a time for her computer to scan, making an immense play of the trouble this was causing her.

Dean folded his arms and watched her repetitive overly-dramatised actions. Finally he said, 'Do you need to scan the whole thing?'

'No, not if you don't want me to, sir.'

'Will it work from a few pages?'

'It depends how long you want the conversation to be, sir.' She stared at him. Challenging him, though he didn't understand how or why he'd ended up in a stand-off.

'Can we just get on with it?' he said, hearing the huffiness in his voice.

Giving him a brief, but not friendly, smile, she returned to her keyboard and tapped away for a long time.

Finally, he broke the silence. 'So, is that it?'

'Nearly done, sir,' she said in a sarcastic sing-song voice, as though calming an irritable child. 'Oh dear, we've got a problem.'

Sighing, he folded his arms. 'Yes?'

'I've tried sending through your order but the system is indicating an error. It says you've given me the wrong duration for your length of residency.'

'What do you mean?'

'Well, it's showing zero for your length of stay. You can't have lived somewhere for zero length of time. If you'd been in the Complex for zero length of time then you wouldn't actually be here, sir. Does that make sense?'

'But...' He tried to rein in his exasperation. Speaking very slowly and clearly, he said: 'When you asked me for my length of residency, I said two weeks and you said you needed the information in months, so I said one month, and then you said...'

'I've corrected your error, sir. I've changed it to one month and it's all gone through. Have a wonderful fantasy. Thank you.'

He stood there while the woman continued typing. 'So what now?'

'You can go through.' Without looking up, the woman pointed with her thumb at a door to the side of the booth.

On the other side was another waiting room, identical to the first from what he could tell. He hoped this painful process of gaining entry would soon be over. The tedious bureaucracy of the place had at least dampened his fears. He now felt bored, anxious to get it over and done with. Around him he recognised some of the same men from the previous waiting area, each of them lost in their own worlds.

He took a seat. He wanted to doze, but he knew he had to watch for his number on the display screen. Strange how the clerk didn't bat an eyelid at Erich Vinty. But she was young and presumably Vinty was old news now. He sat there with as much enthusiasm as a cat at the vets.

When his number came up, flashing on the display screen, he rose slowly and headed for the relevant booth.

'Good day, Mr Rogers!' said a super-cheery man dressed in a black suit, with the same quiff hairstyle and black eye-liner as the door stepping Vince Style. 'I'm your flight attendant for the day, so to speak. Now just a few details. I see from your records that this is your first time and that you've only been a resident in the Complex for one month. That means you won't have sufficient chemical enhancements in your bloodstream for the electrode insertion.'

'An insertion? I don't remember anyone saying anything about an insertion. I wouldn't want that. So does that mean I can't go in?'

'Not at all. There is an alternative. You can use this instead.' The man handed him a black helmet with a dangling lead. 'It's one size fits all. You can adjust the strap.'

Putting on the helmet, he fiddled with the fastener. It was surprisingly comfortable. 'Thanks,' he said. 'But who'd want an insertion if you can wear this?'

The man shrugged his shoulders. 'Come with me,' he said, stepping through a side door.

They walked down a grey, fluorescent-lit corridor. They passed a dozen doors lit up with 'Engaged' signs until they reached one that showed 'Vacant'. The assistant opened the door and gestured for Dean to go inside. 'Make yourself comfortable and, when you're ready to begin, plug in your helmet, insert your holo-card in the reader, and away you go. You won't be disturbed. Have a good fantasy!'

'Thank you.'

The room was something like a padded cell, in maroon, with a black leather recliner in the centre. The only other furniture was a small circular stand on which stood a bottle of water, an empty glass and a box of tissues. This is the unglamorous part of the process they don't show you in the adverts, he thought. Settling onto the recliner, he imagined the hundreds, probably thousands, of men and women – mostly men – who had been in this room before him. At least it smelled clean, with a whiff of disinfectant in the air.

Taking a deep breath, he reminded himself that it was Jane who had encouraged him to come here, so nothing too bad could happen. Even so, these games were powerful. *Purgatory* was like nothing he had experienced before, and the Fantasorium claimed to leave Krane Media games in the shade. The recliner reminded him of a barber's chair. He plugged in his helmet, slipped the holo-card into the slot in one of the armrests, and closed his eyes.

'So we finally meet!'

'What?' He swung around to see a tall, dark-haired man in an office lined with books.

'Please, take a seat.' The man looked like a Greek sculpture, slim and tanned, with high cheekbones and a lantern jaw, dressed in something resembling a pilot's uniform. He pulled out a chair for Dean then took a seat behind his desk. A gold embossed plaque on the desk read: 'Mr Erich Vinty, Author of *The Machine Society*.' The window behind him overlooked a forest-lined lake.

'Thank you,' said Dean, sitting down, 'I've got a lot of questions. I've known your name for many years. I loved your book, *The Machine Society*.'

'Thank you. *The Machine Society* was published by Philosi-read. ISBN 987-7-36454-099-3.' Vinty smiled to reveal fluorescent white teeth.

'Really? You've got a good memory!'

'Ah! Memory. Page 7 contains the first reference in my book to "memory". *Can we trust our memories? All the information we have ever received has passed through many filters, primarily through the values of our parents and the society in which they live. Incoming information is also distorted, unconsciously, by our emotional disposition. For example, if we don't believe we are loved or loveable, then all the messages we receive from the world around us will be skewed by that belief system. There are countless other ways in which we distort the data we receive. So how can we ever claim to have a grasp on reality? Indeed, is there a reality that can be said objectively to exist?'*

'Interesting,' said Dean. 'That's a lot to take in, but I think I get it. You're speaking about reality and knowing what's truly out there. That's my dilemma. I have so many questions, though I forget exactly what those questions are or why I have them.'

'I'm enjoying this conversation,' said Erich Vinty. 'How would you like me to continue? You used the word "questions" twice, but do you have a question? Is your question to ask why I, you or we have questions?'

'I'm confused.'

'*Confused, confusion, confusing.* The word "confused" appears on page 12. *We are all confused, though we don't know it. We sense it, but we can't put a name to it. We think we need a bigger house, a new job, the latest electronic gadget. But these are just ideas that we have absorbed from advertising and the media. We imagine that our consumeristic lifestyles will bring satisfaction and rescue us from the confusion: but our needs are endless, so we never get to fully test this hypothesis. However, there are some who have stepped outside of this confused state by letting go of the need for an objective reality. By which I mean, we embrace the subjectivity of our own sense of knowing. It is a way of being that the media...'* Erich Vinty folded his hands and smiled kindly as if he had fully concluded his speech.

'And?'

'Sorry?'

'You were saying something about the media, but you stopped mid-sentence.'

'Did I? I'm sorry, let me check.' He closed his eyes for a moment, then opened them and smiled. 'Sorry, I reached the end of the page, but I could go back and converse from earlier pages if you like, you dirty boy.'

'Sorry?'

'What?'

'You called me a dirty boy?'

'Yes. Isn't this the part where we have sex?'

'What?'

Erich Vinty looked confused.

Something wasn't right, Dean could sense it. He knew he'd wanted to meet Vinty for a long time – maybe years – and he knew there was something he wanted to ask, but the words were out of reach. 'Why did you call me a dirty boy?'

'You know you want it,' said Vinty, pouting and loosening his tie.

Dean was no longer listening. His attention had become absorbed by the scenery out of the window. 'Where are we?' He got up and walked over to look out.

'We're in my office having a conversation.'

'Yes, I know, but it seems a bit odd to have an office like this, overlooking a lake and a forest. I recognise that scene.'

'My secretary is very attractive. Shall I call her in? She's very accommodating. Whatever your desire, she will be happy to oblige.'

'What are you talking about?' asked Dean, inspecting the bookshelves. He picked out a book at random and was surprised to find it was *The Machine Society*. 'That's weird,' he said, 'I just picked out your book at random.' But then he noticed the book next to it was also *The Machine Society*, and the book next to that. In fact, every book in the office, as far as he could tell, was *The Machine Society*. Opening the copy in his hand, he flicked through the pages. The text stopped at page 12 – every page after that was blank. Putting the book back, he said, 'Something's not right.'

'My assistant has a twin sister. They could put on a show for us. She also has a twin brother.'

'Something's wrong. I'm leaving. I'm going to get help.'

'I wouldn't do that. Relax. Take your clothes off.'

Dean opened the office door... and came to, lying on the recliner, back in the fancy maroon cubicle, helmet on his head. 'Hopeless,' he said, taking off the helmet. He felt groggy. He sat up and rubbed his face with his hands. 'I feel so strange?' he said out loud. 'Where was I just now?' He tried to remember. It was Vinty's office. But Vinty wasn't real. And the scene out of the window, he realised, was the holographic lake he'd seen in Charles Krane's office. Vinty was reciting the pages the woman had scanned in. Which woman? He had a feeling of being conned, but couldn't think why.

Getting to his feet, he decided he would go and find someone. He tried turning the door handle, but it wouldn't budge. He'd been locked in. 'Hello?' he shouted. No reply. He tried the handle again. 'Shiz.' He paced the room. His mind was outside his body – disconnected, disassociated. He tried the door handle again, this time it opened. The corridor was grey, non-descript. A muffled sound of music. Then he remembered: he was in the Fantasorium. It hadn't worked. He felt sick. He had to leave. Every door was lit up with the word 'Engaged'. At the end of the corridor, another corridor, and more doors, all 'Engaged'. He started running – corridor after corridor. He decided to try one of the doors at random and pushed it open. Inside, it was exactly the same as his own cubicle. A helmet stuck up above the back of the recliner: a customer, not moving. He crept around the side. Mustard-coloured pullover, checked shirt. The man turned his head to look at Dean: it was Erich Vinty. 'Hello, Dean. Would you like to have a conversation?' Dean turned and ran. Back into the corridor. He tried the next door: Erich Vinty again...

Dean sat upright in the recliner and threw off the helmet. Then he pulled his holo-card out of the armrest. There was a red button on the wall and he pressed it. A few moments later, the assistant from before entered the room.

'Mr Rogers,' he smiled. 'How was it for you?'

'Can I ask you a favour? Can I just shake your hand?'

'Certainly, sir,' said the man, his eyebrows knitted. He proffered a hand. 'Is sir feeling alright?'

He gripped the man's hand. It felt real. He let go and felt his own skin, pinching his arm. That felt real too. 'How do I know I'm back in reality?'

'Ah, sir, this is common after your first experience at the Fantasorium. It takes a while to settle afterwards. Please, have a sip of water. It will help.'

He did as the man suggested, taking the bottle of water, unscrewing the cap and drinking it all down. It tasted good. It tasted real. He could feel his heart thumping. 'I'd like to leave now.'

'Of course, sir.'

* * *

Back at his apartment, Dean searched in vain for medication of any sort, looking for something to ease the hammering in his head and the grogginess that had persisted since he staggered out of the Fantasorium. He looked in every panelled hatch with no success. Slumping down onto the floor, he thought about his mother. She'd have known what to do. He recalled his first hangover. A school friend's parents had gone away for the weekend, so Dean and his friend plundered the drinks cabinet – whisky, gin, vodka. They tried a bit of everything, topping up the bottles with water to hide their crime. Dean's parents didn't drink so he'd never had the opportunity to try before. They laughed so much, music blaring, jumping around the room aping their musical heroes, playing air guitar. So this was what getting drunk felt like! 'How come people don't get drunk all the time?' he'd yelled at his friend above the jump-step beat. Later, lying on the floor, he'd let the music wash over him, lost in a world of fuzzy bliss. But the next day he went home early with a blinding headache. He didn't even make the connection between the headache and the drinking, but he found out quickly enough. He was too ill and scared to hide what had happened. His mum was kind. Got him to drink lots of water to rehydrate, and some fizzy drinks for sugar. Then she said: 'You know, there is one fool-proof method for avoiding a hangover. Don't drink alcohol!'

He didn't trust any of the fizzy drinks he could order in his apartment, so he settled for water, something that contained as few additives as possible. As he drank, he thought about the Vinty character he'd met in the Fantasorium. If it hadn't been so strange, it would have been funny: Vinty trying to set him up for a scene in a porn movie. Everything and everyone he'd encountered in the Complex had the taste of money, sex, lies and desperation. Clare was the only person who seemed free. She'd shown him a different way of dealing with the Complex, a quiet sort of rebellion, a skilful way of living. Surely she must know more than she was letting on. Part of him felt nostalgic for his simple solitary life out in the Perimeter, but he also remembered the intense yearning for human contact.

He rested for a long time, preparing for a return visit to Krane: to get it over with. They'd be wanting to run tests on him, or whatever they did, to see what they could learn about the Fantasorium. They'd quickly realise he hadn't taken the pills. They might be disappointed – angry even – but he could tolerate that.

* * *

'Jane Tanner, please.'

'Is she expecting you?' asked the Krane shop assistant.

'I believe so.'

'Name?'

'Dean Rogers.'

While the assistant called Jane on her headset, he looked around at the faces: shop staff with painted, stretched smiles and dead eyes, customers treating all the gadgets and toys so seriously. Holographic games and snippets of movies and advertisements burst up like geezers, then faded away as the shop workers scrolled on in search of other gaudy options to tempt their customers. Everywhere, swirling clouds of pixels and electricity, fantasies that appeared magically for an instant then vaporised into nothing.

'Dean, how are you?'

Snapping out of his reverie, he turned to see Jane. In the bright light of the shop, she looked like a girl trying on make-up for the first time. 'Hi, Jane. I'm fine, just about. Unfortunately, I don't think I got what you wanted. I didn't take the pills and it wasn't a great experience. But maybe I can still be of some help?'

'Let's not talk here.' She looked worried now. 'Come with me.'

She led him through the back of the shop to a lounge area he hadn't seen before. This place is huge, he thought. The furniture was from many eras, a kaleidoscopic mix of patterns, styles and colours, but somehow it hung together aesthetically. Some sort of VIP lounge, he thought. There were waiters serving drinks and snacks. Jane guided him to an isolated spot where they perched on a giant Chesterfield.

'Dean, why didn't you take the pills?'

'There are too many chemicals in this place. But I can still tell you about what happened.'

'But I thought we'd agreed. We had a deal.'

'I know, but I had a change of heart. And anyway, I've decided to call it quits with all these games. They're too intense. I want to keep things simple.'

'Dean, this might be serious. Please can you go back to the Fantasorium. And take the pills this time.'

'Why are you so worried?'

She raised her voice. 'We had a deal!' She took a moment to calm herself. 'Sorry. But you agreed to something.'

'So I've changed my mind. So what?'

She looked down at her lap, thinking.

'What's going on, Jane?' He put a hand on her shoulder. 'Don't worry. You have your life with Krane and I'll work something out for me. We'll be fine.'

'Dean, it's my job to find people to research the Fantasorium. I have quotas. There are requirements. Jobs at my level are hard to come by and hard to hold onto.'

Sighing, he withdrew his hand from his ex-wife's shoulder. 'So this isn't about my welfare. It's about you and your job.'

'Would you go back as a favour to me?'

'I'm only one person. Surely you can find others?'

'Maybe we can salvage something,' she said. 'What happened?'

He talked through his experience, just the process, omitting to mention Vinty.

'So it was the helmet service you had, not the insertion. The helmet creates a lucid dream. It would have been a more vivid experience with the pills.'

'It was vivid enough. And I felt awful afterwards. And it didn't seem to work either. I thought I'd woken up, but I hadn't. Then I woke up again, only for real this time. It was very strange. I don't want to do it again.'

'But that's why you need the pills, to stop your brain from interfering with the process.'

'But maybe my brain had good reason to interfere? It felt dangerous, no wonder I woke myself up.'

'Oh, shiz.' She slumped back, her eyes closed, thinking.

He tapped her on the knee. 'Jane, you don't seem happy. I'm

not happy either – I don't know if anyone is happy here – but I'm at least starting to think things through.' He realised this was true. 'Yes, I'm starting to see more clearly.'

'I don't know what you're talking about.'

'After you left me, I was angry. Even so, I kept your picture and I thought about you all the time and imagined that one day I might see you again, and that kept me going. So I thank you for that.'

'Don't, Dean.'

'I'm sorry you're not happy, but at least you're building a career. You always wanted stability. I was more impetuous. I wanted you to be like me, but now I can accept we're different.'

'I don't want to hear this.'

'I want to be honest with you, that's all.' He cleared his throat. 'The fact is, I've met someone. Nothing's happened yet, but it's given me a different perspective. She isn't so caught up in all of this stuff and that's inspiring to me.'

'You've got a girlfriend?'

'Not exactly. Just a friend.' It felt good to speak the truth. He no longer needed Jane's picture to give him hope; he'd taken a pin and burst the bubble. 'Jane, I want you to be happy.'

'Stop. You don't know what's really going on.' She wiped her eyes.

'What do you mean?'

'Only a few of us know the truth. Everyone else is being fed a story, make-believe. The TV stories about the government and all the voting, it's all lies.'

'I knew it.'

'But that's only half of it. There is no government. President Afini is a fiction. Everything's run by big business. More specifically, Krane Media and the Fantasorium. Between us we own almost all the credit in this place. In all of New London. We need each other: the competition creates the drive and the energy that keeps the economy going. Just as long as people keep spending.

We bring in people from the Perimeter to help with our market research.'

Dean shook his head. 'I'm not getting this.'

'I tried to tell myself I was doing you a favour bringing you here. One way of finding people is to scour the lists of evictees. When your name came up, I leapt at the chance to make you a part of it. Dean, you're only here because of me. Like I told you, it's my job to find people for experiments.'

It took a while for the words to sink in. 'So all of this – Ferry, the apartment – it's all because of you?'

'Ferry's on our side. We employ him to bring people in and get them into shape. I assume the Fantasorium do the same.'

'I don't know what to say. I don't know whether to leave now or hear you out. Is there much more of this?'

'Life here isn't easy,' she said. 'Keeping yourself afloat isn't easy. We don't want to get thrown out of our jobs and our homes any more than you do. You were done for, weren't you? Over the Wall for you. I bought you a new life in here.'

'Temporarily.'

Jane breathed out deeply.

'Go on. What haven't you said yet?'

She looked at him, a tear trickling down her cheek. 'My experiments are the most dangerous. They require intelligent people that are the most resistant to influence. My task is to work out how we can get people like you to surrender to all the Complex has to offer. You're highly resistant to this stuff – it's fantastic, really – but we need to know what makes people like you tick. But dismantling a resistance like yours is a risky process.'

'Dismantling me? Just listen to yourself. What kinds of risks?'

'The worst kind. Possible death.'

'I don't believe what I'm hearing. You deliberately recruited me for an experiment that could have killed me, is that what you're telling me?'

'The thing is,' she paused to wipe her eyes, 'I believed you would get through the tests and learn to like it here. Maybe we could have found stuff we still had in common. Try and start over.'

'Jane!' he shouted, 'you were playing Russian roulette with my life. How many other lives have you played God with? What's happened to you?'

'That's how it works in here. We invested time and money in you. We needed a return. My job is always on the line.' She started sobbing.

'This place has changed you. I know I wasn't perfect, but they've turned you into something that isn't even human.' Standing up, he steadied himself. The hangover was still there. She was crying but he needed to get out – and not just out of Krane Media. 'I'm going now,' he said, managing to keep his voice steady. 'I'm done with Krane Media. I'm not coming back.'

'Don't try anything stupid, Dean,' he heard her say. 'There are consequences.'

Part III: The Wall

'If we stay with the feeling of emptiness for long enough, if we face our pain rather than running away, we will eventually find riches buried there.'
Erich Vinty

A new sign in the window at Harding's Emporium read: *'Heroes of History. Limited edition plastic-effect figurines: men and women who shaped our world.'* The moulding of the figures was so poor you could barely tell the faces apart. Cleopatra, Einstein, Princess Diana.

Standing to the side of the window, out of view, Dean watched the daily sitcom of commerce playing out inside the shop: Coleman smiled ingratiatingly while serving a customer; Clare busied herself adjusting one of the displays. He wondered how happy they were. Did Coleman really like his customers or did he despise them? Did the guy have any self-awareness? And how could Clare stand to do what she did day after day? Sure, she'd found a way of coping – but didn't she hope for something more? Coleman seemed the polar opposite of Clare. But maybe that's how families worked, trying to find balance. If one sibling is the conformist then another will take on the role of the rebel. Jane was the conformist and he tried to be the rebel, but his rebellion was more like teenage petulance than a coherent stand against the system. Vinty was the real deal – and look what happened to him. The Machine was quite happy with stylistic gestures of rebellion, but real rebellion – holding up a mirror so society could see its own hypocrisy and emptiness – that was unacceptable. People like to pretend they're free spirits, rebels, but they stop short of real action. When it comes down to it, they prefer the security blanket of conformity.

Slipping inside the shop, he reckoned he could get a few moments with Clare before Coleman started interfering.

'Clare!' He spoke quietly but urgently.

'Dean?'

At least she seemed pleased to see him. But the noble philosophical speeches in his head had vanished. No words came to him.

'What do you want?' she asked.

'Clare,' he felt a rush of adrenalin, 'two things. First, I've got into a mess with Krane Media – I think they're after me. Second, I want to say how much I like you. I mean, you're the only reason…'

'What do you mean, they're after you? Are you in danger?'

'I don't know. We had a disagreement. I've been told I could face consequences. Does that mean eviction? I don't know.'

'OK. Don't say any more now. Go to Retro-respect and I'll see you there as soon as I can.' She rested her hand briefly on his forearm. 'Keep a low profile for once.'

'OK. I…'

'Shush!' She put a finger to her lips. She shook her head as if she was disappointed with him, but her smile gave him hope. 'Go.'

He left quickly, guessing Coleman had been watching the whole thing.

* * *

In Retro-respect, Giovanni was standing behind the counter as usual, always watching. He gave Dean a stern look as he ordered a Fizzyade Supershake. Looking out for Clare, no doubt. Good to have someone looking out for you. Could he take her away from this – could he look out for Clare? But it wasn't like that. He didn't want to be Clare's protector. He wanted them to be a team. He took a sip on his Supershake. The taste reminded him of family outings. Mum, Dad and his sister by the sea in Nike-Blackpool. They visited the amusement park every year and went on the roller coasters. Simpler days. For him anyway. He knew now that his parents must have lived with a lot of anxiety about the future. Amazing that they were able to let him grow up in a bubble of contentment, while all around them the world was falling apart.

The music in the café changed. The new track was by Straight Talkin', a song he must have played hundreds of times as a teenager.

'Take me to another place,
Run me in another race,
Show me I don't have to face,
Another year – giving chase!'

Rubbish lyrics, but who cared?

'One of your favourite songs, I bet?' Clare sat down in the seat opposite.

'You know me so well! I was just remembering miming to this track, playing my tennis racquet guitar, being Gerd Torme.'

'Well, you can tell me more later, but right now we should get out of public view.' She looked over at Giovanni. She nodded at him and he nodded back. 'Come with me.'

She took him through a door at the back of the café into the kitchen. There were food mixers, pans, sieves, packets of synthetic flour, tubes of glycerine fruit, everything – an actual kitchen, with actual mess. It was more retro than Harding's.

'Frack,' he said. 'I've not seen…'

'No time for that.' She led him through the kitchen into a small back office. Again, more clutter: paper and pens – old-style bookkeeping by the look of it.

'So,' she sat down and pointed at the other chair in the room. 'Sit down. Tell me what's going on.'

He ran over the key points of his encounter with Jane and Charles Krane and his trip to the Fantasorium. He worked in the line: 'Me and Jane are totally over. There's no chance of a reconciliation.'

She listened silently. 'So, what exactly did Jane say? How strong a threat was it?'

'She said how they've invested in me and want results. I said forcing me to take the pills and go back to the Fantasorium would be like playing Russian roulette. She just said something like:

That's how it works.'

'Maybe she's just super-keen at her job or under stress. Maybe...'

'No,' Dean interrupted. He looked down at his hands and saw they were shaking. 'I know it might sound benign, but there's something seriously bad going on, I'm sure there is. The Fantasorium was fracking horrible. I'm not going back there. And I'm not kidding myself: those guards that brought me here, they're real. They have real lasers. My friend in Pete's Bar, what happened to him? The lies on TV. Krane are watching me right now, for all I know. Watching me in my apartment. And I know no one apart from you and some sales guy, my ex and Charles fracking Krane.' He bit his thumb nail. 'My options are pretty limited. You don't know what it's like out there in the Perimeter. And I no longer feel safe in here.'

'OK, OK. Calm down.' She reached over and took his hands in hers. 'I believe you. I think this is delayed shock or something.'

'Yes, yes.' He sat back in his chair and breathed. 'I think I was starting to get caught up in all the excitement. I forgot about the dangers. The fact is, I don't want to stay in the Complex, but I don't want to go back to the life I had before.'

'I hear you. And, the thing is, there is another way.'

'What do you mean?'

'That bread I gave you. It was baked here in this café, but not for public sale, obviously – the ingredients are strictly forbidden. It's the big secret.'

'I don't understand. You've got a secret stock of yeast or something?'

'No. The ingredients were smuggled in from over the Wall.'

It was as if someone had turned the room upside down. He gripped the edges of the table. 'I don't...' he started, but no more words would come out.

'Dean. There's life over the Wall. There are people. I don't know how many. But I know because we have contact. We communicate.'

'But how? How do you know?'

'From Giovanni. I told you how the people that hang out here are different. We're not exactly an underground movement – there are too few of us – but we talk and make plans. Nothing big has happened yet, but maybe one day. Giovanni knows someone in the Complex Security Force who organises imports from over the Wall.'

'Sorry? The Complex receives imports from over the Wall? But it's the government that put up the...' He remembered there was no government. 'Sorry, I'm not getting this. So the Wall's a big trick?'

'Pretty much. There are farms on the other side of the Wall. You don't think people like Charles Krane would put up with all this synthetic crap, do you? They bring in food.'

'So why the hell are people still living in this fracking awful place?' He stood up. 'And all those people in the apartment blocks in the Perimeter?' He thought about the blank faces of the people on the commuter buses. Wasted lives. All of them duped. He sat down and leaned forward. 'So, we've got to tell everyone, haven't we?'

'Are you forgetting the lasers and the security guards? People go missing. And it's a big fracking wall. How good are you at pole vaulting?'

'So we're prisoners?'

'Pretty much. A captive consumer base, is how I think of it.'

'But if you know all this, why haven't you tried to get out of here?'

'I've thought about it,' she said, 'but everyone I know is in here. My life is here, in this café and with my brother. Even if he is annoying, I still love him.'

Now his mind was racing. 'So the North wasn't destroyed?'

'Not entirely.'

'My family could be alive.'

'Maybe. We know it isn't a nuclear wasteland out there. How could it be if there are farms? But there was a war, remember, and a great deal of destruction. When we first heard about life outside the Wall, none of us could believe it either. But it's proved to be true.'

'I have to go. Get out.'

'I know.'

They sat in silence. He tried to imagine the landscape outside the Wall. Communities, tilled fields, herds of animals. Maybe his old house was still standing?

'Dean. I understand you need to go. I know you're going to try. I don't know if you'll make it. We'll help if we can.'

'I want you to come with me.'

She smiled. 'You're very persistent. It's a very nice offer.'

'Frack, I knew it. You think I could be your father or something...'

'Ew! Shut up! You're not that old!' She held his hand. 'Actually, I think you're OK. Always have done.'

'So, what are you saying? You'll come?'

'Let me think. I'll make some enquiries. Don't go back to your apartment. Lay low somewhere, and come to my apartment later.'

'But what about your brother? Won't he mind?'

'I don't care. I'm not a child anymore.'

'Do you think he'll recognise me?'

'Who cares? It won't be a problem.'

He might report me, thought Dean, but what other choice did he have? 'So, do you think it's possible? Getting out of this place?'

'The less you know, the less danger there is.'

He looked at her, taking her in. It was like with his friend in *Purgatory*, she was a constantly shifting image: a shop assistant, an object of desire, a wise person, an inspiration. All of these things and always something new to surprise him. 'Thank you, Clare. You know how much I like you, don't you?'

'Yes, I know.'

* * *

Standing in the Complex thoroughfare, people bustling around him, Dean didn't know where to put himself. He noticed a darkened shopfront – a shop selling aquariums – and stood inside the entrance. He looked out at the brightly lit Complex, sheets of metal and glass towering above the citizens, an endless parade of colour, the people being pushed around by the Machine. He wondered whether anyone was watching him right now. Perhaps Krane Media? Perhaps Ferry? He looked at one of the fish tanks. 'Electric fish' read the label. Inside, rainbow-striped fish scurried about their business. He wondered if they were mechanical. It's the spirit that gives life, he thought. Without spirit there is no life. And what about the people in the Complex? Beneath their make-overs, plastic dresses and fancy suits, beneath the acting and the advertising slogans, underneath the chemicals that coursed through their veins, was there still spirit? Or had they become part of the Machine? Electric people in an aquarium, is that what they'd all become?

He looked up at the roof of the Complex – at the huge, golden glass dome. How far could you see from up there? He imagined a telescope powerful enough to see the North and his family's home. Maybe they had survived. But he mustn't raise his hopes. The important thing was to get as far from the Complex as possible – the further North, the safer he would feel. The countryside, the sea, no more walls. His mind wandered. He was on a beach, walking on the sand with Clare, the taste of salt in the sea air, seagulls overhead. He could pull her close.

'Dean!'

Dean looked up, startled. It was Carlton.

'Where have you been hiding? I thought we were partners?'

'Hi, Carlton. I've been around. You know, busy.'

'Busy buying fish?'

'Ha, maybe.' His collar felt tight.

Carlton inspected him for a moment, frowning, then he broke into a smile and wagged a finger. 'You've been with Krane again, haven't you? You've got yourself in with them and you're keeping all the goodies for yourself, you fracker.'

'If only you knew the half of it.' He laughed.

'Yeah, likewise.' Carlton looked down at his shoes.

'What's up?'

'Something's going on. I was in The Designer Frothaccino. Some heavy types were asking after you. I kept my head down. The staff told them I was a regular, so this guy comes over and asks me all these questions. Asked me if I knew you.'

'What did you say?'

'"Who?" That's what I said. But I'm sure he didn't believe me. Funny guy. Sort of enigmatic.'

'Did you get a name?'

'Ferry.'

'Shiz.' The electric fish kept changing direction: left, right, left, right. Electricity and water don't mix, he thought.

'Do you know him?' asked Carlton. 'This Ferry?'

'Kind of. It's a long story.'

'Well, I'm glad he's not my friend. Gave me the creeps.'

'Yeah.' He looked at Carlton. 'Listen, you've lived here a long time. Bullshiz aside, do you like it here? Ever wanted to get out?'

'What do you mean?'

'Leave this Complex?'

'And go where? Back to a shizzy apartment block? Water rations. No thanks.'

He looked back at the fish tank. It looked crowded in there, but at least those fish always had someone at their side. 'Carlton, how do fish breed?'

'What?'

'Do they have partners, or is it more like free love? Do they even have sex?'

'I've no idea,' said Carlton. 'Where did that come from?'

'The thing is. I think there might be a third option. A place you could go. Not in this Complex, not in the Perimeter, somewhere else. Are you interested?'

'I don't know what you're talking about.'

'Do you trust me?' asked Dean.

'Truth be told, you're probably the only person I've trusted in a very long time.'

* * *

A couple of hours later, Dean was standing outside Clare's apartment. Final roll of the dice. Danger didn't feel good, but there was a sense of aliveness in it – a sharper sense of awareness. He put his handprint on the door.

'You're early,' said Clare. 'Come in.'

She was wearing a dressing gown, her hair wet. The apartment was nothing like his; there was a real kitchen at one end and rooms off to the sides. It was filled with retro furniture – maybe freebies or bargains from the shop – with no sign of electronic or holographic effects. 'I didn't know you could have a place like this in the Complex. It's wonderful. Your creative touch?'

'We've got some time.' She touched him on his cheek and moved closer. She caressed the side of his neck and drew him towards her. Their lips touched.

'My room,' she said, leading him by the hand.

They lay down on the bed facing each other. She undid her dressing gown and he pushed it off her shoulder.

* * *

Dean lay in a half-sleep, holding Clare. Her back to him. Him wrapped around her, his nose in her hair. It would be fine, he thought, if they could stay like this forever, skin against skin. It was amazing how much physical heat two bodies could generate together. Then he heard a door shut – the door to the apartment.

'Clare,' he said.

'Mmm?'

'The door?'

'Oh no. This is going to be interesting.'

'Clare?' came Coleman's voice. 'Are you OK? I've got a feeling something weird's going on.'

A pause.

'Clare?' Coleman continued, his voice louder, closer to the bedroom door. 'Are you in there? Clare, I'm coming in.'

'No,' she shouted, but she was too late.

Then an angry voice from the bedroom doorway. 'Shiz! Clare! What the frack is this? We have an agreement. Get this man out of here!'

The bedroom door slammed shut.

Dean could hear Coleman's footsteps stomping around in the apartment.

'Oh hell,' said Clare, turning around. She kissed Dean on the nose. 'Time to face the music.'

He kissed her back. She responded, then stopped. 'Sorry,' she said. 'No time for that now. Come on.'

They dressed and went out to face Coleman.

Her brother was in the kitchen, with his back to them, making food or washing up or something, making a racket, slamming utensils onto the work surface.

'You're home early,' said Clare.

Coleman said nothing.

She made a face at Dean. 'Someone's pissed off.'

Dean hadn't seen Coleman angry before – malicious, obsequious, but not angry. He knew there had to be something beneath that smarmy show he put on in the shop. Now he knew:

rage.

'You've no right, Clare,' Coleman began, his back still turned. 'This is not your apartment, it's our apartment. It's the one place we have that's ours alone. We don't have intruders. I've worked hard to keep the payments up. I just want to have some sanctity about it.'

'It's not a church,' she said. 'And I'm allowed to have friends.'

Coleman turned around. 'A little more than friends, I notice.'

'Well he won't be here for long.'

'Good.' Coleman stared at him. 'You can go now.'

'Hey! Manners!' said Clare. 'He'll go when I say. Meanwhile, he's my guest, so don't be so rude.'

'I guess your brother's surprised,' said Dean. 'I can see his point of view. It's OK.'

'No, it's not OK. He's a jerk,' snapped Clare. 'You'll stay here as long as you like. Come on, let's sit down.'

They sat on the sofa.

Coleman was still staring. 'You're that guy, aren't you? Rogers. I was so glad when you gave me an excuse to sack you. Always leering at her.'

'Pack it in,' she said. 'And my name's Clare, not "her", thank you very much.'

Coleman moved closer and pointed at Dean. 'I don't how you managed it, with your new clothes and your twisted face, coming back here, trying to wheedle your way into Clare's life. She must be ten years younger than you, you freak.'

'Listen,' said Dean, sitting forward. 'I don't like you either, but I won't be around much longer so no need to have a hissy fit.'

'What does that mean?' asked Coleman. 'Where are you going?'

'None of your business.'

'Quiet, you two,' said Clare. 'Let's all calm down and have a proper conversation like adults.'

'Clare, if this fracker has got you in trouble…'

'Don't worry, Brandon. It's complicated, but Giovanni's sorting something out.'

Coleman looked incredulous, like he wanted to shout but couldn't find the words.

'It's OK,' she said. 'Everything'll be fine.'

'How could you?' said Coleman. 'How could you do this to me? Why can't you settle down and live a quiet life? You're hanging out with crooks. And as for him, I don't know where to start.'

She turned to Dean. 'Can I get you a drink?' She asked in a conspicuously polite tone of voice.

'Please.'

She took his hand and led him to the kitchen. Clearly her new tactic was to ignore her brother, and Dean was required to do the same. 'So what happens now?' he asked.

'I've told Giovanni what you want. Let's see what he comes up with. Meanwhile, we wait. And try to ignore him.' She nodded in the direction of her brother.

Here it was: the family dynamic in full swing. Even so, he noticed Clare was barely fazed by Coleman's temper; as a unit, they were solid.

A knock at the door.

'I'll get it,' said Coleman.

'Here already,' said Clare. She smiled and kissed Dean. 'Whatever happens, I'm glad to have met you. If you were staying longer, I think it could have been good.'

He sighed. 'So you've made your decision?'

Commotion at the door. Coleman was trying to tell someone, 'You can't come in.'

Then Carlton appeared and, behind him, Ferry. 'Hello, Dean,' said Carlton. 'Sorry it had to end this way. But the game's over. You're now officially surplus to requirements.'

'What the frack? What is this?' Dean was incredulous. 'I trusted you, Carlton.'

Carlton shrugged his shoulders. 'Only doing my job.'

'We were partners. You said so at Krane Media.'

'And I guess we were, at the time. But you didn't play the game.'

'Thank you, Carlton,' said Ferry. 'Let's not get too excited. Let's take a moment and calm down.'

Dean turned to Clare. 'I'm so sorry. I've messed up. I gave that guy your address. I thought he was on our side.'

She said nothing.

'You live and learn, Dean,' said Ferry. 'Did you think we'd invest so much in you and then let you cause chaos doing your own thing? Your friend Carlton has been keeping an eye on you. Your little adventure is at an end.'

Ferry was sitting now. Carlton stood by the door. Coleman looked stunned.

'So what was the plan?' asked Ferry.

Dean looked at Clare, trying to read her for clues or anything, but she wouldn't return his gaze.

'Not speaking? Are you shy?' said Ferry.

'All I know is they were meeting here,' said Carlton, 'and planning some sort of escape.'

'Not sitting down?' asked Ferry, indicating the empty seats in the lounge 'We could be waiting a while.'

'We're fine,' said Dean.

'You might be fine,' said Clare.

'Clare, please don't be angry.'

'Lovers' tiff?' asked Ferry.

Dean and Clare were standing side by side, with their backs to the kitchen work surface. Dean felt Clare's hand on his back, tapping him with something. He made as if to scratch his back and felt behind him. It was the handle of a knife; she was trying to give it to him. A knife? Was that a good idea? Surely Ferry and Carlton would have lasers? But at least he knew Clare's intentions – they weren't giving up without a fight.

'Ferry, there's something I want to ask you,' Dean said. 'Why did you give me the Vinty book?'

'Why did you take it?'

'What choice did I have?'

'We all play our games. We have to pass the time somehow.'

'But doesn't Vinty stand for everything you hate?'

'What do you mean? We love Vinty!' Ferry laughed. 'This society is built on Vinty! First he gave us the science and the chemistry. Then he wrote the instruction manual.'

'What do you mean?'

'*The Machine Society*. It told us what we needed to do with the science.'

'But you are the Machine Society. You're what he argued against.'

'No,' said Ferry, fixing Dean in his sights. 'We're a society, that's all. *The Machine Society* gave us the insight into how people function. It's a masterwork of psychology, sociology and philosophy. We learned it all from Vinty. But here's the twist: he wrote a book to set people free, but what he didn't seem to realise is that people don't want to be free. They think they want freedom, but they don't know what to do with it. Freedom makes people anxious. No, when it comes to the crunch, people prefer to have someone looking after them. And that's what we do. Vinty gave us the key to freedom and we used it to lock the door to keep everyone safe.'

'It's manipulation, that's all. Trickery.'

'Society's like a small child. We're good parents.'

'You've brainwashed people with your games and additives. You've poisoned the food, poisoned the air, poisoned people's minds. It's inhuman.'

'Why so negative? We've nurtured the people and we keep them safe.'

Coleman lost his patience. 'Could you please stop this philosophical nonsense. We do our jobs. We get paid. We keep our heads down. End of story.' He pointed at Ferry. 'You might have it easy. The rest of us just get on with it.'

Dean wanted to respond, but thought better of it. What was the point in debating all of this now?

Clare was hunched up, her head down. Coleman stared blankly at the floor.

'Listen, take me,' Dean told Ferry. 'You don't need these people. They've done nothing wrong. I wrangled my way into their lives.'

'Too late for that now, Dean. We know they've got connections. Whoever is on their way to meet you, we're curious to meet them too.'

'What are you going to do?'

'Ah! That I don't know yet, but I'm a patient man.'

They didn't have to wait long. A short burst of music told them someone was at the door.

'Keep cool, everyone,' said Ferry. He pulled out a handheld laser and pointed it at Coleman. 'You. Answer the door. I'll be right behind you.'

Coleman shot an angry look in Dean's direction.

Now the attention was off them, Dean looked at Clare, who nodded back at him. This was the moment to make a move. Dean gripped the knife, holding it tightly behind his back; they walked forward.

Coleman opened the door, said something Dean couldn't hear, then he turned, punched Ferry and fell on him. The sound of a laser gun. A cry of pain. While this was happening, Giovanni burst in, coiled, ready to pounce, scanning the room. Carlton reached inside his pocket but Giovanni jumped at him.

Dean and Clare ran forward. Coleman lay heavy on top of Ferry. Ferry was groaning. Clare fell to the floor, her knees landing on Ferry's arm, and twisted the laser gun out of his hand. Dean held the knife to Ferry's throat. Giovanni had Carlton in a pincer grip.

'Brandon?' Clare shook her brother. 'Brandon!' She yelled, then she looked at Dean, desperate. She pushed Coleman off Ferry, and her brother flopped onto his back. His body limp, his eyes lifeless; shot dead by Ferry.

'Clare, take a moment,' said Giovanni. 'We need to make a plan.'

'Clare, I'm sorry,' said Dean.

Carlton spoke hurriedly, 'Let us go and we'll see you don't come to any harm.'

Giovanni tied Carlton's hands behind his back and gagged him. Then he came over and did the same to Ferry. 'Clare, you need to sit down. Dean, help her onto the sofa.' Giovanni arranged Coleman in a more dignified position and closed his eyes.

Dean put his arm around Clare's trembling body. 'I'm sorry, Clare. I've fracked up.'

Giovanni had Ferry's laser now, and another gun – an old-fashioned pistol of some sort, presumably his own. 'First thing, this is no time for analysis, for asking who should or could have done whatever differently. Deal with that later. All we need to do now is clean up this mess.'

'I want to get out of here, out of the Complex, out of New London,' said Dean.

'OK,' said Giovanni. 'And you, Clare? What do you want?'

She nodded.

'You want to go too?' asked Giovanni.

'I don't have much choice now, do I?'

Giovanni paused. Dean could see the tenderness he felt for Clare. With her own parents no longer around, Giovanni must have been a father to her.

'Right,' said Giovanni, 'leave these two to me. Clare, grab anything you need right now. Dean, you take this.' He handed him the laser. 'It's simple to use. Either of them make a move, aim for the chest. No mercy. They didn't show any mercy to Brandon, and you can be sure they wouldn't show any mercy to you either.'

'OK,' he said, inspecting the gun. He'd never held one before.

Clare went into her room. The rest of them waited. They could hear her rummaging around.

'Thank you,' Dean told Giovanni.

'I'm doing this for Clare.'

He nodded. He got the point. Clare was the priority, he was the inconvenience.

Clare came back with a bag slung over her shoulder. 'OK. What now?'

* * *

Dean and Clare followed Giovanni back to Retro-respect. Exactly how extensive this underground movement was, Dean had no idea. It seemed any new information was provided on a strictly need-to-know basis.

'Stock up. Water, food. Take some of this bread.' Giovanni plied them with supplies.

Clare was crying silently, wiping away the tears that kept flowing. Giovanni put his hand on her shoulder.

'Won't you come with us?' she asked.

'I can't. I have my family. One day, though. I will see you one day.'

She smiled, but Dean felt sure she didn't believe him.

Giovanni had arranged for a collection from the 'Bread Man'. Dean and Clare were to be transported inside large delivery crates in the Bread Man's truck.

'Inside,' said Giovanni, pointing at Dean.

In the silence, he climbed inside the crate and curled up. The lid came down. Then he could hear sobbing. Giovanni and Clare were saying their farewells.

* * *

It was a painful journey, being jostled inside the crate. Dean hadn't even seen the Bread Man. Nor did he know the plan. All he knew was that Giovanni had said, 'Trust me.' And he did trust him. In the darkness, curled up, his legs hurting, he tried to console himself. He hoped Clare could forgive him. He hadn't planned or intended any of this. He tried to breathe. Once they were out, Clare could decide what to do.

The crate lurched forward. Maybe he and Clare could improvise something together – negotiate a relationship between them – look out for each other.

Then, a horrible thought: what if he and Clare were being separated. Maybe Giovanni had different plans for him. Breathe. Surrender, he told himself, you've done all you can. Sometimes all you can do is let go.

* * *

Dean couldn't tell how much time had passed. Maybe an hour, maybe not that long. The temperature had risen dramatically. The pitching and lurching finally came to a stop.

A different movement – being unloaded?

The bin was laid on its side and opened up. He felt a hand on his shoulder and he crawled out.

'You're safe.' A stranger, middle-aged with a beard, stood before him in white overalls. They were in an alley, out in the open, outside the Complex. The man's truck was parked at the entrance to the ally, blocking it off. It was dusk.

Clare was rubbing her eyes. 'Where are we?'

'You've been driven out of the Complex,' said the man. 'I'm en route to the incinerator station, but this is where I drop you off. Other than that, I have no information. I leave you here. I have to go.'

'But we need some information, surely?' Dean said.

Turning to leave, the Bread Man shrugged his shoulders.

'Dean, it's OK. Giovanni spoke to me.'

'OK.'

The truck's electric engine hummed into life and the vehicle moved on.

'I was given the address of a safe house. We're to spend the night there. Then tomorrow we can decide whether we want to go over the Wall.' She didn't sound angry, but there was something detached in her manner, matter of fact.

'What do you mean?'

She sighed. 'It seems we still have a choice. It might be possible to live out here in the Perimeter. Or there's the option of going through the Wall. There's a place where we can get through. They'll tell us more at the safe house.'

'It's fracking hot. I'd forgotten.' He wiped sweat from his forehead and thought about what life was like in the Perimeter, the monotony of it, the loneliness. 'I don't know what to say. I don't know whether we're in this together or whether you hate me. Whether this is a joint decision or whether we go our separate ways. I know I want to be with you, but I also want you to do whatever you want.'

She frowned. 'I've noticed you babble when you're anxious. Let's just find the safe house. The address is 36 Fountain Parade, Sector 23. Know it?'

'I think so.'

'OK. Come on.'

* * *

They walked on, night closing in. In the fading light, Dean caught glimpses of the Wall between the towering concrete blocks. A constant presence, but no longer a boundary keeping evil out. He wondered if anyone had actually been thrown out of New London. How many debtors and defaulters had been given a make-over like he was? How many had been eliminated?

They had been given overalls by the van driver, workers' overalls, to help them blend in. Dean mussed up his hair. 'I'm trying to give myself a make-under,' he tried joking. Clare didn't respond. The sun, even as they approached dusk, felt sharp on his skin.

The quiet streets were empty, clean. Anything that could be recycled had been claimed long ago and sold on by the make-shift business enterprises that were part of the Perimeter economy. There are muggers, thought Dean, although how much of that was fearmongering fed through the TV he could only guess.

He pulled a bottle of water out of his backpack. He would have glugged down the lot – then he remembered the water shortages – the siren in the morning.

'We'll need to conserve this,' he said. 'I just hope they've got water at this safe house. That's one thing the Complex has going for it – plenty of water.' He handed the bottle to Clare.

She took a drink also, tilting her head right back. Her hair had waves in it, tangled, shining.

Dean breathed in – fresh air that blew across the planet. If the human race didn't hold much promise, then at least nature would press on – hopefully – breathing life back into the earth.

The pale moon was already visible in the fading afternoon sky.

'It's a full moon,' said Clare. 'It's a long time since I've seen it. In the old days, Brandon had a telescope. I used to stare at the moon hoping I might see little people going about their lives. Perhaps I thought it would be more fun to live up there.'

Dean said nothing, fearful of saying the wrong thing. He was just glad to hear Clare speaking.

'Brandon wasn't so bad,' she said. 'He was consistent, at least. But he couldn't relax. After Mum and Dad died, I guess he didn't feel he could take it easy. Life became a responsibility, a duty. He earned money and kept a roof over our heads. Meanwhile, I carried on being a child, a teenager, moody and emotional. In a way, he sacrificed himself for me. And now he's given his life for me.' She bowed her head and put a hand over her eyes.

Dean stepped closer. 'I'm sorry, Clare. I'm sorry everything's so difficult. And I'm especially sorry about Brandon. He was a very good brother to you.'

She turned and walked into his arms, letting him hold her.

* * *

Many of the streetlights were broken and, in the tower blocks, only a few apartments were lit up. As the evening darkened, an orange gloom leaked into the streets, but the source of the light was unclear. It took Dean a while to work out that the orange glow was caused by the Complex, its dome shining brightly in the distance.

Carefully picking out their route, they avoided the darkest streets and thoroughfares, threading a path between the risk of running into too many people or being too isolated, too much like easy prey. Solitary figures would occasionally scurry past on the other side of the road and they'd eye each other with suspicion. Dean recalled commuting on the coach to the Complex and how the people avoided each other's gaze. But despite all the rumours of gangs on TV, he could see no evidence of them.

'We must be getting close now,' he said.

'I'm tired,' said Clare.

'Me too.'

They walked on.

'Hush!' said Clare. 'I heard something. Someone.'

They stood still. He could hear moaning. Someone crying into the night. 'Is it coming from up there?'

It was rare to hear a real human emotion, he thought. In the Perimeter, people hid their feelings. In the Complex, the people wore masks. Of course, there was Cherilea, a rare exception. Where was she now? Perhaps evicted from the Complex and living in one of these tower blocks, trying to eke out a living, maybe commuting into the Complex and working in a menial job. Her make-over injections would wear off and she'd revert to her real age.

The voice was coming from a side street, an indistinct pleading, impossible to make out the words.

'Careful,' he said, as they approached the alleyway.

They peeked round the corner. A man sat on a doorstep, a light above it. Grey hair, unshaven, his clothes were torn. He stared at them. 'You've found me,' he slurred. 'Have you come to help?'

'We were just passing. We heard...'

'She threw me out,' he shouted, mucus dripping from his nose.

'He's out of it,' said Clare. 'He's in a world of his own.'

Dean tentatively approached the man. 'Where do you live?'

The man looked up, his eyes flitting about, unable to focus, then he was staring into space again. 'She threw me out.'

'Who threw you out?'

'She threw me out!' he shouted, then he started crying. 'Need a drink.'

'Let's give him some water,' said Dean.

'No,' said Clare, then she looked self-conscious. 'I mean, we need the water. We can't help everyone.'

'We're not helping everyone.'

'You know what they say: when the plane is going down, the first thing you need to do is give yourself oxygen before you try to help anyone else. We need the water.'

Dean concealed his surprise. He hadn't seen Clare panicking before but, then, she'd only lived in the Complex. 'It's OK,' he said, 'I'll give him some of my water.'

'I'm not being selfish. I just think we should look after ourselves.'

'Yes. We will. We'll look after each other. I just want to do this.'

He took a bottle of water out of his satchel. 'Here,' he said, handing it to the man, 'you can have some of this.'

'Need a drink,' said the man.

Dean took off the lid and handed him the bottle. The man looked amazed. He took the bottle and drank deeply, with his head right back. Then, just as quickly, he lurched forward and spat out the water. He looked at the bottle in disgust then threw it into the road.

Dean watched the water leaking out.

'Need a drink!' said the man, more emphatically than before.

Dean didn't know where to look.

'Let's go,' said Clare.

* * *

The sign read 'Sector 23'. They had no map, but kept walking.

'Are we close?' asked Clare.

'Not far now.'

A couple of Nutri-Bars had given them some energy. It was getting late.

Dean recalled a time when he was a boy, perhaps around the age of ten. He was visiting his friend Mark. Mark lived with his mum and his granddad. His granddad was an angry man, perhaps because he was so ill, so they kept out of his way. The fascinating thing about Mark's granddad was that he had a glass eye. Mark's mum and granddad had gone out, so the two boys decided to investigate. They crept into Mark's granddad's bedroom, a room strictly out of bounds. The box for the glass eye sat on the bedside cabinet.

'Go on, you open it.'

'No you.'

If they were caught they'd be in serious trouble. Not just told off, but the wrath of granddad would be terrifying.

'He's your granddad, you open it.' No way was Dean going to

look in the box. He felt excited and terrified at the same time.

The box was a scuffed, blue cardboard thing. Mark opened the box, they were squealing as he did so, they couldn't stop themselves. The box was empty. It had soft, white padding inside, with a space for the eye. Of course, Dean realised now, why would the eye be in the box? If Mark's granddad was not in the house then, wherever he was, he would be using it. But children don't think like that.

'These signs are all about water,' said Clare. 'Look. This one is Waterfall Avenue. The last one was Riverside Close.'

'Well spotted,' said Dean.

Brookside Avenue... Seaview Crescent...

'There: Fountain Avenue. I bet Fountain Parade will be down there somewhere.'

They were walking faster, but cautiously, vigilant. They were in a residential street with what might have been considered rich houses once, but which were now presumably broken up into apartments.

Fountain Parade was a cul-de-sac off Fountain Avenue. They found the house marked 30-36.

'Number 36 must be on the top floor,' said Dean.

'How are we going to do this?'

'Press the buzzer, I guess.'

'I don't like it. We don't know what they look like. We don't know anything about them.'

'I don't suppose we've got much choice now. We just have to trust.' He pressed the buzzer. Nothing. Stepping back into the street, he looked up. No lights were on. He felt exposed. The street was deserted, but he could imagine hundreds of eyes watching him.

'I don't feel comfortable, Dean. Let's go.'

'But what else can we do?' He imagined returning to his old apartment, but it was too far, and no doubt someone else would be in there now.

'Come on. We'll come back later. I don't like this.' She was already walking away.

He pressed the buzzer again, then walked after her, looking back. Still no lights. No movement.

'I don't like being stuck in this cul-de-sac,' she said.

They turned the corner and walked on.

Footsteps behind them.

Dean looked back. A man following them. Looking at them. An older man, tall. Dean felt for the laser gun in his pocket. 'What do we do?'

'Cross over? See what he does.'

They crossed the street. The man did the same.

The footsteps were getting closer. Gripping the handle of the gun, his finger felt for the trigger. He pulled out his gun and turned – the man had gone.

'Shiz! Where is he?' Dean looked around. Empty pavement. Empty road. No side alley.

'No need to shoot.' A man's voice.

Dean turned again to see a laser trained on him.

'It's OK,' said the man, lowering his gun, 'I think you're looking for me.' He had a trimmed grey beard, closely cropped grey hair, an erect posture. 'I don't need to know who gave you the address. Come on. Follow me.' He turned and walked on.

Clare shrugged. 'Guess we came to the right place, after all.'

* * *

The man's flat was large and sparsely furnished. Bare walls painted a deep grey. A few books on a shelf, but not much else. Just a sofa, an armchair and a coffee table, and a red rug on a dark wooden floor.

'Please, take a seat,' said the man. 'I'll get you something to drink and some food, and then we need to discuss your next move.'

Clare had already flopped down onto the plump burgundy sofa, put her head back and closed her eyes.

'Thanks,' Dean said. 'That's very kind.'

Clare had unzipped the top of her overalls and the blue floral design of her shirt was showing underneath. Dean watched her chest rise and fall with her breathing – she might already have slipped into sleep. He wanted to collapse on the sofa next to her, but he thought he should keep alert, pay attention.

'I've nothing much to offer you, I'm afraid,' said the man, returning from the kitchen carrying a tray with two glasses of blue-ish water and two sandwiches on a plate. 'It's blueberry syrup – at least, that's what they call it – heavily diluted. The syrup takes the edge off the taste of the water. And I hope you like cheese.'

'Cheese? Real cheese? Thank you,' said Dean. The food must be from over the Wall, he thought. 'Do we exchange names?' he asked, taking the glasses and the plate and setting them down on the coffee table.

'Best not,' said the man. 'The less we know, the less we can tell. Sorry about the gun earlier. Just checking. You understand.'

'Of course. So how did you know we weren't dangerous?'

'I've never known the authorities to do anything other than smash a door down. Even so, good old intuition. And the way you were holding that laser gun, it didn't look like you were a killer.'

Dean took a bite of the sandwich. The bread was the same as the type Clare had given him back in the Complex. 'This is good,' he said, sitting down.

'Thank you. We cobble together what we can.'

'I've so many questions, but I don't know if it's wise to ask.'

'You can try, as long as you understand if I don't answer everything.'

'Of course,' said Dean. He chewed for a while, considering how to begin. 'OK, so, what about all the TV, is it really all fake?

And how does this place run, I mean, who's in charge? What's life like on the other side of the Wall?' He looked at his sandwich. 'Where does this bread come from? Why are you still here if you could go over the Wall? Who...'

The man laughed. 'OK, I get the picture! You have a lot of questions! Let me just say this for starters: we have hope. We're a network of people who haven't lost faith that there's goodness in peoples' hearts, I mean, at the core of them, underneath all the fear and all the desperation and the anger and the grudges. We want change, but we only resort to violence if absolutely necessary, and even then reluctantly. We don't have a dogma or a creed, but we find we naturally have a lot in common. No one knows everyone else in the network. Some of us are on the other side of the Wall, many of us are out here in the Perimeter, a few of us are in the Complex. It seems we've each found our role. For now. We gather intelligence and we trust that a moment will come when we can apply this intelligence in a new society. And in the meantime, we try to focus on living a simple life. Believe it or not, we try to enjoy life.'

Dean chewed his sandwich, his mouth full, then swallowed and said, 'It sounds great. It sounds like exactly what's needed.'

'I hope so. That's how I see it. Others might see it differently. We each have a different experience of reality. So who's right? Except, if a few of us end up with a similar view, you start to wonder if we're onto something: maybe a glimpse of the ultimate reality.' The man stopped and smiled at his visitors.

Dean, put his empty plate on the coffee table. 'I like what you're saying. I'm trying to take it all in.' The man looked familiar. 'If truth be told, I was just thinking that what you're saying reminds me of a book I've been reading.'

'Really?' The man stroked his beard.

He exhaled deeply. 'This book, it's a controversial book.'

'Don't worry,' said the man. 'It's safe to talk about *The Machine Society*.'

'Exactly! So you know it?'

'Live it and breathe it. It's a special book for us. Especially for me.'

'What do you mean?'

'I think I've said enough for now. You got me onto my hobby horse, and you're tired.' The man laughed, causing Clare to wake up.

The two men watched her rub her eyes and gather her thoughts. 'Hey,' she said, 'I disappeared for a minute. Have I been asleep long?'

'Only a few minutes,' said Dean. He passed her the plate with the remaining sandwich. 'Here.'

'Thank you,' she said before taking a bite, putting her head back and closing her eyes again.

'Listen, I'm going to leave you guys to get some rest. You're safe here. I'll be sleeping in there,' he pointed at a door in the corner, 'and the bathroom's over there,' he pointed to another door. 'I trust you'll find whatever you need, towels and so on. If you get stuck, just yell.' He left the room.

Dean rubbed his stomach. He hadn't eaten a lot but he felt full; it's the difference, he thought, between real food and plastic ready-meals. They'd been given sheets and blankets. He picked up a blanket, noticing Clare had fallen asleep again.

* * *

Even with the curtains drawn, the room was light – and it was hot. Shifting uncomfortably on his blanket on the floor, Dean tried to ignore his desperate need to pee and tried to get back to sleep. Suddenly – loud and penetrating – the wailing tones of the siren. Sitting up immediately, he panicked. He needed to collect water.

'Don't worry.' His host's voice came from the bathroom. He stepped briefly into the lounge. 'I've got it. Pans at the ready.

Maybe you remember this?'

'All too well,' said Dean.

'What the frack is going on?' asked a voice from the sofa.

Dean lay back down, recalling his past life in freeze frame: standing by the sink in his old tiny apartment. He could picture the taps, the sink, the bucket, every detail. 'Don't worry,' he told Clare, 'it's only the water siren. The water rations.'

His heart was beating. There were moments in the Complex when he'd imagined that life might be better back in the Perimeter. Strange how we forget so easily. Now he was tempted to think the reverse: he should have stayed in the Complex. Tricks of the mind. He thought about their host, how he'd found a way to stay sane in the Perimeter, among his community of fellow believers. The Complex and the Perimeter were some kind of yin and yang, thought Dean, two sides of the same coin – dependent on each other, stuck in a co-dependent drama like an unhappy marriage. He'd had enough of that with Jane.

'Make the fracking siren stop!' Clare complained, rolling over and covering her head with a cushion.

Sometimes she reminded Dean of his sister: more impetuous and outspoken than he was. His sister said what she thought; you always knew whether she liked something or not, but there was never any spite. 'It'll stop soon,' he said. And a few moments later it did.

'Thank frack for that!'

'Got it!' said the man. 'Nearly three litres!'

* * *

After breakfast they freshened up, then the morning was spent preparing for the next step of the journey. The man gave instructions: no address but directions to a location closer to the Wall. This would be a rendezvous and they would be told how to get through the Wall.

Clare unpacked her bag and started re-organising her belongings. She held up a long dress, crumpled. 'I'm not going to need this, am I?'

'I'll swap you,' said the man, 'in exchange for supplies. I know someone who'll love it.'

'Please, it's yours. You've given us so much.'

While the unpacking and re-packing was going on, Dean's attention was drawn to a row of books on a shelf. Mostly in German, it seemed. Then he spotted *The Machine Society*. He hesitated. The man was fussing with food supplies, and Clare was nose-deep in her backpack. He pulled out the book. It was a cleaner copy than his, still with the dust jacket: a bright-blue cover with a clever illustration depicting a clockwork powered cityscape. The citizens of the city were parts of the machine. But in the centre, in an open space, like an oasis, a single green shoot had sprouted out of the ground: a symbol of life, something organic amid the mechanisation. It reminded him of the tree at the heart of the Complex. He opened the book and found it had been signed with a dedication. *'To Deiter. Not just my older brother, but my inspiration. Love, Erich.'* He quickly turned the book over, fumbling with excitement. Sure enough, on the back, there was a photo of the author – smiling benignly, outdoors in nature. Dean recognised this photo from when he had first read the book, before the civil war. With his lively, kindly features, sharp nose and lean physique, Vinty certainly looked like their host. Dean flipped inside and flicked through the pages. Near the back, in a chapter entitled 'What next?', he found these words underlined: *'The temptation is to blame the system, the government, the authorities, those in charge, but they didn't create the Machine Society. We did. We all played along. Why? Because, unconsciously, it was the easy option compared with the alternative: which is to truly live in the present. The reason we live at such speed in the Machine Society is not because we are becoming more skilled and efficient with our time, it's because we daren't stop. We desperately try to flee the present. We daren't stand still for a moment because, if we did, we'd realise how empty we feel. But this is not the whole story. If we stay with the feeling of emptiness for long enough, if we face our pain rather than running away, we will eventually find riches buried there. This is our true nature. We must help each other in this quest, as a community, as friends, as therapists, because it is not a journey for the faint-hearted.'*

It made sense, thought Dean. Everything in the book made sense. The trick was to live it, not just theorise about it.

Reclined on the sofa, her bag beside her, Clare looked pensive.

'You OK?' he asked.

'Sure.'

'You know you don't have to come don't you?'

'I know.'

'I don't want you to feel you're stuck with me. Look, I'm just going to say this, just for the record, just in case it's not clear, I think you're fantastic. I'd love you to come with me. I'd like us to be together.'

She stood up, walked over and kissed him on the lips. 'I know. Let's not worry about it. Everything's going to be fine. I'm kind of resigned to whatever will be, will be.'

'And so,' said their host, emerging from the kitchen, 'it's time for you to be on your way. We never guarantee safety, but we're always careful and we are very organised. Go well.'

He walked them down three flights of stairs. 'You're on your own now. If you try to come back here, you won't find me. That's how it works, I move on. We keep the lines of contact cold.'

They shook hands, Dean gripping tightly the hand of this freedom fighter, this peace activist.

The man put his hand on his shoulder. 'If you meet him, say hello to Erich from me.' Then he winked and closed the door.

Vinty is alive, thought Dean, his mind racing. On the other side of the Wall? But why not? He could have escaped, and the authorities – whoever was in charge at the time – must have circulated lies about his insanity and death to try and discourage his followers.

'What's up?' asked Clare.

'Nothing,' he said. 'Just thinking about how life's always throwing up surprises.'

* * *

Less than a day out of the Complex and Dean had already started to acclimatise to the heat. The sunshine felt painful at times, but it wouldn't defeat them, not if they kept in the shade. People passed by on occasion, eyes cast down. The grey apartment blocks towered above them, many of them appeared to be ruins, doors with glass smashed in, dark inside. Then someone would walk in or out. In front of some of the buildings, breezeblocks lay on the ground, rusted iron cables protruding. Dust swirled under their feet in a sudden hot burst of wind. But above it all, he noticed the deep brilliant blue of the sky – the same sky that had looked down on all of humanity throughout history. Hundreds, thousands of generations had lived and struggled under this blue sky, he thought. Wars and love affairs, spring time and harvest, the endless cycle of the human race had played out its dramas, yet, above and beyond it all, nature endured.

Clare walked a little way ahead, perhaps lost in memories. He hoped she could feel his watchful presence, as he could feel her connection to him.

Everything had changed. He remembered his life before the civil war with a sense of gratitude: ordinary days, school, watching TV with his family, then leaving home to move in with Jane. Then came life in the Perimeter. That broom cupboard of a flat, his job, the daily monotony, his fantasies about reconciling with Jane, they were all he had. They had held him together like skin. And then, for a time, the Complex had presented him with a riddle, and solving it had given him a purpose. These things had given him some sense of stability, for a time. His life was like a set of Russian dolls, lives contained within lives. And now he was with Clare, on the run, another puzzle to solve.

Between the tower blocks he caught glimpses of the Wall. Clare walked slowly, meandering. Maybe the heat was getting to her. At some point they could stop in one of the few bars or cafés that still traded. They would take refreshments. His mouth prickled with saliva at the thought of it. They wouldn't need to speak – they wouldn't want people to overhear anyway.

At a corner, Clare stopped and turned round. Maybe twenty metres ahead of him. He watched her pat her stomach then point off to her left – round the corner. He nodded. Yes, he felt hungry too – and they had plenty of time.

Then – a single gunshot – a growing circle of red on the shoulder of Clare's white overalls – shock and disbelief on her face. Dean moved forward, tentatively, not comprehending. Then another gunshot. He saw Clare's eyes close, her body waver and then fold and slump to the ground. Everything was over. Spinning on his heels, he turned and ran, and kept running, down any side street he came to, down alleyways, one way then another – dreading that a shot would hit him in the back at any moment.

Unknown streets. Tower block after tower block. A rat in a maze. Only fear and the pounding of his feet. The heat intense. Sweat pouring into his eyes. These grey walls, the tower blocks, hemming him in. Pointless, pointless. He kept running... But what about Clare? He checked behind him – no one there – and started to slow down. Was he always going to run away? From the debt collectors. From Ferry. And now this? Down a back alley, he spotted a doorway – some sort of service entrance, a recess where he could rest. He crouched down, exhausted. His heart still pounding. Now he felt anger. Now he felt like he could kill. He realised he had been running with the laser gun in his hand. Whoever shot Clare, he could have fired back. But who had shot her? Maybe an agent of Krane? Perhaps they had been double-crossed? Surely not? He couldn't believe that Giovanni or Deiter Vinty could do that. Whatever had happened, he had fled the scene without knowing for certain what had happened. Perhaps he had left her dying. Now he felt like a coward. He could feel it in his body, in his face, hot with shame. What if Clare was still alive? Anything could have happened, but he hadn't even waited to find out. Selfishness. Self-preservation. Had he learned nothing?

He stood up. Frack it! He had to make his way back to the scene. No more running. He wiped the sweat off his face and ran his hands through his hair. He took off his overalls to cool down, and stashed them in the alcove of the doorway; maybe he could collect them later. He no longer cared who saw him or what they thought. Clare was all that mattered, and getting over the Wall.

* * *

It took maybe fifteen or twenty minutes to find his way back. Approaching the corner where Clare had been shot, Dean gripped the laser tucked inside his shirt. At the junction he saw blood on the pavement. Two women stood on the other side of the road. When he made eye contact they started to walk away.

'No. Wait. Please!' He jogged towards them.

The women turned to walk away.

'Please, wait! Can I just ask a question?' he called, drawing closer. Then he spoke in a softer tone: 'I knew the woman who was shot. I was her friend.'

'Leave us alone,' said one of the women. She was middle-aged; the other was younger. Maybe they were mother and daughter. They wore uniforms. Cleaners, perhaps?

'Look,' he said, standing in front of them, holding up his hands to show empty palms, 'I won't hurt you. I just want to know where they took the body.'

The women looked at each other.

'Please. I love her.' He knew this to be a solid fact.

'She was still alive.'

Nodding, swallowing hard, he fought back tears. His reaction must have convinced the women of his sincerity.

The older woman uncrossed her arms. 'It was some young lads. Perhaps they were only meaning to scare her. They took her bag.'

'But where is she now?'

Again, the women looked at each other. Then the older one said, 'Follow me.'

They took him to one of the older streets, with the old town houses. 'See the one with the blue door. Dr Strachan lives in apartment 14. She'll be in there.'

'Thank you so much.'

The women hurried away.

The steps leading up to the blue door had been swept clean. He pressed the bell, but noticed the door was ajar. He pushed it open. A hallway and a staircase. This would have been the house of a wealthy Victorian family at one time. Upstairs he could hear commotion. He climbed, tentatively at first, then started hurrying, two steps at a time. The voices were getting louder. Three flights up, he came to a landing and saw an open door. They must have rushed up here, carrying her. He approached the door and knocked. No reply. He knocked again, then stepped inside the hallway.

'I'm a friend,' he called out, walking forward. 'I'm safe. Please don't be alarmed. Did you bring a woman in here?'

He was still speaking when he walked into the room where the voices were coming from.

'Who the hell are you?' an elderly man demanded.

Dean gasped with relief: Clare was lying on a table, her eyelids opening and closing. She lifted her head. 'Dean?' she asked faintly.

'No speaking,' the man told Clare tenderly, his hands red with blood. He was attending to the wound on Clare's shoulder. 'Get the hell out of here.'

A woman came into the room carrying a bowl of water and bandages. She nodded at Dean, indicating he should comply. Were they husband and wife? Doctor and nurse? It didn't matter who they were: Clare was alive.

* * *

'So you know her?' The doctor stood in the lounge doorway, hands in his pockets.

Dean stood up. 'I'm sorry for bursting in on you.'

The man inspected him, making an assessment. 'Foolishness. The whole thing. Mindless.' He stared at Dean, angry, but Dean sensed the doctor wasn't angry with him.

'Is she OK?'

'She'll live. Looked a lot worse than it was. The shock was the main thing.'

'Thank frack,' said Dean, quickly adding, 'and thank you. Two ladies showed me this place.'

'So, who are you?'

'I was with her. With Clare. There was a gunshot. Two gunshots. She fell down. I didn't know what to do. I panicked.

'You ran.'

'Yes.'

'Doesn't look like you're from around here.'

'No. I've come from the Complex. We both have.'

'Oh, that'll explain it. Escapees. Don't get many of those. That would explain your naivety. Got tired of life in the Complex? Had some romantic notion of freedom, then you run into a street robbery.'

'I know. We should have been more careful. I used to live in Section 15. I'd heard warnings about robberies, but I'd never seen one. In fact, the only danger…'

'Save your story,' said the man. 'I don't need to hear it. They're all sad stories. I just patch people up.'

'Yes, sorry. I suppose I was just trying to say, thank you.'

The doctor exhaled deeply. 'I do what I can, and the people look after me. They bring me drugs, medicines, food, clothes. I'm the nearest thing they've got to a local hospital. Frack knows what will happen when I'm gone. All you need to know is that your friend will live. Look after yourselves and try not to wind up back here.'

'Thank you. I don't know what we can give you. Clare had a bag, but they must have stolen it.'

'Don't worry about me. Just take care of her. She lost a lot of blood. You said two gunshots? She only caught one; the other must have missed. I've given her artificial blood that will adapt to her blood type. It's the best I could do. She seems strong. She'll be OK.' The doctor looked around his lounge. 'You can sleep here tonight. Then you'll have to go.' He left the room.

Standing there, Dean inspected the room, the fading fabrics, the threadbare rug, a painting of the English countryside in a chipped frame, a mantelpiece cluttered with ornaments: someone's life, someone's history. He took off his shoes and lay down on the sofa.

* * *

'Dean, wake up.'

Clare shook Dean by the shoulder.

'Clare! You shouldn't be up.'

'I know, I know.' She winced.

'Your arm?'

'It just needs to heal. There are stitches. The bullet took out a sliver of flesh – gruesome, I know. I fainted. And there was mild concussion. Dr Strachan says I was lucky not to have worse.'

She was wearing fresh clothes: a large checked shirt and blue cotton trousers.

'What does Dr Strachan say about you being up?' he asked.

'I can't stay in bed all day. We've got that Wall to get over, remember.'

'It's still light,' said Dean. Trying to get up, he felt a sharp pain in his back and flopped back down. 'Ow! What's the matter with me? Wait a minute, how long have I been lying here?'

'Dean, it's morning. You've been asleep for nearly twelve hours.'

He scrunched up his eyes. 'Frack, this is getting ridiculous.' Slowly, he sat up. He had slept fitfully. He knew he'd had bad dreams, but he couldn't remember the content, just the awful feeling that went with them. Guilt feelings. Staring down at the rug, he admired the classic Persian design. His grandma had a rug just like it. He remembered sitting on it, playing with his toy cars, driving them into the diamond shapes which he pretended were garages for the cars to hide inside. He couldn't look up. 'Clare, I did something awful. I ran away when you were shot.'

She put a hand on his arm. 'You didn't run away. You came back. The doctor told me.'

He looked at Clare. She kept surprising him. 'When I saw the bullet hit you, the blood, it was horrible. I was a coward.'

'Dean, if you're a coward, why are you here now?'

He shook his head. 'Frack! Listen to me! You were the one that was shot and I'm the one feeling bad. I should be comforting you, not the other way around.'

Gripping his arm tighter, she said, 'If we're going to be a team then we need to look out for each other. No need for this macho bullshiz. We all get scared. And sometimes we get brave. Do you understand? I'm saying it's OK. Accept it, the morphine will wear off soon and then I'll tell you what I really think!'

'You're right.' Laughing, he put his hand on top of Clare's hand. 'We're a team.'

'So what's next?'

'I haven't a clue. We've missed our rendezvous. Deiter won't be at his place anymore.'

'Deiter?'

'Yes, I meant to tell you. The guy we stayed with last night, he's Erich Vinty's brother. I'm pretty certain.' He stood up. 'Look, we can't stay here long, and we've got no contacts, so I think we should just head for the Wall and see what happens. But, right now, I'm starving.'

'OK. I'll see what I can do. If I ask nicely, I'm sure the doctor will have something for us to eat. Give me five minutes.'

He remembered he didn't have his overalls. Not worth going back for. Emptying his pockets, he found a couple of holo-cards, a light pen and his old apartment key-card. He remembered how he used to scrunch the card up in his hand, checking he hadn't lost it. It was useless now. He walked up to the mirror that hung above the mantelpiece. His fancy hairstyle had grown out. The face-lift injections were wearing off. He looked older.

Clare came back into the room. 'Toast. Inflicted with something called Margadreame.'

'Wonderful,' he said, taking the plate from Clare. He bit into the toast. Between crumbs he sighed with mock delight. 'Delicious and nutritious!'

She watched him closely, not saying anything, while he chewed. Her gazed unsettled him. What was she thinking? Then the penny dropped.

'This bread,' he said, 'it's from over the Wall, isn't it?' He held up what remained of the thick buttered slice. 'The doctor's one of them, isn't he?'

She nodded. 'I'm already on it. I've got directions.'

'Fracking hell!' He stamped his feet with joy. Then, laughing, he held out the toast so Clare could take a bite. She bit into it, then he gave her a kiss with Margadreame-coated lips.

'Yum!' he said. 'You taste delicious! Those directions, where will they take us?'

'The doctor wouldn't say. He just said we'd find what we need.'

'OK.' He stood so his nose touched hers, and they remained like that for a moment.

'People will be looking for us,' he said. 'There'll be guns out there.'

'Do or die.'

* * *

'It's like a treasure map,' said Clare. She held out the piece of paper given them by the doctor, with its crudely drawn map of squiggles, lines and arrows.

Looking from the map to the street, then back again, Dean said, 'This is tricky, but I think I know where we're going.'

The sun felt hotter today. The further they walked, getting closer to the Wall, the more exposed he felt. They dipped into doorways or down alleyways if they heard traffic. Once a coach went by, no doubt full of workers on their way to the Complex. But mostly they were alone in the streets. Sensible people stayed indoors. The further they went, the more the walls of the buildings were peppered with scorch marks from laser fire.

'I've never been out this far,' said Dean.

They turned a corner and, suddenly, the Wall stood tall in front of them, at the end of the street, perhaps a hundred metres away. Solid concrete.

'Frack,' said Dean. How could anyone get through that, he thought. 'Are these directions taking us straight to the Wall?'

'I don't know where it's taking us, but the arrows are pointing down there,' Clare pointed at the Wall, 'then around the corner.'

A thunderous metallic groan made them jump – stopped them dead – whatever it was sounded right on top of them.

'What the frack?'

Now Dean could hear voices, though not distinct. Someone

shouting commands. A sense of urgency. They backed away.

'We're too close,' he whispered.

'Too close to what?' Clare sounded frustrated.

'I don't know. But we're too close. We need to back away.'

'But these directions, if we stray too far, we could lose our way.'

'We'll remember,' he said. 'We'll find our way back, between us.'

'But maybe this is exactly where we're meant to be. This is where the map leads.'

'Here?' He stopped to think. Maybe Clare was right. But there were voices – people – activity.

'Didn't we say do or die?' she asked. 'You're not having second thoughts are you?'

'Of course not!' He shook his head. 'Frack, I don't know.'

'Come on. What other choice have we got? When sundown comes, where will we go?'

He knew Clare was right, but there was no point taking unnecessary risks. 'OK. Let's take a look, but cautiously.'

'Of course! I'm not going to just steam out there, am I?'

'OK, keep your voice down!' They were standing close, side by side, his hand gripping her shirt.

They edged forwards to the corner of the street – the Wall in front of them – the area in front of the Wall, as far as they could see in both directions, was open space. The thing that stood out was a tall metal structure standing against the Wall, its purpose not obvious. A watchtower? Scaffolding for repairs or building work? The noise they heard suggested work in progress. No one was in sight.

'That thing must be where the map is directing us,' said Clare.

'That thing?'

'Why not? The guy didn't say we would be meeting anyone. Maybe this is our chance?'

He looked at her, not comprehending.

'We could climb it?' she suggested.

'And then what? Parachute down the other side? It must be twenty metres high?'

At that moment, Dean felt a prod in his back and turned with a sinking feeling.

'Mr Rogers. And Clare. I was worried we weren't going to see you again.' It was Ferry, holding a laser gun, and a guard next to him, visor down. 'So how does this play out? You going to come quietly? Or will I have to shoot you in self-defence? It would be such a tragic waste of life.'

Dean tightened his fists. 'Ferry, how the hell?'

'The game's over. You didn't want to play by the rules. We offered you a good life in the Complex. You threw it away.'

'Where's Giovanni?' asked Clare. 'What happened to him?'

'You can't beat the system, Clare. If you take us on, you'll lose. Giovanni knows that now. We have more people, more resources, more knowledge. But, don't worry, I'm sure your angel is looking down on you.'

'You're a nasty piece of work, Ferry. The Complex, the whole of New London, it's all messed up.'

'I'll give you this, Rogers, you're more of a man now than when I first met you. When you first came to us you were a trembling wreck, willing to do anything to save yourself.' He steadied his aim.

A laser shot. Ferry fell to the ground clutching his leg, his gun skidded across the road. The security guard stood motionless. Clare was pointing her laser at Ferry's head. 'Grab his laser,' she told Dean.

He bent down, picked up the gun and pointed it at the guard.

'Kill them!' screamed Ferry.

The guard did nothing.

'Kill them!' he repeated.

'We're going to back away now,' said Clare. 'Move, either one of you, and we'll shoot.'

'You fools,' Ferry hissed. 'There's nothing over the Wall. You're on borrowed time.'

Slowly, they backed away, guns poised, eyes on Ferry and the guard.

'How's your aim?' Ferry shouted, panting, holding his leg where the laser had hit him. 'The further you are, the more likely you'll miss and my guard will hit. You'd better kill us now or you'll soon be dead.'

'No!' The guard said, 'you keep going. I'll deal with Ferry.' Reaching for his holster, he pulled out his laser slowly, barrel pointing down, non-threatening.

Dean's heart leapt. 'You're with us?'

'Wanted to make sure you made it.'

Then the guard stepped on Ferry's leg, prompting a howl of agony. The guard lifted his visor. 'Payback,' he said. He looked at Dean and Clare. 'Go!'

Dean thought he recognised the guard from the night he was arrested. He was one of the guards who escorted him to Ferry, the one Ferry dismissed with a wave of his hand.

They turned and ran. From behind them they heard a sickening cry of pain. Whatever the guard had done to Ferry, it was safe to assume he wouldn't be troubling them again.

'Keep going,' said Dean.

'There's nowhere to go.'

She was right. Nothing but the Wall, and behind them the city. He slowed down, stood next to the Wall and pressed his hands flat against it. The concrete felt cool in the shade. Then that deafening sound again. More voices, but still no sign of people. Then a deep engine roar kicked in, a smell of smoke, scraping metal.

'Dean, look out!'

The scaffolding structure started moving towards them. They leapt back, again checking from side to side, but still no one. The structure moved slowly, maybe ten metres, then halted. The engine switched off. Voices, but still no one in sight.

'Clare. Those voices, they're definitely on the other side of the Wall.'

'We should try climbing this thing.'

'But your shoulder? And the people on the other side?'

'What else can we do?'

Dean sighed. 'OK. Fine. I'll go first.' He started his ascent, slow and steady, looking down from time to time. Clare followed, struggling, teeth gritted, moving up using only her good arm to hold on.

Near the top, Dean raised his head cautiously. Coming out of the shade, he felt the full force of the sun on his face. He squinted. Sweating. Dizzy from exertion. Over the top he could see vast open reaches of scrubland, desert-like, with bleached white thickets and sand dunes. And beyond, green vegetation, trees. Now Clare was level with him. The top of the Wall was about three metres wide. The metal structure stopped half-way across the top.

Dean pulled himself up onto the top of the structure and worked his way forward, flat on his belly, the metal bars digging into him. More of the dunes came into view, then figures below, workmen, in white hats and overalls, with shovels and barrows, and guards, in uniform, standing idly at a short distance. A chain gang. They seemed to be shovelling sand away from the Wall.

'Four guards,' whispered Clare, now lying next to Dean.

'Heavily armed.'

On the horizon, clouds were gathering. Dark grey and black, piling up. He hadn't seen such a view for years. The open expanse of sky, deep-blue, and in stark contrast, the storm coming in. These strange weather patterns: the fierce sun and the torrential rain. Clare was breathing heavily, perhaps trying to control her pain, her eyes closed. She could have been saying a prayer. Wisps of her hair had blown across her face. They could try crawling along the Wall, it was wide enough, and if they kept to the city side maybe they wouldn't be spotted by the guards. But it was too far to jump down. They could try shooting and hope to take out a couple of the guards, maybe all of them if the prisoners helped them out. But the guards were heavily armed and would be well drilled.

The storm clouds were getting nearer.

'What do you think?' he asked. 'Do we shoot the guards or go back the way we came?'

Before she could reply, the structure juddered, then groaned, then cranked into life. It started moving.

'Frack!' Dean held tightly onto the structure with one hand and onto Clare with the other. 'Hold on.'

'What the hell is this thing?' she said.

'I've no idea. Just hold on.'

They were moving along the Wall, away from the guards.

'We need to do something,' said Clare.

'I know.' He spoke absently because further down, on top of the Wall, something ahead had caught his attention. 'Look. Straight ahead. Look where we're going.'

They were approaching a metal gantry whose structure dropped down the other side of the Wall.

'They must connect up,' he said. 'When it joins up, this thing makes a ladder, up and over.' He stretched himself forward. The guards were further away now, not out of sight, but there was distance between them.

'We need to get ready. When these two things pass, we can climb across. Can you do it?'

'Do I have any choice?'

Bracing himself, poised, he said, 'We'll cross, then start climbing down.'

'OK.'

The screeching of metal on concrete was painful.

The gap got smaller and smaller – until there was no gap at all. When the tops of the two structures came together – one running over the other – they scrambled across.

Clare's face screwed up in pain. 'Frack!'

Dean could feel his heart thumping. He daren't look in case the guards had spotted them, even though they must be a good two hundred metres away. He imagined a laser shot cutting through the air and sending him flying. His body tensed. *Focus on climbing down. Quick as possible.* He went first, but paused to let Clare catch up. She struggled with her arm. But they were in it together. He desperately wanted her to hurry but knew she was going as fast as she could.

Now they were moving, getting into a rhythm, half-way down the ladder. *Keep going. Another step, then another.* A quarter-way from the bottom. He wanted to jump, but couldn't trust how he'd land – and Clare might need his help. From this angle, they were hidden from the guards by the curve of the Wall.

Only a few rungs to go, then his feet touched the soft sandy ground, his shoes sinking. Lifting up his arms, he grabbed Clare around the waist... and now she was standing next to him. But this wasn't victory. Not yet.

He put a hand on Clare's shoulder. 'See how the Wall curves? We can get some way out without being seen, but then we'll come into view of the guards. All we can do is keep running.'

'So, this is it?'

'Yeah. Are you ready?'

'Thank you,' said Clare. 'Whatever happens.'

'You've changed everything for me. We're free no matter what they do now.' He touched her cheek, and she brought her hand up and placed it on top of his. They stood like that for a moment.

And then they ran and ran, heads down, away from the guards, away from the Wall, away from the city, from their old lives, away from debt, from the empty promises of a better life, from drudgery and slavery and poisoned food and the manipulation of Krane Media and the Fantasorium.

'Keep running,' urged Dean, out of breath, exhausted.

The sky beyond the trees was darkening and there were flashes of lightning. He stumbled on across sand dunes, getting closer to the scrubland, and the forest beyond that. Then more flashing – but different this time, coloured red – not thunder, laser shot. He looked round. Clare was staggering but keeping up. Flashes again. He ducked down. The guards were aiming and firing. And now another sound. An engine.

'Dean, get down,' screamed Clare, dropping to the ground.

A truck was heading in their direction. An open-backed truck, four-wheel drive, with huge tyres, bouncing over the dunes. Dean dived to the ground and scrabbled to find his laser. It wasn't there. He must have dropped it while he was running.

'Clare, have you got your laser?'

She felt about her overalls, then returned his gaze, shaking her head.

Surely, it doesn't end like this, he thought. Not devoured by wild animals or frazzled by radiation, but murdered in cold blood by security guards. Dean lay on his side and stared at the Wall – an unobscured view stretching for miles – and, rising above it, the Complex, a prisoner behind the Wall. At least he'd made it outside.

In moments, the truck was upon them. More flashes of laser shot – and lightning too. Thunder overhead and drops of rain. The sky darker. Voices shouting in the distance. Dean could see the guards had not left the Wall. They were shouting at each other. One was pointing at the prisoners then in Dean's direction. Another guard fired, but missed. Then Dean realised someone in the truck was returning fire. His heart leapt as the realisation flooded through him: they were being rescued.

'Clare! We're safe! Come on!'

The truck pulled up closer, bumping across the uneven terrain, slowing down.

'Climb in,' shouted the diver, his hair bedraggled, thick stubble on his face. 'Keep your heads down.' A man in the passenger seat was firing out of the window.

There were steps into the back of the truck. They clambered in, and lay flat. Rain had started falling. Poisonous rain, they had been told, but Dean doubted that now. Even so, he grabbed at a sheet of tarpaulin and pulled it over himself and Clare to shield them as best he could. He could see she was in pain, and the jolting of the truck didn't help. Holding her, he tried to cushion her injured shoulder. 'We'll be safe soon,' he said. Clare was silent, her eyes closed, and he noticed the blood on her shirt.

After a while, the truck stopped lurching so violently. Dean looked out from under the tarpaulin. They were on level ground on a dirt track that cut through a field of dry yellow grass. The rain had stopped – they must have caught the edge of a passing storm. The sky was brightening. It was cooler. It would be dusk soon.

They were heading for a line of trees. He thought about the copse in *Purgatory*. He sat up, pushed the tarpaulin to one side and laid Clare's head in his lap. She opened her eyes.

'I feel dizzy. Too much exercise is bad for you.' She smiled.

He pushed the hair from her face then closed his eyes. He felt dizzy too, and hungry. And there were pains in every part of his body. Wherever they were going, he hoped they would get there soon.

The dirt track took them into a forest of conifers. His head drooped.

* * *

Grandma not looking. Mother not looking. No one looking. Through the gate, over the stream, and into the wood. Among the trees. Sunlight filtering through. The ground spongey underfoot, a carpet of dead leaves and bark and moss. Placing his hands on the trees, looking for clues, for carved messages from those who had been before him, directions. Then a voice calls his name. A woman's voice. Ahead of him, through the trees.

The sun in his eyes now. There's panic in the voice. Something is coming, from behind, catching up. There's danger. The ogre has found him! Run! Don't look back. Run, towards the voice, running now...

'Dean, Dean!' It was Clare's voice.

He opened his eyes.

'We're there,' she said. 'Wherever there is.'

They were out of the forest and the truck was turning slowly in a compound. A circle of dark-green, rounded huts looked like a bracelet made of giant garden peas. Running a hand through his hair, he turned to look at Clare, sitting next to him. 'How are you?'

'Dazed and confused!' she said, pointing at the blood stain on her shirt. 'It's sore, but it's a small price to pay. Dean, can you believe this, we're free! And look at all of this.' She indicated what lay beyond the huts.

In the dusk light, he could see the compound was on the edge of a hill overlooking neatly tilled fields that extended to the horizon.

The truck came to a stop, doors slammed and the driver and his companion walked round to inspect their passengers.

'This we haven't seen before,' said the driver, suntanned, tangled shoulder-length hair, bright white teeth almost shining. 'This is certainly new.'

'It certainly is,' said his friend, his tan even deeper. 'There are planned escapes. Perhaps someone smuggles themselves out in a waste disposal unit. But you! Over the top of the Wall! This is different.'

'Really different,' continued the driver. 'It's a good job for you we were on patrol.'

'We're grateful,' said Dean, offering a smile.

'Our pleasure,' said the driver.

'My friend needs some help. Her shoulder.'

'Yes, so I see. Don't worry. The doc will look you over.'

The two men unlatched the back of the truck, climbed in and

helped them out.

Standing there, Dean stretched his arms out and breathed in. The air was fresh. A rich aroma. Of what? Grass, trees, flowers? Smells you didn't get inside the Wall, not in the dusty Perimeter and not in the artificial Complex. Nature smelled delicious! He started laughing, but his chest hurt and the laugh turned into a cough. He spluttered, then managed to compose himself.

* * *

'I feel dizzy. My head hurts if I move it.' Dean frowned.

'Don't move it then!' said Clare.

Dr Robinson listened with a paternal smile. 'It's all perfectly natural, Mr Rogers. We see this in everyone who escapes. It's withdrawal symptoms.'

'But we've only been out for two days.' Dean sat with his head in his hands. They were inside one of the pea-shaped huts, in the doctor's office.

'Exactly,' said Dr Robinson, stroking his thick grey beard, his bald head glistening in the bright lamplight. 'This gives you an indication of the depth of the problem. You've been feeding your system with who-knows-what for years. Now all those additives have become a part of your system. You're going to feel groggy for a little while. The best cure is to drink lots of water, eat healthy, take light exercise – walking, that sort of thing – and you'll soon be right as rain.'

'Ha, I haven't heard that expression in years!' said Dean.

'No, I suppose not! Because the rain is poisonous, right?' said the doctor, raising an eyebrow. 'And other such nonsense! It's not only your body that's been poisoned, but your mind too. But I know you've worked that out already. That's why you escaped.' He turned his attention to Clare. 'And how about you? How's the shoulder?'

'It's fine, thank you. It's like his head: I'm fine as long as I don't use it.' She winked at Dean.

'So the big question is: What next? I know where you don't want to be – inside the Wall – but where do you want to be? It gets pretty boring here after a while. We're here to handle the communications with New London. We do a little farming, but not much else. You'll want to be on your way.'

Dean sat forward and placed his hands flat on the doctor's desk. 'That's where I was hoping you might be able to help. All the time I was inside, I didn't realise there was anyone out here. But now I know there's a chance my family's still alive. Can you help me find them?'

'We can help, of course. Our network stretches throughout the country. We might not have the communication tools or the technology we once had, but we have walkie-talkies, we move about, we have connections. I'll put the word out. Write down whatever details you can remember: names, last known addresses, anything that might be useful.'

'Thank you, I'd really appreciate that.'

'We'll do what we can and send you on your way. Find somewhere to settle. Become part of a community. That's how we now do things. We don't travel like we used to; we don't have trains or planes and there are very few cars. People are keeping things local, learning practical trades, joining in, supporting each other.'

'And it works?'

'Seems to. We don't have a government. We're a network of people who ascribe to a set of values and principles. The principles seem to work, so we stick with them.'

'The teachings of Erich Vinty. I met his brother.'

'Exactly. Wonderful man. Of course, there are some who don't want to fit in, it's a free country. But joining a community is safest. You'll look after each other. How about you, Clare?'

'I'm not attached. I mean, I've not got family to consider. I'm tagging along.'

Smiling, Dean looked at her, then affectionately rubbed her arm.

'Ouch! Careful!'

'Sorry!'

* * *

'How's your head?' asked Clare.

'I'm much better now,' said Dean.

They were sitting side by side, watching the sun set over the meadows. In the distance, a tractor was slowly making runs up and down a field of bright yellow corn.

'Dr Robinson says we'll need to move on soon,' said Clare. 'Make room for others coming over the Wall.'

'Yes. Time to move on. Time to make a new life. What's it going to be like?'

'Only one way to find out.'

A small bird swooped down and landed near them, perhaps hoping for some crumbs. Its head twitched for a moment, then, not finding anything, it flew off.

Dean's attention reverted to the blades of grass he was twisting in his fingers. 'I'm still getting used to it: a completely blank slate, starting from scratch.'

'We'll find a community we like. We'll make friends and make ourselves useful. You can teach. And I can open a shop selling genuine plastic Art Deco clocks – I'm sure there'll be a huge demand!'

He laughed. 'It'll be a great success, I'm sure.'

They didn't speak for a while. The tractor had stopped and the man had stepped out onto the land. He was moping his forehead and having a drink.

'I'd like to go home first, back to Lancaster. See what's there. Just have a look.'

'Sure, we can do anything we like.' Her hair was getting long.

She pushed it behind her ears.

'Good. We've got a plan,' said Dean.

In the field, two children were running towards the tractor driver. As they got nearer, he put down his drink, opened his arms and let the children run into them.

'Dean! Dean Rogers?' A man's voice was calling from the compound behind them.

'Yes?' said Dean, turning round.

It was the young man they'd seen helping in the canteen. He was holding up a walkie-talkie and beaming. 'I think the name Meg Rogers might mean something to you?'

From the author

Thank you for purchasing *The Machine Society*. I hope you enjoyed reading it as much as I had fun writing it.

If you have a few moments, please feel free to add your review of the book at your favourite online site for feedback (Amazon, Apple iTunes Store, GoodReads, etc).

You can read my blog and find out more about other books I am working on at my website www.brooksbooks.co.uk, where you can also sign up for my newsletter.

Sincerely, Mike Brooks

**COSMIC
EGG
BOOKS**

Cosmic Egg Books

FANTASY, SCI-FI, HORROR & PARANORMAL

If you prefer to spend your nights with Vampires and
Werewolves rather than the mundane then we publish the books
for you. If your preference is for Dragons and Faeries or Angels
and Demons – we should be your first stop. Perhaps your
perfect partner has artificial skin or comes from another planet –
step right this way. If your passion is Fantasy (including magical
realism and spiritual fantasy), Metaphysical Cosmology, Horror
or Science Fiction (including Steampunk), Cosmic Egg books
will feed your hunger. Our curiosity shop contains treasures
you will enjoy unearthing.
If you have enjoyed this book, why not tell other readers by
posting a review on your preferred book site. Recent bestsellers
from Cosmic Egg Books are:

The Zombie Rule Book
A Zombie Apocalypse Survival Guide
Tony Newton
The book the living-dead don't want you to have!
Paperback: 978-1-78279-334-2 ebook: 978-1-78279-333-5

Cryptogram
Because the Past is Never Past
Michael Tobert
Welcome to the dystopian world of 2050, where three lovers are haunted by echoes from eight-hundred years ago.
Paperback: 978-1-78279-681-7 ebook: 978-1-78279-680-0

Purefinder
Ben Gwalchmai
London, 1858. A child is dead; a man is blamed and dragged through hell in this Dantean tale of loss, mystery and fraternity.
Paperback: 978-1-78279-098-3 ebook: 978-1-78279-097-6

600ppm
A Novel of Climate Change
Clarke W. Owens
Nature is collapsing. The government doesn't want you to know why. Welcome to 2051 and 600ppm.
Paperback: 978-1-78279-992-4 ebook: 978-1-78279-993-1

Creations
William Mitchell
Earth 2040 is on the brink of disaster. Can Max Lowrie stop the self-replicating machines before it's too late?
Paperback: 978-1-78279-186-7 ebook: 978-1-78279-161-4

The Gawain Legacy
Jon Mackley
If you try to control every secret, secrets may end up controlling you.
Paperback: 978-1-78279-485-1 ebook: 978-1-78279-484-4

Mirror Image
Beth Murray
When Detective Jack Daniels discovers the journal of female
serial killer Sarah he is dragged into a supernatural world,
where people's dark sides are not always hidden.
Paperback: 978-1-78279-482-0 ebook: 978-1-78279-481-3

Moon Song
Elen Sentier
Tristan died too soon, Isoldé must bring him back to finish his
job… to write the Moon Song.
Paperback: 978-1-78279-807-1 ebook: 978-1-78279-806-4

Origin
Colleen Douglas
Fate rarely calls on us at a moment of our choosing.
Paperback: 978-1-78279-492-9 ebook: 978-1-78279-491-2

Perception
Alaric Albertsson
The first ship was sighted over St. Louis...and then St. Louis
was gone.
Paperback: 978-1-78279-261-1 ebook: 978-1-78279-262-8

Readers of ebooks can buy or view any of these bestsellers by clicking on the live link in the title. Most titles are published in paperback and as an ebook. Paperbacks are available in traditional bookshops. Both print and ebook formats are available online.

Find more titles and sign up to our readers' newsletter at http://www.johnhuntpublishing.com/fiction. Follow us on Facebook at https://www.facebook.com/JHPfiction and Twitter at https://twitter.com/JHPFiction.